Do Dreams Come True?

JM Dragon

Do Dreams Come True?

JM Dragon

An Affinity Romance

Affinity
eBook Press
NZ
2015

Do Dreams Come True?

Affinity E-Book Press NZ LTD
Canterbury, New Zealand

1st Edition

ISBN: 978-1-927328-89-7

This is a work of fiction. Names, character, places, and incidents are the product of the author's imagination or are used fictitiously and any resemblance to actual persons living or dead, businesses, companies, events, or locales is entirely coincidental

Editor: Ruth Stanley
Proof Editor: Alexis Smith
Cover Design: Irish Dragon Designs

Acknowledgments

I'd like to thank Mel for all her hard work in the beta process. For lots of reasons this wasn't the easiest book to work on for either of us. We got there in the end.

Thanks also to Ruth for her editing skills; my work is forever polished and ready for the reader with the help of a fine edit.

Thanks, Alexis, for the proofing. As always that eye for detail is crucial.

Nancy, as always, thanks for the help with the cover. Couldn't do it without you.

Thanks go out to the wonderful team at Affinity for their attention to detail and continued professionalism and humour when the going gets tough, and believe me it can when writing a book.

Dedication

To my wonderful array of pets: cats Katie, Mr. Ginge, Shadow, and Max. The numerous chickens, that refuse to make it easy for me to find their eggs, and my two Alpacas, Cherokee and Comanche. You make my world a brighter place to live in.

Table of Contents

Also by JM Dragon

The One
Letting Go
Circus
Falling Into Fate
The Fixit Girl
In Name Only
Death is Only the Beginning
Lonely Angel
Echo's Crusade
A Window in Time
Waterfalls, Rainbows and Secrets
The Dragon's Halloween Collection
Incantations – A Collaboration
Affinity's Christmas Collection 2010
Christmas Collection 2011
Christmas Collection 2012

Define Destiny Series

Define Destiny
Haunting Shadows
In Pursuit of Dreams
Actions and Consequences
All Our Tomorrows
Two Steps Forward One Back
A World of Change
When Hell Meets Heaven
Fatal Hesitation

With Erin O'Reilly

Earthbound
Echoes of the Past
Paradox of Love
Quest For Love
The End Game
Requiem
New Beginnings
Atonement

Chapter One

Laurel rapped hard on her apartment door knowing it was futile. Sidestepping her belongings packed in cardboard boxes and piled haphazardly outside the door, she attempted to peek through the spyhole in an attempt to find out if Ronnie was home.

"Damn you, Ronnie, this is my home too. You can't do this." Rage fought its way through her normally docile manner and she clenched her fists. With a sigh any ogre would be proud of, she gazed at her possessions. "Thank God I left most of the bulky stuff in the storage unit Mom had in Breckenridge at Limetree Estate."

"Laurel, what the hell?"

Laurel looked at Carol Bannister, whose apartment was on the floor above. "Hey, Carol. I don't know about hell but I think this time it's the end." Unable to squash the tremor in her voice or the tears that fell, she looked away from her friend and neighbor. Carol was tall, lean and plain-featured with the most gorgeous auburn hair that was slightly lighter than her own.

"Let me help." Carol bent her lanky frame to collect one of the boxes.

"It's okay, Carol, I have this."

Carol shrugged. "What's a neighbor for?" She picked up a box with ease.

What the hell. She's being nice and the help would be good. Laurel had no clue as to where she would go. She glanced at the closed door—number fifty-five—that would be forever etched in her brain. "Thanks, Carol," Laurel said. She frowned as she looked at the closed door of the broken elevator.

"Do you have someplace to go?"

Laurel bit her lip. It was embarrassing enough to have one of her neighbors find her in this predicament and quite another to admit she had no place to go.

"I'll find a hotel for the night and work it out tomorrow." Laurel smiled.

Carol frowned. "Jacs is away until the weekend. Why not stay at our place until then. You know Jacs will arrange everything once she's home. She's good at that." Carol chuckled.

Laurel laughed and could feel a little of the building tension regarding her situation dissipate. Jackie Carruthers, Carol's partner, was a life coach and a fine organizer when it came to finding a place to live in Chester.

"I couldn't impose. Besides, it's the same building…"

"Oh, forget maggot face. I'll deal with her if she turns up. Although Rose in eleven told me on the way up that she was leaving for Paris or was about to. Did you know that?"

Carol seemed to grow five inches taller to Laurel as she spoke. "No. No I never knew that. I guess she was keeping some pretty big surprises for me." Laurel shook her head. "Maggot face?" In the circumstances Laurel felt the name appropriate. "If that's what you called Ronnie, what did you call me?"

Carol grinned. “Laurel, we never called you anything…okay maybe we did have a nickname. I’m sure you did the same with everyone in this building that you know.”

“No,” she said, shaking her head. “I never did that.”

“Oh.” Carol scratched the back of her neck and Laurel figured she was embarrassed.

“Well maybe, Mrs. Kolchonsky. I never opened the door to her on Halloween. I swear she has vampire running through her veins.”

Carol laughed. “Stay please, Laurel. I’d love the company.”

Laurel considered the offer seriously this time. “Thank you, Carol. Your offer is a godsend.”

“Great. Let’s get your stuff moved. We will have to make a few trips since that darn elevator is out of order again.” Carol, with the box in hand, made her way toward the staircase.

“I’ll find another place to stay tomorrow. How hard can it be?” Laurel picked up a box and followed Carol. “So what do you and Jacs call me?”

Carol chuckled. “Angel.”

Christen Jamison glared at her brother, Hank. “I’m not going to waste my breath on that explanation,” she said.

Hank Jamison rapped his fingers on his desk and gave Christen an icy stare. “The company needs to downsize, Chris.” He folded his arms. “Do you want me to let you go?”

“If that’s necessary then sure. What you are proposing is a cheap way of saving money for a few months—maybe weeks—and then you'll be recruiting again for Thanksgiving. Stupid is what I call your plan."

"Fortunately, I don't have to listen to your advice to get it by the board. They already agree. Tough luck, sis. You will have to stomach doing all those severance paychecks and seeing those upset employees. For the life of me I don't know why you want to be personally involved in every one we sever employment with." Hank shrugged and flicked on his computer screen. "Lola invited you over for dinner this Saturday."

Christen moved to the door. "Why? We haven't been together for dinner since…oh yeah, the deal with Rayburn fashion."

"Whatever it takes, Chris, whatever it takes. Remember it's *our* inheritance. Don't you ever forget that," Hank snarled.

"How could I, Hank? You drum it into me at every tick and turn." Christen opened the door. "I'm busy Saturday."

Hank growled as she left the room and pressed the intercom. "Get me David on the line. Now!"

†

"Chris, there's nothing you can do. Mom's coming home sometime in the next six months." David Jamison drummed his fingers on the table in the store canteen.

Christen flicked her brother a wild look before shutting her eyes and drawing in a deep breath. "Mom hasn't been home since the accident that killed dad. So why is she coming back now? When I talked with her on the phone a month ago she didn't mention that she was coming home."

David did not lift his eyes from the table. "In a word…"

"Oh please, don't tell me Hank invited her," Chris hissed. "I find that hard to believe under the present circumstances he'd do that."

David shrugged. "Maybe she knows something we don't." He flicked the simple menu card across the table. "Let's eat. I have a feeling it is going to be a long day."

"Long day? It's going to be a long week. Do we have any idea if she's coming in six months or earlier?" Christen took the menu and seeing nothing that appealed to her put it back on the table. The current news shredded her appetite.

"According to Hank, there wasn't a specific date mentioned. Why not call her and ask?"

"She'll think it odd if I call her sooner than the usual three months." Christen bit her lip.

"I call her every month at least." His brow furrowed. "That's a bit harsh, Chris."

Christen glared at him. "She doesn't give a damn about us, David. She's made that plain by being away so long."

David took Christen's hand. "Chris, are you worried about not telling her about your breakup? She will understand."

Christen scowled and drew her hand away. "That I lied to her for the last ten years…give me a break, brother dear."

"For the life of me I never understood why you lied. It happens to me regularly. I'm going to have a BLT what shall I order you?" David stood.

"I'm not hungry. I think I'll go back to my office. I have lots of stuff to prepare before tomorrow's debacle. How the hell did he manage to get that decision by the board, or did you know about it before I did, too?" Christen quietly asked.

David shook his head. “I didn’t know. Look, I’m free tonight. I’ll be over with carryout unless you tell me otherwise.”

“Oh, you have no rendezvous planned? That’s not like you, David,” Christen said. She stood facing her brother.

He chuckled. “I think I’m getting too old for this philandering nonsense. Maybe I should find myself a nice girl and settle down just like George Clooney.”

Chris laughed aloud and several faces in the canteen turned to them. “Hmm, I won’t hold my breath on that one.”

“I can change. You wait and see. I met someone once a few years ago and we had a couple of dates but I finished it because she scared me.” David turned away toward the counter service area.

Christen frowned, wanting to know more, but people were still looking at her. When she cast her glance around the room they quickly turned away. With a thunderous expression mirroring her mood, she stomped out of the canteen. “Today is not a good day,” she muttered.

Chapter Two

On the bench outside the store where they had both worked since leaving high school, Laurel scrunched up next to her best friend and colleague, Andrea Forrester.

"How was the evening with dishy Rick from accounting?" Laurel asked.

Andrea rolled her eyes, reminiscent of a dice throw. "Terrible. All he wanted to do was take selfies of himself everywhere we went."

"Isn't that the idea of a selfie?" Laurel chuckled.

"Not when he's out on a date with me. Where has all the romance gone, Laurel? There was a time when a guy asked you on a date because he wanted to spend time finding out about you. Not now. It's all about them," Andrea moaned.

Laurel bit the inside of her lip as she contemplated her own failed relationship. "Not sure, Andy. I know there is someone out there just waiting to meet you and knock you off your feet."

"Well, I hope that's not literal." Andrea shrugged. "At least you found someone who still has romance in her bones. Your partner is a wonderful artist who paints fabulous romantic scenes from around the world."

"Yes, but it doesn't necessarily correlate." Laurel contemplated her feet.

Andrea gave Laurel a sharp look. "Are you okay? Is Ronnie okay? You sound miserable."

"We had a disagreement and it's too late to talk about it now. Tonight after work we'll go to Jones's and have a drink and I'll tell you all the details." Laurel glanced at her watch and stood. "We will be late if we sit here gossiping any more. Shaver was in a real bad mood this morning."

Andrea stood and linked her arm in Laurel's. "Sounds like a plan. I think bad moods are catching. Helen bit everyone's head off yesterday and then locked herself in her office. Haven't seen her yet today. I hope she got up out of the right side of the bed this morning."

Laurel laughed. "Thank God we only have to deal with grumpy customers most of the time. Come on, let's go. We can have a coffee together if you can take a break at three?"

"I'll make sure I do. I want to know all about this disagreement. What a way to leave a conversation. It's like a cliffhanger in a really good book." Andrea giggled and they headed inside the five-story building toward the main store elevator.

Laurel thought about Andrea's last words. Yep, *cliffhanger* was right, but she was the one on the precipice. *You are a real stinker, Ronnie. Why did I ever fall for you?* Her dad knew Ronnie's true colors after meeting her for the first time. Darn him. He should have been the first one she turned to but it's way too far for a commute. She'd be on the train for three hours there and back each day and she wouldn't have any money left.

Andrea took the only place available in the staff elevator to the fourth floor, where the women's department was located. Laurel waved as her friend disappeared behind steel doors. She waited a few seconds and pressed the button for the elevator. She turned to take in the backdrop of the canteen located near the entrance to entice customers and reveled in the delicious smells that wafted in her direction. Her stomach grumbled at that point and she placed a hand on her belly. Breakfast hadn't been high on her list that morning.

The bacon and eggs aroma was quickly replaced by a musky perfume that reminded Laurel of the sea. She turned and schooled her features to prevent the look of surprise as she came face-to-face with the Dragon of finance—Ms. Jamison. In all the years she'd worked at the store this was the closest she had ever come to the woman personally. The picture of her in the staff newsletter didn't do her justice. She was simply stunning.

"Have you pressed?" the woman asked.

"Yes," Laurel whispered.

"Good."

Laurel tried not to stare but couldn't help herself. Christen Jamison was a woman who could never be lost in a crowd. From her willowy height, shining brunette hair, and flawless pale skin she was hard to miss. Her angular features seemed to be carved out of stone in the best possible aspects. So lost in the images of the woman, Laurel was surprised when she spoke again.

"Are you getting in or just loitering with intent?"

"Loitering? No. No! Sorry." Laurel scrambled into the elevator along with the other woman as the doors rapidly slid shut. *Where is everyone else?*

"You need to select a floor unless you are going to the top?"

Laurel wished the floor would open up and swallow her. She jabbed at the button glowing three and then sank against the cool steel wall as the elevator took off.

When the bell pealed her floor, Laurel shot forward. "Have a great day, Ms. Jamison," she said over her shoulder as she skipped out before the doors slid shut. She swore she heard the reply, *Highly unlikely.*

God, everyone from the top down is cranky. I wonder what's going on. Laurel marched off in the direction of the staff room to change.

†

David Jamison sank into the supple leather sofa in his brother's conference room. It was inviting but businesslike at the same time. He had always applauded Hank for this chink in his otherwise callous mindset. On the other hand, was it a chink or a way of making his adversaries comfortable before he took them apart? Adversaries was mild since his brother would take down anyone, including family. He ran a hand through his wavy blond hair that reached his collar and relaxed his shoulder muscles.

The door opened and Hank strolled in. "Oh, it's you. What do you want, David?"

David raised his eyebrows. Even as kids Hank never had any time for his siblings. "You wanted me to be here remember."

"Right." Hank glanced at his watch, his bushy eyebrows twitching. "Want some coffee?"

"Are you allowing me that long an audience? That's refreshing?" David smiled.

Hank glared at him. "Bring in two cups of coffee," he barked into the intercom.

"Do I get any clue why you requested my presence? We went over the monthly sales figures two days ago." David sat forward and gazed at his brother. Hank needed to lose a few pounds. He was becoming pudgy rather than stocky, and at his age he was better off without the extra pounds.

"It isn't about the store," Hank growled.

"Really," David said. Now his brother had his attention and that hadn't happened since Hank stole his first girlfriend.

"I want to talk about Christen. She is being more difficult than normal. What's the deal?" Hank sat opposite David.

David knew Hank only called her Christen when he was annoyed with her. *Way to go, girl.* "Chris, difficult? I'm surprised you even noticed a change. For the record, she's upset at Mom coming home and you sending her a vague email. The question on our lips is why did she only contact you?" David watched closely as Hank seemed to shrink at the question.

Hank drew out his chest. "Mom emailed me out of the blue. I didn't have anything to do with it. The last time we had any correspondence was two years ago. I thought it was you or Christen. Now is not a good time. I hope she doesn't arrive in the next couple of weeks."

David frowned and shook his head. *Two years. Really?* He thought Chris was bad about staying in touch with their mother but Hank took the cake on that one. "Because you are going to kick good people out of jobs for the sake of a few dollars. Dad would be turning in his grave and Mom certainly wouldn't approve." For the first time in years David felt that Hank wasn't as in control as normal and he wanted to take the advantage for as short a period as it lasted.

"It's business. She will understand. Her allowance is as much as it is because we keep tight control of the finances and the seasonal dips."

The door opened and Hank's PA walked in with the coffee. She placed the coffee on the table and left as quietly as she'd arrived.

"David, Christen needs to be less aggressive about the board's…my decisions. I want you to have a word with her. Stop her attending the exit meetings." He narrowed his eyes. "It isn't good for our image."

David frowned and got up off the couch. "Chris is her own person, Hank. I will not coerce her into anything she doesn't think is right for her. That goes for me too. When is it a bad thing that a Jamison is around when people lose their jobs? I applaud her courage. You and I take the easy option."

"You and she were always linked at the hip." Hank snorted. "You should have been twins."

"We are mentally. I thought you would have figured that out when we were kids and always beat you at any board game." David grinned.

"Enough. When Mom arrives I want business to be the one thing we don't talk about. Do you get me?"

"Mom isn't stupid, Hank. She will ask…no in fact, she will want to visit the store. It was her life for years."

"I'll deal with that. You deal with Christen. We both know that if she doesn't toe the line I will ensure Mom knows the lies Christen has told her over the years." Hank smugly looked at David.

"You wouldn't do that, Hank. She's your sister, for God's sake."

Hank stood and wandered over to the picture window.

David glared at the back of his brother and wondered how their parents had ever brought such a person into the world. "I'll tell her, but don't expect her answer to be pretty." David turned and left the room, slamming the door behind him.

†

Christen threw her pen down with so much force it bounced off the desk onto the floor. She stared at it in disgust. The door to her office opened and a towheaded man grinned at her with his crooked white teeth gleaming.

"Christen, Mr. Jamison wants the files and you in personnel within the hour. Those are his words, not mine."

Christen allowed a smirk to tug at her lips. "I know that would not be you, Barry."

Barry Craig grinned. "Well, is that going to happen or do I need to make an appointment with my stylist for tomorrow when The Lord and Master cuffs my hairstyle." He emphasized his coiffured look with a wave of his hand.

Christen chuckled softly. "You are such a queen. I'll be there on time." Christen sighed.

Barry entered the office further and walked up to her. "Pity your brother isn't into me. I'd show him that treating people like he does doesn't work." Barry twirled.

Christen laughed. "Yeah that's a pity, Barry. Look, I need to ask you something personal."

"Sure, boss, go ahead." Barry straightened to his five-foot-six stature and folded his arms.

Christen loved the man. He had been her best friend since her first year in college. *God, that's nearly twenty-five years ago. Where has the time gone?*

"I'm waiting?"

"Sorry. Did you know that we met twenty-five years ago to the day almost?"

Barry placed a finger to his full lips and pursed them. “Please, Christen, don’t count years. It has merely been a blink of the eye.”

Christen shook her head and smiled. “Have you had contact with Macy recently?”

Barry’s eyes flared and he stroked his chin. “Why?”

Christen shifted in her chair and stared at the pen on the floor. Then she drew back her head. “Mom’s coming home.”

“Fuck…oh. Hell, what are you going to do?” Barry fluttered around the room.

“I figured that I could offer Macy a financial incentive to play along for a few days. Mom isn’t staying long—at least I hope she’s not.”

Barry shook his head adamantly.

“Bad idea?” Christen looked at the man, frowning.

“She’s married, Christen. Her wife is due to give birth any day now.”

“Married? You never said…then again why should you,” Christen quietly said.

Barry moved closer and placed a gentle hand on Christen’s shoulder. “It’s been ten years, Christen. You didn’t exactly part on good terms. I decided that it was better to let things slide. What exactly did you want her to do?”

Christen frowned. “Nothing. I’d better get going. We can’t have Hank mussing up your hairstyle, can we?” She stood and collected the folders on her desk.

“Your mom is ace, Christen. Just come clean. She’s your mom. She might be hurt you lied but don’t parents always forgive? Especially the youngest.”

Christen squared her shoulders at the comment. “Did yours when you told them you were gay?” Christen threw Barry an understanding smile at his hangdog expression. “I need to go to the bathroom." She walked past her friend and left the office.

†

Laurel closed a sale with a customer and then swiftly went over to one of her co-workers in the hardware, that doubled as the furniture, department.

"What's going on, Glor? I just saw Stanley leave like someone with a hive up his ass."

Gloria Richards raised pencil-lined eyebrows and Laurel grinned. "Sorry. But what is going on?"

Gloria frowned. "Rumor has it that there are firings and today is the day."

Laurel gulped down the bile that entered her mouth. *Please, God, not me.* Hadn't she suffered enough in the last week. "Really," Laurel nonchalantly replied.

"You don't sound worried, but then you have been here for years. You are most probably safe." Gloria sniffed the air.

Laurel didn't like the sound of her patronizing tone but ignored it. "I doubt anyone is safe. Even Mr. Stanley. You don't think…"

"I doubt it is old Stanley. He's like one of the fixtures here, besides he'd crawl up anyone's ass if it meant he saved his job." Gloria twisted her lips.

Laurel didn't exactly like her manager, Reginald Stanley, but he didn't deserve that comment. "That's uncalled for, Gloria. What has he ever done to you?"

"Done to me? Done to everyone is more like it, unless you are the only one who hasn't been screwed over by Stanley. Do you have a hankering for him? He's old enough to be your grandfather. Maybe that's why he always gives you the best hours." Gloria smirked and turned when an irritated voice asked if anyone could get served in the store.

"Sorry, madam. What can I do for you?" Gloria asked with a smile.

Laurel frowned and looked at the clock. It was two forty-five. Dare she take her break if what Gloria said was correct? *Damn.* She wished she could use the internal store phone for private business. She could have called Andy to ask if she had heard the rumor.

She slowly went back to her counter and smiled at a young woman who looked confused as she stared at bedroom furniture.

"Hi, do you need any help?"

The young woman shrugged. "This looks wonderful but expensive. I'm on a budget. My mom is coming to stay for a month and I can't have her books and lamp on the floor. She loves to read at night before she goes to sleep."

Laurel smiled. *Don't we all.* "What's the budget and when do you need it?"

"I can only spare fifty dollars. I'm a waitress and I depend on tips to get by. She arrives in three weeks." The woman flipped her hands wide.

Laurel looked at the piece of furniture. All were a hundred dollars minimum. Nothing came cheap in the store. "I totally understand. It's a beautiful piece but…if you go to this website," Laurel quickly wrote an email address down on her notepad and handed it to the woman, "you will find something similar at a price you can afford, and it's good quality too."

"Wow. Should you be telling me this?"

Laurel shrugged. "Hey, I say a good turn every now and again doesn't do anyone harm. Besides, you might end up in a great job in the future that can fund the store prices." She grinned. "It's a win-win."

"You are wonderful. I hope your bosses appreciate you. Thank you," the woman said and rushed off.

Laurel reflected on her advice. It was all true. *Well, maybe not the bosses understanding*. She grinned.

"Laurel." Laurel shivered. It was Reginald Stanley's voice. If he heard her she'd be in big trouble. She turned and faced the man. "Hi, Mr. Stanley. What can I do for you?" She gave him her best smile. It only took seconds for her to realize the man looked uncomfortable.

"Personnel needs to see you. Now."

Laurel felt like her life was passing before her in seconds.

Chapter Three

Frances Roche took a position at the side door of the boat house and silently observed her mother. At seventy-five her mother looked at least ten years younger and was fitter than her. Her hair was the shade of burnt copper, and sure it was colored, but close to the original shade she'd been born with. Her stature was the same as her height, five-five, and was nothing like the boys or Christen—they took after their dad. Her features were lined and her mom called them her emotional lesson lines. She wasn't classically beautiful but when she smiled the whole room lit up.

"Mom, you look pensive," Frances said, moving to her mom's side.

Samantha Jamison turned. "Pensive, darling? How absurd."

Frances wrapped an arm around her. "Mom, you and I have been through a lot together, and I know these things and you look pensive."

"It's been fourteen years since I've gone home. Do you think your brothers and sister will be happy with my return? I did abandon them."

"Mom, you didn't abandon them. We are a flight away and they love you. Whatever ax they have to grind, if any, you can take." Frances hugged her mother.

"You have a beautiful soul, darling. I just want them to understand, after your father…"

"Dad made decisions that affected us all. He hurt you the most, both mentally and physically. I know you have never told them the truth. Maybe this visit is the time."

"How can I? They worshipped their father. I just want to see that they are happy in their lives. That is the most important thing to me."

"Hey, family, am I missing out on something important?"

Frances looked at her husband of thirty years and grinned as she disengaged from her mother and straightened. He still had the same boyish charm she had fallen for at eighteen and married in a whirlwind affair a few months later. He had never been the person you would expect to be a United States diplomat at twenty-five but he was. Studious and interested in making the world a better place.

"Nothing, you incorrigible boy."

"I love you too, Sam," Danny Roche said. Then he placed his arms around his wife and kissed her on the cheek. "Okay, so it's a girl thing then?"

Frances chuckled. "No silly, we were talking about Mom's travel plans to see the Jamison clan."

"Ah."

"Is that all you can say, darling?" Frances turned and Danny dropped his arms allowing her to face him.

"How long has it been now? Ten years?"

"Fourteen, but who's counting," Frances flippantly replied.

Danny shrugged and pulled at his tie.

"Daniel, I'd appreciate your opinion and please don't pull any punches," Samantha said.

Danny pursed his lips and then quietly said, "If it was my mom and she hadn't been home for that long I'd have grievances."

"Mom is in touch by phone and mail. She sends presents and cards at birthdays and Christmas." Frances glared at Danny.

"Don't get upset with Daniel, Frances. He's right. There will be issues. Not with Hank but…" Samantha did not finish.

Frances sighed. "David and Christen are happy in their own worlds, you know that. Chris sends you messages about how happy she is with…Mary, or whatever her name is. David is…well David. He's a philanderer like…" Frances turned away.

"Macy. Christen's partner's name is Macy. David does have many of Carlton's traits when it comes to flirting with women. At least he had the sense not to marry and make someone's life a misery," Samantha slowly said.

Frances returned to her mother's side and hugged her tight. "Christen and David will understand, trust me. Hank was always a loner. He probably hasn't realized how long you have been away and frankly won't care—sorry, Mom, but that's Hank. It's all about him."

"I'm a little afraid, Frances."

"I know, but it was your decision, Mom. If you want to change your mind…"

"No! Absolutely not. When are Oscar and Leia due home from college? I miss them."

Frances and Danny laughed at the subject change.

"Only a doting grandmother would ever miss teenagers. They'll be here this weekend and want to see you too. Not their parents of course…we are just the money machine," Danny said with a grin.

"They are no longer teenagers, Daniel. The twins would be horrified to hear you say that. We will be celebrating their twenty-first birthdays. Where has the time gone?" Frances winked at her husband.

"Well, ladies, I have a conference call with Washington in fifteen minutes. How about tonight we go out and have a lavish meal at David Toutain's? It's on me." Danny grinned.

"Well, I'm for that. It's one of the most lavish restaurants in Paris. Have you already made reservations because you can't turn up on spec," Frances said, smiling.

"Absolutely. See you in a couple of hours." Danny strode away toward the main house.

Neither women spoke for a few moments.

Frances felt her mother's hand squeeze hers. "He has never changed from the moment you brought him home for the first time. He has been the most genuine person I have ever met in my life. I'm glad for you, darling."

"I'm very lucky that I was able to see the measure of the man when I was eighteen. It would have been so easy to pass him over as too intense back then. Do you remember I was dating Tony Montgomery at the time?"

"Do I remember that football jockey?"

They both laughed.

†

Christen deposited her jacket and purse on the hall table of her apartment and then entered her living area, throwing herself on the bright red sofa. The leather groaned at the sudden weight. Kicking off her shoes, she closed her eyes. It had been one hell of day.

Her doorbell pealed.

"For God's sake, can't I have any peace?" she grumbled before standing and going to the door. She took a quick glance through the security spyglass before she opened the door. "What the hell, David."

"Hey, that's no way to speak to your favorite brother." David grinned before holding up the carryout.

The distinct aroma of Chinese food soothed Christen's irritation. "I hope you have king prawns."

David chuckled. "Absolutely."

"I'll let you in then." Christen moved back toward the living area. "You know where everything is," she said before sinking back down on the sofa.

"I most certainly do. Dinner will be served in a thrice."

"In a what?"

David laughed. "It's an old English term, probably got it in the wrong context, but I liked the sound of it. It's better than in a jiffy."

Christen rolled her eyes. "Yeah, whatever."

Five minutes later they were tearing apart the two bags of food that David brought.

As they began to consume the food, David waved his chopsticks in the air. "How many this time?"

"Do you want to know?"

"Yes," David said, sadly.

"A third of the staff, and we had to let people go who had been working for us for years. Right now, I hate Hank." Christen sank her teeth into a king prawn, the garlic sauce bursting onto her tongue.

"He says it's for the good of the company, Christen. Is he right?"

"Hey, it's mid-October and Christmas is around the corner not to mention Thanksgiving. Have you ever known a time when we haven't had to employ extra staff for that time period? He is wrong, big-time. Damn him, David. He doesn't have to see these people lose their livelihoods."

David put down his chopsticks, reached across, and touched her hand. "You don't have to do it either. We have a personnel department for that."

"You sound like Hank."

"Hey, I take exception to that remark. I have much better taste in women and looks."

"It isn't funny, David. A member of the Jamison family should be there when we destroy their lives." Christen placed her chopsticks precariously on top of a carton.

David gave her a caged look. "Christen, one of the things I love about you is that you care so much about our employees. It is a business, though, and things like this have to happen. It happened in Dad's time too."

Christen considered her brother's statement. Had it happened with their dad? *Maybe, but not like this. Something didn't sit right.* "Perhaps. Anyway, tomorrow we have the final ones to go. The woman's department is next up."

David choked on his food. "The woman's department…who?"

"What does it matter?" Christen picked up a prawn cracker and munched on it.

"It doesn't I guess," David sheepishly answered.

They continued their meal both lost in thought. At least Christen knew she was. David, on the other hand, was eating as if he wasn't sure of a meal tomorrow. He'd always been the same crazy kid when it came to food.

"Today there was a woman who broke down in front of the panel. I didn't know her, but I got the feeling that she didn't do that sort of thing. Her partner had just kicked her out of their apartment and within twenty-four hours she had lost her job too. How do you come back from that, David?

We've been fortunate. Even if Hank sacks us, we have a little set aside for a rainy day and we still have some financial resources. This woman doesn't have anything…at least not that I know of." Christen sighed.

"Speak for yourself. I'm mortgaged to the hilt. However, some people never get a decent break. It sounds like that woman certainly needs one." David shrugged.

"She'd worked for the store for fifteen years, was a great worker, never any trouble. Always on time and never sick. Tell me, David, how did she end up on the list?" Christen stood and walked over to the window that overlooked the main road. *It's vibrant here and it makes me feel alive. I need that, especially tonight.*

David went to his sister and placed an arm around Christen's shoulders. "I love you, sis, and it will all work out…even for that unfortunate woman."

Christen looked at her brother and gave him a tight smile. "Strange thing was I met her this morning and shared an elevator with her. How ironic is that."

"The world works in mysterious ways, Christen. Maybe this is fate telling the woman to move on to new and better pastures." David shrugged.

"Perhaps."

"Come on, let's finish our meal and then we can discuss your predicament with Mom coming home," David said.

†

Laurel took comfort in the hug she received from Carol and snuffled as her nose began to run in competition with the moisture flowing from her eyes.

"You can stay here as long as you need, Laurel. Jacs won't mind." Carol brushed aside Laurel's bangs and gave her a smile.

"I can't." The words caught in her mouth.

"Yes, you can. In fact, I'm going to go and see Ronnie. She is so wrong in what she did and you should be compensated. I bet you kept her for years."

Laurel held up her hand. "No! Please, Carol. I want nothing from Ronnie. This is my mess and I'll take care of it." Laurel blew into a tissue.

"But…"

Laurel gave Carol a sharp glance.

"Okay. What about your friends? Are any of them in the same boat?"

Laurel nodded. "Some, although they are not good friends. I only have one of those and she is safe for the moment. I guess they decided to get rid of most of the old faces and keep the younger ones around."

"If I didn't know you better, Laurel, I'd say you sound bitter."

"Maybe I am." She sighed.

Carol lifted her chin and gazed at her. "I've known you for five years, ever since you moved into the apartment. Things haven't always been a ray of sunshine but you never let it get you down. Remember when Jacs broke her leg and she was stuck in the apartment for a month? You came around every day to cheer her up. If you hadn't I doubt we would have been together now," Carol said, withdrawing her hand.

"Yes you would. You love each other—everyone can see that. Besides this is a little different." Laurel bit the inside of her lip.

Laurel walked around the living area that doubled as a kitchen. It was beautifully decorated in low-key but earthy colors, giving the impression of more space. The pots and pans all matched in a vibrant green and there was an old-style stainless steel kettle on the stovetop. She swiveled around and caught Carol's eyes.

"I'll get a reasonable severance package. That's what the Dragon woman said while I was having my meltdown. It will keep me for a few months. I can contribute to the rent and essentials until I find a new place." Laurel gave a tremulous smile.

Carol shook her head. "Forget about the rent and stuff. As far as we are concerned you are a guest in our home."

Laurel's heart swelled at the generosity of her friend. She knew they were comfortable but not rich. If they were they would live somewhere else. Having someone sponge off you indefinitely wouldn't be in the budget. She didn't intend on doing that and she planned on job hunting the next day. "You are a wonderful friend I'll pay you back when I can. You know that right?" Laurel held her breath. *I'd know if she is giving me lip service out of charity.*

"Your friendship has been worth its weight in gold. Jacs and I are more than happy to help. Now let's see what to have for dinner. We can always have carryout if you don't like what I have to offer. Jacs does all the cooking, not that we do much around here."

Laurel laughed and it felt good to have her face crease into something more than a frown. It was just what she needed. "I'll cook, it's the least I can do."

Carol grinned. "I was hoping you'd say that. Your cooking is to die for. I don't think I've ever tasted food as good outside a Michelin star restaurant. Maybe that's something you could look into for the future?"

Laurel smiled. "Maybe I will." She picked up the kettle and filled it. "Want to give me the rundown on the provisions on hand."

"Absolutely." Carol sauntered up to the kitchen, walked behind the counter, and then opened up several cupboards on the wall.

"Wow, and you don't cook much?" Laurel's gaze took in the array of provisions. *I can cook for an army with this lot.*

"Not my forte, now tell me, I'm fascinated with who *the Dragon woman* is." Carol slid onto a barstool tucked under the granite-topped counter.

"Oh, she suits her name perfectly. Her name is Christen Jamison and she's the financial director of the store. Even when I broke down her expression remained calm, telling me what my severance package would be. Talk about uncaring!" Laurel fumed. *How cruel was life that on that day she met the woman twice.*

"Oh, nasty lady. At least you won't have to see her again. I take it she's a relative of the owners?"

"Her dad owned the company. I'm not sure how the inheritance worked when he died but you don't see a Jamison on the firing list. All I heard is that she has a reputation as being a cold bitch…now I know for sure that's true." Laurel had the image of light brown eyes staring at her when she entered the personnel office. She shivered.

"Typical nepotism. I bet people like that never have the problems we do. Enough of dragon woman. Dare I inquire as to what you will be teasing my taste buds with this evening?" Carol grinned.

Laurel glanced at the provisions and spied her favorite quick meal. "Lasagna Ella vegetarian."

Carol frowned and Laurel laughed. “You have pasta sheets and lots of veggies in cans. Tomorrow we’ll talk fresh produce and meat. It’ll be my treat,” Laurel said forcefully.

Carol scrunched her eyes and then nodded. “This once. Jacs is back tomorrow night, we will say in her honor.”

“Yes, we will.” Laurel selected cans and a pack of pasta and began her preparations.

Chapter Four

"Jamison Department Store, the dream of Carlton Jamison, fresh out of the army, began life as a small haberdashery in 1948. His inexperience in the trade was outclassed by his savvy manipulation of people coupled with the need to be the best at whatever he put his hand to. His war experiences set him in good stead for stories to keep would-be investors—both male and female—happy. In 1952, at the age of thirty, he had increased his holdings. Carlton invested wisely and by the midfifties he was ready to take over the most prestigious store in Chester, owned by the Ridge's, the most prominent family in the area. It wasn't just the store he wanted. Their eldest daughter, Samantha, at eighteen, was the belle of society. Carlton used all the charm he could muster to win her over. They married in 1961 and had four children. At the birth of their first child, the store was renamed Jamison's Department Store in 1963."

Samantha listened intently as Isabella Delfosse, her secretary, repeated the story about how Samantha came to marry Carlton.

"Thank you, Isabella."

"Do you wish to continue today or shall we return to this tomorrow?"

Samantha thought about that for a few moments. "Perhaps we will continue on my return. Are you looking forward to going to the United States?"

Isabella shrieked, "Can't wait. I'm so excited. It will be the prefect trip before I return to the University in three months' time."

Samantha smiled. She supposed a trip to another country would be exciting, though Chester wasn't exactly New York City. Still it is a change.

"I'm very glad you are able to accompany me, my dear. What would I do without my Isabella at my side?" Samantha heard a shy chuckle and nodded slowly with a smile creasing her lips.

†

Autumn in Ridgeway Park was a colorful collection of oranges, browns, and deep greens. Leaves from deciduous trees fell to form a carpet so deep that feet nestled into the organic matter as it would a luxurious wool pile. Tangled branches naked to the afternoon sun basked in their freedom. A park bench with a brass plaque in dedication to a couple called Pearl and Roy Feather settled naturally among the trees.

Laurel kicked a few leaves around as she walked through them and smiled. It reminded her of walking through this park as a child with her parents. So vivid was the image she could have been forgiven for thinking it real. It wasn't. Back then she recalled only happy times. Her parents had always been willing to help someone else worse off than them. A memory invaded her from her teenage years when she was bullied at school by a rich kid…

"Laurel, love, we all have to live together. You can't go around saying you want to kill someone."

"Dad, she bullies me. Do you approve of that? Bet you don't care," Laurel pouted.

"I do, but there are better ways to handle people like that, love. Will you let me handle it?"

"I can handle it. I will look like a loser if I let my parents intervene."

Her dad laughed and his round face began to glow. It always reminded her of the pictures of Santa Claus's face.

"Trust me, love, you will have many years to look after yourself. Why not let your old dad do this for you? I promise not to embarrass you."

"Do you promise?"

"Cross my heart and hope to die."

"You are so dramatic, Dad. Sure go ahead."

Laurel felt tears prick as she sat down on the bench.

"I'm sorry, Dad, that we don't see eye to eye these days. It wasn't my fault Mom died so why can't you talk to me about her? Why can't you just talk to me? I'm still alive," she whispered, staring ahead. Her vision was obscured by tears as she looked down the path to see someone walking toward her.

She snuffled and reached inside her pocket to retrieve a handkerchief. Blowing hard onto the cotton she ignored the fact that she sounded like a trumpet. Laurel couldn't believe when the person sat on the bench.

The person cleared their throat and Laurel looked sideways in that direction. Through shimmering tears, she gasped. *No. Not her. Not here.*

"I'm sorry."

The words floated between them at the same time as a shower of leaves did in the breeze. A few settling on the bench between them.

"I'd rather not discuss it," Laurel said quietly. *Un-frickin' believable. Is she dogging every step in my life since I met her?*

"Fair enough. Do you mind if I sit a little longer?"

Laurel waved her hand at Christen Jamison, who looked so out of place in a pin-striped pantsuit in the middle of a half-deserted park. "Please yourself, it's a free country."

Laurel wanted to get up and run away but her pride forced her to stay.

"Do you come here often?" Christen asked.

"It's a free country to sit here but I don't have to converse with you. You said enough yesterday," Laurel's voice raised sharply. She looked at a couple of teenagers walking hand in hand toward them.

"I'm sorry."

"You said that already. Are you a broken record?" Laurel gave a heavy sigh and looked at Christen, who appeared surprised at her response. "You did your job. I no longer work for the company. Therefore, as far as I'm concerned, you are a complete stranger to me. When I was a kid my dad said never speak to strangers. I figure in your case he was right." Laurel stood and squared her shoulders. "I'll make one exception because my parents told me to be polite. Have a nice day." Laurel strode off.

As she reached the gated exit to the park Laurel realized she was headed the wrong way. "No way am I going back that way," she seethed.

Two blocks later she came across a small bakery and in the window was a flyer—*Assistant Wanted, Apply Within.* Maybe the universe was listening.

Laurel opened the door to the tiny establishment and sucked in the beautiful aromas of freshly baked breads. *Oh, I love this already.*

A woman in a floral apron and the most gorgeous blue eyes she'd ever seen in her life grinned at her. "What can I do for you, love?"

Laurel smiled. "This place is wonderful. Why have I missed it? I used to frequent Ridgeway Park at least three times a week."

"Oh, we are tucked away, love. It takes some finding. What can I tempt you with?"

Dare she say…no. Oh God, what a wuss. Maybe this is what the universe had planned for her now. "I need a job," she blurted out.

"Really. Do you have any experience in baking?"

Laurel frowned. "Not professionally. People say I'm a great domestic cook. I can provide examples if you want."

"Sounds interesting. I'm Maisey Clayton and I own the bakery. What are you doing right now?"

"Nothing, Maisey. I was fired as of yesterday and I need to find work quickly. Bills to pay and finding a new place to stay" Laurel shrugged.

Maisey smiled. "Let's grab you an apron, because in about," Maisey looked at her watch, "half an hour I will be rushed off my feet. Want to help?"

Laurel nodded vigorously. "Wonderful, I hate not having anything to do."

Maisey laughed. "You might regret that." She handed Laurel a pristine white apron. "Now, young lady, what is your name?"

"Laurel Harley Rogers at your service." Laurel took the apron and donned it.

"Parents wanted a Harley in their lives?"

Laurel chuckled. "Yep, but they settled with me." She winked.

"Then, young Harley, that's what I will call you."

Laurel smiled. "My mom used to call me that…she was the only one."

†

Christen sat on the bench in Ridgeway Park wondering how the hell fate had managed to have her there at the same time as someone she'd fired the day before. It was crazy. One thing she instinctively knew by the short acquaintance with the woman was that she wouldn't be out of a job long. She appeared to be the get-on-with-the-future type, complete with a positive vibe, which defied the negative stuff happening to her, even if she had broken down at the meeting.

Wanting to cry, Christen bent and placed her head in her hands. She didn't cry, instead she drew in a deep breath, lifting her head sharply as someone spoke.

"Ms. Jamison, I didn't know you came to the park at lunchtime?"

Christen looked at the woman who spoke but didn't recognize her. *She must be an employee*. Now why didn't she think that it might be a personal acquaintance? *Ah right. I don't go anywhere to have a personal life outside the office.* "It's nice here," Christen lamely answered.

The woman grinned. "Yes it is. I used to have lunch sometimes with a colleague and friend…"

The trailing off was the big black flag to Christen. "She doesn't work for Jamison anymore I take it?"

"Yes. It was a shock. She had an exemplary record. Had worked at the store since high school. I guess I was lucky today."

"How so?" Christen's interest was piqued.

"I work in the women's department and our department was earlier today. I wasn't called. I heard they were going on to the men's department this afternoon."

Christen was puzzled.

"You know who I am yet you seem quite happy to talk to me, though your friend was fired. I have to say I find that odd? Do you mind if I ask you your name?"

"Andrea Forrester. Laurel Rogers is my friend. You probably don't remember her. I have always thought she was too good for Jamison's. I think this is her big break. Sorry, but she's talented so I never understood her keeping the job."

Christen warmed to the woman in a strange way. "I see. Perhaps we should have a ballot in the future."

Andrea grinned. "You wouldn't listen. Not even your reports make a difference. I should be out of door with a flea in my ear for my lateness. Laurel hasn't been late in fifteen years. If you check, she has the perfect record and you still kicked her out. Makes me wonder what message you are giving."

Christen refrained from answering. She was going to find out just what Hank was up to because this didn't stack. "Business is business, I've found. Good to know you, Andrea. Perhaps we will see each other again."

"Oh, I doubt it, unless you personally seek me out or we meet here. Have a great day." Andrea stood and walked away.

Christen pondered what the woman had said. "When I get back, I am going to check on exactly why Laurel Rogers had to go."

†

Christen struck the door of the personnel manager's office with a hefty blow, regretting it the minute the pain from her hand reached her brain. Still with a resourceful determination, she didn't wait for a reply but opened the door and entered.

"Ms. Jamison!" Carl Sylvester exclaimed.

A young man, otherwise unseen in the room, scooted around the desk and, red-faced, stared at Christen.

"Hope I'm not interrupting anything, Carl?"

"No. No, of course not, but I wasn't expecting you for another hour. You always keep to schedule."

Christen gazed at Carl. He was great at his job or so she had thought in the past. Right now he had questions to answer. "Who is this?" Christen flicked her gaze at the young man who seemed decidedly uncomfortable.

"Oh, this is nobody. Get out now. I need to speak with Ms. Jamison," Carl barked.

Christen watched the younger man's reaction. He obviously wasn't happy but fled nonetheless. As the door shut behind him, Christen sat opposite Carl, and then contemplated her nails. "Nobody, huh. How are Claire and the children. You've just added a new addition, I hear," Christen remarked blandly.

Carl flushed. "What can I do for you, Christen?"

"I want to know how a candidate for termination is chosen." Christen stared at Carl who frowned.

"We use a tried-and-tested formula. You have never asked this before."

"True. If I give you a few names can you go through the process." Christen gave Carl a sweet smile. "For my education. My brother tells me often enough that I don't understand the business properly."

Carl shrugged. "Sure, give me the names."

Christen gave Carl three names from the day before.

They went through the process and all seemed reasonable. Bad time keeping, last in first out, bad record, all the ticks in the box.

"What about Laurel Rogers?"

Carl blinked rapidly and flicked over a few pages before he frowned. "Same."

"Same? Enlighten me, Carl?" Christen smiled.

Carl wavered and clasped his hands together. "Well, she…"

"She what, Carl? Had an exemplary service record, no black marks, never late, had worked for the company for years. Tell me, Carl, how was she chosen or has everyone in that department or the store for that matter, worked there for over fifteen years?"

Carl pulled at his shirt collar. "No. There are many people who have limited time at the store and even the department…"

Christen heard panic in his voice. "How many more are there in this unique category, Carl?" Christen stood and loomed over the man.

Carl gazed at the papers in front of him and then gulped. "Your brother wanted us to let go of some of the older employees at each termination session. That way, over a period of time, we will have only short-term employees."

Christen grimaced and balled her hands. "How long has this been going on?"

Carl cleared his throat. "The last four years."

"How many of our employees are long-standing, statistical wise?"

"After this round maybe twenty percent, maximum."

I hate you, Hank. Christen held her temper and drew back her head. "How long have you worked here, Carl?"

"Fifteen years in December. Why?" Carl frowned.

Christen headed for the door and then turned back. "Guess you will probably be in the next round…maybe even this one." She opened the door and left. Christen grinned as she heard an audible gasp before the door shut behind her. Carl was going to have one hell of a day, especially since his new boy toy wasn't happy with him either. *Life works in mysterious ways.* She chuckled as she headed for her office.

Chapter Five

Club Eighty was the only place in town to be on a Saturday night if you were a nightclubbing lesbian. Even if you were straight it worked. Laurel rolled her eyes as Carol and Jacs pushed her forward into the foray of bodies that jived, pushed, and groped their way inside the crammed club.

Music pulsed from the fabric of the building.

"I love this song. Sam Smith is awesome," Carol shouted above the noise.

Laurel had to agree; Sam Smith was great. She listened as he sang, "Leave Your Lover" and became entranced in the song.

She looked around and bodies that had previously been gyrating now closed into each other with barely a space between them.

"Hey, guys, go dance. This is your record for sure. I'll get the drinks."

Carol and Jacs grinned and headed off to the dance floor.

Laurel finally pushed her way through the crowd and found a minute spot at the bar. She hoped that one of the bartenders would see her, and to her great fortune an argument erupted with the couple next to her. Two bartenders appeared immediately.

"Break it up, girls. It's a party night not fight night."

Laurel smiled. She discreetly observed the muscular bartender who could make two of the fighting couple. There was no way they wouldn't comply except they were oblivious to anything else around them. They continued to argue and this time a glass broke.

"That's it, girls. You are out of here."

Almost as soon as the words were spoken a woman bouncer, who looked like she'd gone ten rounds with Tyson, appeared.

Moments later, the girls were hauled off under protest and Laurel assumed they were ejected from the club.

"What can I get you?"

Laurel smiled. "Great work. I…three Buds please."

"Three, hmm, my lucky number." The bartender winked and left to get the drinks.

What seemed like only seconds later three bottles slid along the glass bar. Laurel nearly freaked as she stopped them just before they took a dive off the edge. "Thanks." Laurel reached inside her pocketbook and brought out her billfold. She paid for the drinks and gave a three-dollar tip. She looked at the bartender's hand, a hand that would have looked masculine on most women but actually suited her build. There was a rose tattoo spread across the knuckles, winding around the fingers in blue and red, interesting more than attractive. "Nice tat," Laurel remarked with a smile.

"Thanks. I can recommend the parlor if you need…"

"Oh, no. I'm fine," Laurel shrugged, "not really my thing."

"Pity." Light green eyes surveyed her and Laurel had to admit she didn't feel creeped out about it like she had in the past with Ronnie's weird friends. "If I change my mind I know where to find you." Laurel sucked in a silent breath.

"I'm Laurel. I haven't been in here for years…well at least three." There was a deep chuckle in response and the hairs on the back of Laurel's neck stood upright. *I like that sound, it's sexy.*

"Three is a long time, I'll be back—work."

Laurel smiled as she watched the woman serve the customers, observing her huge grin that was in perfect symmetry to everything else about her.

"Hey, you look miles away," Jacs said as she slapped Laurel on the back before sitting next to her.

For a few seconds Laurel was taken aback at her friend's return. "I bought Bud. Is that okay?"

"Perfect. Wow, is it hot on that dance floor." Jac swished her blond hair away from her face as she took a swig from the bottle.

"Is that the music, people around you, or Carol?" Laurel wriggled her eyebrows.

Jacs chuckled. "All, but Carol will always be hot, even when she's in her nineties and wants me to push her around."

Laurel considered the words spoken freely and without hesitation. She wanted someone to love her like that. Maybe she still had time. "Where is the love of your life?"

"Oh, she met a friend from work. They are doing what I call sorting out the world's problems or at least those at Stephens and Company," Jacs said before taking a drink of her beer.

"How long has she been at the firm?" Laurel asked.

"Hmm, let me think now. Seven years. She won't tell you this but she's being put forward for a partnership. She will be the youngest female ever to make it in that firm."

Laurel's eyes grew wide.

"I know, awesome, right?" Jacs grinned. "My dad will definitely want her in the family once she gets that."

"Your dad doesn't approve?" Laurel was surprised.

Jacs laughed. "Pop Stan, who you've met, loves Carol. He's my stepdad for the record. My parents divorced when I was ten. Daddy Welch is a high-achiever, corporate type. Nothing short of a partnership in a law firm is good enough for his only child."

"Oh." Laurel was sure her mouth struggled to close.

"Hey, it's fine, Laurel. My baby takes everything on the chin and still comes back for more. That's love for you." Jacs drained her bottle. "Right, let's get another." She turned to the bar and lifted her arm to signal for service.

A different bartender arrived and took the order. Laurel was disappointed and guzzled her beer.

"Sorry guys, you know how it is when you meet someone from work…" Carol trailed off. Giving Laurel a guilty look and a wink to her partner.

"I know exactly," Laurel responded.

"Drink. I need a drink. Didn't you think it was hot on that dance floor? They need more air con," Carol said.

"You now have two," Jacs said, pointing to the beers on the bar. She drew her partner toward her. "I love you."

Laurel's cheeks burned at the simple show of affection. In all her time with Ronnie that had never happened. Ronnie said it was bad for her image to show public affection—she knew why now.

"Hey, now I know who the three are. Excellent choice of friends. Jacs, you haven't been here for eons?" the original bartender said as she grinned at Jacs.

Laurel went bright red.

"Fifi, you are such a liar. We came here two months ago…you must have been away," Jacs said before throwing her arms around the bartender and kissing her cheek.

Carol chuckled and Laurel watched in fascination. *Fifi...doesn't compute for this woman.*

"Laurel, this is my old college friend, Fiona Bruce. Fifi and I shared a room for four years and it nearly killed us," Jacs said, laughing.

"You know I hate that name," Fiona said.

"I know, that's why I call you it." Jacs grinned.

Fiona laughed and the sound sent tingles down Laurel's body.

"I'm off at midnight. Any chance you are staying and we can catch up?" Fiona asked.

"What do you think, girls?" Jacs asked.

Carol winked in the direction of Fiona.

Then they all looked at Laurel.

"I guess that's fine with me…except I need to get up at six," Laurel said sheepishly.

"Hey, who knows, you might be so entranced with our company that you don't go to bed." Fiona winked and then left to attend the bar.

"It's a small world," Laurel lamely said.

"You don't have to stay, Laurel. I'll come back with you and leave Jacs and Fifi to chat about old times." Carol smiled.

"She's staying, right, Laurel?" Jacs asked.

"Yeah, I'm staying." Laurel decided she was going to be decadent for the first time in years.

Jacs stood. "Let's go, girls, the dance floor is waiting for us."

†

Laurel hung onto the leather-clad body of her ride to the bakery. It was five forty-five when the Triumph Tiger

800 smoothly set her next to her work building. Laurel pulled off the helmet and shook her head.

"Too much?"

Laurel chuckled. "Nope, it was awesome. I've never been on a motorbike before. Thank you."

"My pleasure. How about coffee tomorrow?" Fiona shrugged. "I won't say today. By the time you've done your shift with no sleep you'll be exhausted."

Laurel smiled. "Strangely, I don't feel tired but you are probably right about later. Where and when tomorrow?"

"I'd have normally said here but as you work here…which incidentally I'm surprised as I've never noticed you here. I come here often, it's simply the best in town. Do you know Van Clefs on Eighth?"

"No, but I'll find it. What time?"

"What time do you finish?"

"Four. I'm on probation. I only started yesterday. My new boss said if it works out I can take over the apartment above the store. The current tenant moves out in two weeks. "

Fiona laughed. "Well, in that case. I have a day off tomorrow, you tell me."

Laurel grinned. "Six okay?"

Fiona winked and revved the bike. "Tomorrow at six, I'll look forward to it." She waved and then sped off down the street.

"Oh, my God, I've got a date. Is it too early after Ronnie—to hell with Ronnie, she's the past." Bemusedly Laurel walked toward the bakery.

†

Christen sat at the same bench she had for the last three months, a ritual she had assumed after her meeting with Laurel Rogers. The woman's predicament had awakened her at last to what she was becoming—an automaton at her brother's behest. Her eyes cast around the park. Icy patches could still be seen under dense foliage where the weak winter sun hadn't managed to work its charm and melt the cold crystals. Trees barren of their leaves looked majestic in a stark kind of way.

She leaned to the left and traced a finger across the name on the plaque. One day I'm going to find out just who Pearl and Roy Feather are. *One day. That's all I seem to say to myself these days.*

Taking out the brown paper bag Barry had given her prior to leaving her office, she glanced inside and smiled. Then pulled out the chicken mayo wrap and unraveled the cellophane wrapper. It looked appetizing as always. Barry never let her down in the food department. Seconds later she bit into the wrap and the delicious chicken and its accompaniment filled her mouth and tantalized her taste buds.

She rummaged in the bag for the small carton of orange juice and took a sip. Then leaned back on the bench and relaxed her tense muscles. However much she allowed her body to relax her mind still worked overtime and on top of the list of things that stressed her was—Mom.

She sipped more of the juice and then scrunched up her face. Reaching inside her pocketbook she took out a small container and drew out two white tablets. Quickly placing them on her tongue she washed them down with the last of the juice. Grimacing she took another bite of her lunch and smiled. The sound of boots crunching on the crisp surface had Christen looking in that direction. She grinned and nodded.

"Christen, nice to see you today. Are you keeping warm?"

Christen smiled. "Overcoat, wool scarf and thick cotton trousers along with boots…absolutely." She pointed to each garment. "You look happy today, Patrick. Did your numbers come up on the lotto?"

"Aye and it would be a miracle if they did as I don't waste money on that kind of gamble." Officer Patrick Armstrong winked and stopped in front of her.

Christen glanced at the police officer whom she'd met over two months ago. He had asked how she was and before long they struck up a conversation. It was almost a daily ritual for them to pass the time together for a few minutes during the work week. "With five children I suspect that money would be tight," Christen said.

"Bless them, they are worth every cent. Now, how is your day so far?" He stared at Christen, his cool blue eyes in contrast to the warmth of the look he gave her.

"Nothing new, just the usual. What about yourself? Any plans for your day off tomorrow?"

Patrick shook his head. "Special time with my lovely lady and the youngest."

Christen smiled. "Always good to be with the ones you love when you can."

"Aye it is. Right, must be going or I'll be called slowpoke by the boss. See you on Thursday, Christen." He tipped his hand to his hat and walked away.

Christen consumed the rest of her lunch and sighed. *Time to go back to the madhouse.* She stood and walked toward the gate leading to the sidewalk across from the store.

Chapter Six

The cold sniffed at Laurel's face and traveled to find a way inside her warmly clothed body. It failed. Huddling into her overcoat she grinned, the tingles of the lovemaking from the night before providing extra heat.

The bus she took to the bakery had broken down three blocks from her destination. Her boss Maisey had called her on her day off telling her she was sick and needed help. Alighting from the bus she headed to the park entrance since it was the quickest way to the shop. Her eyes took in the beauty of winter; its stark and naked display of nature. Walking quickly, she crossed the park, slowing unconsciously as she looked over the railings to Jamison's store.

"God, has it been three months. It seems like a lifetime," she whispered.

Her steps seemed to, by their own volition, head toward the bench where she and Andrea used to have lunch most days. In the distance she saw a woman. "Oh no, it couldn't be her again." As she came closer the woman seated on the bench stood.

"Not who you were expecting." The stranger grinned. "Hope your friend turns up." The woman gave Laurel a smile and continued her journey.

Laurel smiled weakly. She wasn't expecting to see anyone. *Well maybe...darn her.*

Sitting in the vacant spot Laurel contemplated all the scenarios she had thought about if she ever met Ms. Jamison again. Then it dawned on her. "I was so insignificant in the big picture she probably doesn't even remember me." She hung her head. A few moments later she valiantly rose to meet the cold breeze that had suddenly whipped around her. "She's not going to spoil my day. The Jamisons and all they stand for no longer control my life." With her head held high, she headed toward the gate that would take her to better things.

†

There was a commotion outside her office. Frowning, Christen moved from her contemplation of the park below and popped her head out of her door. Fully expecting to see Barry, she was surprised when David stood there with his arms folded in that 'I'm only doing what I want' stance he'd had since he was a kid. Opposite him was a woman, one she vaguely recognized but could not quite recall.

"Is there a problem?"

David glared at her and lowered his bottom lip. It was another facet from his childhood when he wanted to be petulant about something. "No, it's my business," David replied before switching his gaze to the other woman in the room.

"Really? In my assistant's office. You work on the next floor, David. If you have issues with an employee take it to your office not mine." Christen snorted and allowed her eyes to travel over the woman who was definitely familiar but...*Ah, yes I remember her now.*

"I wanted to speak with you, Ms. Jamison."

Christen was intrigued. "About what?"

"Isn't your business, sis, leave it alone. Andrea doesn't understand how things work around here," David blustered.

"I do too! You are way too arrogant, David. Typical. I knew you would chicken out at the last minute. It's what you've been doing since I met you three years ago. I thought this would be different this time around." Andrea threw her hands in the air and headed to the door.

David moved like lightning and placed his larger hand over Andrea's to prevent her from opening the door.

Christen watched as David whispered something to her that she wasn't close enough to hear. Andrea's body seemed to relax as she turned and looked at David. "Promise?"

He nodded and smiled.

Well, she's suckered now. That smile has charmed every woman he's used it on since he was out of diapers. Christen waited. "Are we done here?" Christen asked, breaking the awkward silence.

Andrea gave her a shamefaced nod. "Sorry for the intrusion, Ms. Jamison. It won't happen again."

"Yes, sis, it won't. Look, Andrea, go back to work. We will talk about this later. I promise," David said.

Andrea nodded and left the room.

"Do I get an explanation? You made a lot of promises there?"

David ran a hand through his hair and touched the graying sideburns. "A misunderstanding."

Christen nodded and moved into the room fully and walked up to her brother. "Why did she want to see me?" At his sheepish look she wagged her finger. "Don't bother to lie to me, David. We both know it never washes. Out with it."

"It's complicated." David sighed.

"Then uncomplicate it for me. I'm beginning to realize that we Jamison's have an aptitude for complications when the easy way would be so much better."

"Where's the fun in life being easy," David replied with an impish grin.

Christen drew in a slow breath and exhaled. "I don't know about you, David, but I'm tired of beating about the bush and being something that I'm not. Now spill. Tell me what the problem with Andrea Forrester is and we can go about our day."

"You know her? Have you spoken before?" David asked.

"Actually, yes, but to save you further questions, not well. So what's the problem?"

"Mom," David said and pulled her into a hug.

Christen knew in the work environment she should repel his familiar touch of comfort but decided to ignore Hank's protocol. "She's one of the problems, now tell me about Andrea."

"Oh it's nothing. Andrea was working on an idea for a sales collection. She thought you had more power than I did and could get it to her superior through you."

Christen smiled inwardly. Her philandering brother was a great liar normally. He'd had to be with his womanizing past. This was pathetic.

"That's crap, David, and we both know it. You have one more chance to salvage this or I will talk with her myself and find out the truth."

David ran a hand around the pale purple collar of his shirt.

"I know you like this woman, David. In fact, it must be the first one I can actually say I'd approve of." Christen smiled as David's previous shifty look turned to one of surprise.

"She's beautiful isn't she, Christen. I think I love her," he announced with pride.

Christen laughed. "Good for you, David, but I'd say that with more clarity. Especially to her. You do love her, not think it."

David shrugged but the biggest grin she had ever seen on her brother's face made her heart pound in happiness for him.

"Will you come over to Andrea's for dinner tomorrow night? I know it's short notice and I was supposed to ask you three weeks ago but...sorry." David shrugged.

Taken aback at the invitation, Christen wasn't sure how to reply. "Am I supposed to bring a date?" *Hell, why did I say that.*

David grinned.

"Sis, just having you at dinner will be enough. Unless, of course, you've found someone since we chatted last week?" David winked.

"No. Give me the details and I will be there. What time?"

David jumped three feet off the ground and pumped his arm in the air. "Yes," he shouted.

Christen raised her eyebrows.

"Seven and I'll pick you up. You are the best, Christen, no matter what other people say about you." He kissed her cheek and left the room.

Christen stood there and frowned. "I can just imagine what other people say about me." She shook her head and entered her office.

†

Andrea Forrester fussed around the table set for six and clasped her hands together. *It will work, it will; it has to. I love him too much to let him down.*

The doorbell sounded and Andrea glanced around her apartment one more time before she went to the door and looked out of the spy hole. She grinned and opened the door wide.

"Laurel, you're early, this is great. You can tell me if everything looks good." Andrea hugged her friend.

"It always looks good. You should open a restaurant," Laurel said. "By the way, dessert as promised. Maisey wasn't up to it but I managed to come up with one of my grandmother's recipes for an exotic chocolate truffle tart."

"You are the best. What would I do without you?" Andrea smiled at Laurel.

Laurel laughed. "Hopefully you will never have to find out for a long, and I mean long, time."

Andrea laughed. "Yep, you and me, sharing anecdotes when we are in our eighties. Sorry Fiona couldn't come. Was she called in for an emergency shift?"

"Not sure, she just said something came up. It's too young a relationship right now for me to demand an explanation. Next time for sure she promised," Laurel answered.

There was a subtle note in Laurel's voice that Andrea picked up on. It reminded her of how she used to explain away Ronnie's absences and now she knew why they were never good.

"Look, no problem, but you know I think you could do better." She watched Laurel frown. "Sorry, I know I have been secretive about Dave. Tonight's the first night for a lot of people to meet him. My parents included." Andrea laughed at Laurel's raised eyebrows. "It was never the right time, Laurel. Tonight I know will be just perfect for everyone."

The doorbell rang.

"Can you answer that, Laurel. It's probably Dave and his sister. I need to check on the roast." Andrea headed off to the kitchen. "I'm crossing every goddamn toe and digit on my person for this to go okay. Please let it happen. I love him so much." Andrea sucked in a deep breath and listened as Laurel announced her parents.

A minute later her mother entered the kitchen.

"This must be one important dinner if you asked your dad to wear more than a track suit," Sandra Forrester said before hugging her daughter.

"Mom, you know it's important. He's the one for me. I just have to convince him that my parents are right for him." Andrea smiled as she looked at the roast lamb. Perfect.

"Darling, it doesn't matter about the peripheral family members, you are the most important person. If he doesn't like you, regardless of kin or friends, he shouldn't be in your life."

Andrea closed her eyes and knew deep down that her mom was right. Except sometimes, it helped that everyone got on. "Yes, I know, Mom. Please, just for me, ask Dad to behave."

Sandra chuckled softly. "Your dad has been sworn to be on his best behavior. Andrea, let's face it, you're in your late thirties. He wants grandkids." Sandra shrugged. "Can I help?"

"I'm only thirty-eight and yes, check the veggies." Andrea grinned at her mom.

The doorbell rang again and Andrea closed her eyes. *This is it. Please let it go smoothly.*

†

David fiddled with his tie for the eighth time since they had entered Andrea Forrester's building.

"The tie looks fine," Christen said. Her eyes cast around the lobby. It was old, but clean and comfortable. There was a bowl of recently cut New England asters in blue, pink, and white adorning a rather misfit clay vase on a small coffee table that looked a DIY effort. It was pleasant though.

David turned to her and wriggled his fingers. "Are you sure? I could change…" David delved into his jacket pocket and held a black tie out.

Christen shook her head. "For God's sake, David, we aren't going to a funeral are we?"

"No, absolutely not…no." He hung his head.

Christen pressed the button for the elevator, surprisingly it came within seconds. The polished doors slid open and they went inside.

"She loves you, I love you, what are you so nervous about?" Christen asked.

The elevator jerked and they both cringed.

Then she noticed the sweat on her brother's brow. Wow, he really is nervous, because he sure isn't afraid of cranky elevators.

David lifted his head and his smile was the one that could charm anyone, absolutely anyone. It had on her since they were five. "Nothing, now that you are here with me. I love you, Christen, and thank you. This means a great deal to me. I owe you big-time."

Christen laughed. "What? For going to dinner? Please. As you know anything is better than microwave food during the working week."

The elevator stopped and they stepped out. Chic but shabby was all Christen could think as they alighted the steel box. A little update in paintwork and it would rival her lobby.

David grinned and pressed the bell of the apartment immediately in front of them. “This is going to change everything I know,” David quietly said.

Christen raised her eyes. “Sure it…”

The door opened and Christen was not sure whose mouth hit the floor first. All she knew for sure was that hers was definitely inches from the pale gray carpet. The next words reassured Christen that she wasn’t the only one in shock.

Chapter Seven

"My God!" Laurel couldn't believe who was at the door. It surely had to be a nightmare since no one had this number of cruel coincidences.

"Sorry, the name is just David. Andrea has never called me that to my face, more likely the opposite." David chuckled.

Laurel stood there for a moment in stunned silence then opened the door wider. "I'm sorry. Come in, please." Laurel's hand shook as she held the door.

"Thanks, you must be Laurel." David held out his hand and she shook it limply. "Andrea has told me a lot about you. She calls you her go-to girl for everything." David shrugged. "She also told me that Jamison's had to let you go a few months ago. I hope you don't hold it against me…us." David turned and winked at his sister.

"Things happen for a reason," Laurel whispered as the siblings walked past her.

Christen Jamison gave her a guarded look. "Hello," she said quietly.

Laurel drew in a deep breath as the woman walked past her. Her nose wrinkled as the spicy perfume Christen wore wafted in her direction. The woman herself might be suspect but the perfume she was wearing smelled great on her. *I wonder what it is?*

Andrea chose that moment to appear. She rushed over to David, embracing him before kissing him.

Laurel turned away. Her friend's display of affection was a little more intense than she wanted to experience. She looked at the others in the room and saw Andrea's parents blush and Christen Jamison was actually smiling.

"Everyone, this is my David," Andrea announced, turning to face the group.

Andrea's parents smiled.

"Mom, Dad, this is David Jamison."

"I guess you didn't know the who," Christen commented quietly.

Laurel turned and was surprised to find the woman on her right less than a foot away. "No. No I didn't. She never really said anything other than he was very special…had always been special," Laurel softly replied.

"If it helps, I didn't know either. At least I knew who Andrea was. I didn't know about the relationship part until yesterday." Christen frowned and shrugged.

Laurel had the distinct impression that Christen Jamison was floundering. "Don't sweat it. Maybe next month it will all be over and he can go back to his philandering ways," Laurel harshly replied.

Christen gave Laurel a look that sent a shiver go down her spine.

"You don't agree?"

"My brother is a philanderer, or was in the past. I have a feeling that Andrea tamed him." She looked at the smiling couple. "Big-time, in my humble opinion," Christen said.

Laurel watched the woman for any evidence that she was being supercilious and didn't see any outward sign.

"Laurel, Christen, please come over here. It's a party." Andrea looked at David. "Actually it's more than that. Right David?"

David appeared uncomfortable at being put on the spot. Laurel had heard in her time at Jamison's that when big decisions had to be made he didn't want to upset anyone so he usually made a joke. Her jaw dropped at his next words.

"Everyone, Andrea has accepted my humble offer of marriage. We are engaged," David said with a grin.

At the news, screams of delight from Andrea's parents filled the room.

Laurel hugged Andrea. "Congratulations. I am so happy for you." She could feel her heart soaring in happiness when she saw Andrea's glowing expression. When she looked at David with Andrea nestled close to his side she saw pride and happiness on his face.

A few moments later, Laurel saw Christen maneuver her brother from the festivities to one side. *Bet she never expected that.* She speculated that the woman probably hated the thought that her gene pool was going to be infested with a normal working-class gal.

"I'm sorry I couldn't tell you about David," Andrea anxiously said. "He swore me to secrecy. Laurel, do you forgive me?" Her white features puckered waiting for the response.

"There's nothing to forgive, Andrea. I understand completely. Just when did you fall for him?" Laurel hugged Andrea close.

"Oh, I've loved him from a distance for years but I always thought I wasn't good enough for him. I didn't want to be a notch on his bedpost either, we dated a couple of times a few years ago but he called it off. I know it's only been a short romance but it's right, Laurel. It really is."

Laurel drew Andrea into a position so she could look directly into her eyes. "If he makes you happy then I'm happy. Now when is the wedding?"

Christen pulled David aside after his unexpected announcement. David grinned at her and she looked into his sparkling blue eyes and softly laughed. "Got to say this wasn't expected. You could have warned me."

David hugged his sister tight then released her. "Christen, this is different. I love her so much it hurts especially when I couldn't ask her over for dinner with the family. It isn't right, is it? We love who we love right? Social standing shouldn't matter."

"Hey, I approve wholeheartedly. This comes at a great time. Mom will be so caught up in your news she won't bother with me losing a partner while she's been gone."

David shook his head. "Christen, Mom has her own issues. We both know Dad was more of a cad on a rather larger order than I ever was."

"You are not a *cad* like Dad. He didn't care. David, you have done the love-them-and-leave-them but never married and left them with children without regard. Today…today I can see that you are so different around Andrea. That's how I know it is genuine." Christen pulled her brother into another hug. "Go slay the in-laws, her friend, and most important of all, Andrea," Christen whispered into his neck.

David hugged her hard. "I love you, Christen, more than anyone." David smiled at the raised eyebrow. "Okay, except for Andrea."

"Go slay the dragons, brother dear. After all, you have me to pick up the burnt pieces if necessary." Christen winked at him when he released her.

"Tie worked wonders, yes?" He flicked the tie and smirked.

Christen grinned. "Yes."

She watched David move back into the excited throng of Andrea's family and her heart went with him on his very important journey. *Good for you, brother.*

†

Laurel approached Christen, who stood to the side of the room appearing to be contemplating the contents of an almost empty glass. "It was a surprise, wasn't it?" she asked.

"For me yes…perhaps not for you."

"What do you mean by that?" Laurel bristled.

Christen shrugged. "Best friends and all."

"I had no idea. In fact, I didn't know she was even dating your brother. It came out of the blue," Laurel said, frowning.

"Perhaps you aren't the best friend you thought you were," Christen said before turning away.

Laurel grabbed her arm. "I take offense at that remark."

"Okay, go ahead and take offense, but ask yourself why you didn't know if you are such good friends?"

Laurel hated this woman for all the things she did and didn't do and every damned thing in between. "I guess I'm not the only one then. Your brother didn't tell you either. I heard you two are like twins." Retaliation could bring its own satisfaction but the stunned and hurt look on Christen's face weirdly hurt Laurel too.

"He had his reasons," Christen quietly remarked.

David clinked a glass with a spoon and both women turned their attention to him.

"This is our pre-engagement dinner. My mother is due to ascend these shores from Paris in a few days' time and I'm arranging a Jamison/Forrester family get together." David grinned at Andrea. "Yes, my love, for you."

Laurel felt like a spare part as Andrea's parents applauded the information. She moved into the kitchen and allowed the sadness of being alone to encompass her as tears pricked her eyelids. "Crap, this has been one hell of a year."

"Need any help?"

Laurel closed her eyes at the voice. What was it with the woman? She seemed to be everyplace Laurel went. "I was going to open another bottle of wine to toast the happy couple. Not that it will be champagne but…" Christen gave her a look that Laurel decided was thoughtful.

"Check the refrigerator," Christen suggested.

Laurel grimaced but did just that and lo and behold on the bottom shelf were two bottles of champagne and the good stuff too—Moet Chandon. "Good call. I suppose you…"

"No, I didn't know but I suspected. Your friend is very thorough. From my limited experience around her, she fights her corner and those of others with her," Christen said.

Laurel clenched her fist. "Did you really not know about this tonight?"

Christen shook her head. "No, I didn't."

"What if I said I didn't believe you."

"Then don't. It isn't as if I'm important in your life."

Laurel once again saw Christen flinch and the somber expression on her face touched her heart. "We might never be friends but the glasses are behind you in the cabinet. Let's enjoy this moment for the people we love." Laurel, her words surprising her, took out a bottle of champagne.

"Excellent," Christen said and turned in the direction of the glasses. "Oh, does Andrea have siblings?"

Laurel chuckled. "You want me to answer that?"

"Yes, please," Christen said.

Christen's intent gaze floored her. "An elder brother Jack and younger sister Fawn. Does that help."

"Yes, thank you. Though I'm surprised they are not here."

"Jack is stationed in the UK, a place called Lakenheath. Fawn is visiting there at the moment, Jack's English wife Sarah gave birth to their first child a month ago. Andrea's parents are due over there in a couple of weeks so this is good timing."

Laurel watched as Christen presented a row of six glasses on the counter for the champagne.

"Thank you. I appreciate the info on her siblings." She frowned. "We need a tray."

"Sure, I'll get it. Why don't you go and be with the family since Andrea is going to be part of yours soon. I'll bring in the tray." Laurel nodded in the direction of the door.

Christen gave a tight smile. "Yes, I suppose she is. Thank you."

Laurel watched her go. Christen's legs appeared to be endless. She gazed at Christen's tight backside, encased in black trousers, before reluctantly drawing her gaze back to the task at hand. It wasn't every day that you had champagne and she was going to make the most of it.

†

Christen picked up the nearest fork, a pastry one. Then flicked it against her wineglass, filled with a very nice sauvignon blanc. She applauded David's taste as always in that area. Glancing around, everyone else appeared to be drinking the California Merlot, which she was sure was also David's choice. All eyes turned to her and she cleared her throat quietly.

"As the only family here from David's side, I'd like to propose a toast. To Andrea and David, not to overuse a tried and trusted cliché, I wish you every happiness in your future and hope that your only problems are little ones. Andrea and David." She raised her glass.

The others around the table mimicked the action, with a resounding "Andrea and David."

Christen smiled at the happy couple. She wished she had a special someone in her life. It would make the life she was living worthwhile. Right now all she did was to eat, work, and sleep. *What a life.*

Unaware she was being observed, Christen suddenly looked across the table at Laurel Rogers. The woman's gray gaze didn't flinch but she did turn pink. *She has beautiful eyes.*

"That was a nice speech," Laurel said.

"I can be nice once you get to know me," Christen softly replied.

"Forgive me if I'm skeptical in that area. Our experiences together have been drastically bad." Laurel shrugged.

"Drastically bad." Christen pursed her lips. "Yes, I guess you could say that. In my defense, I was doing what I was told." Christen twiddled with her pastry fork.

"Really? I find that hard to believe. You own the damn company," Laurel lashed out in a whisper.

Christen looked around the table and sighed in relief that the others were engrossed in conversations. "Some things are deceptive. If you want to call my office tomorrow perhaps I can help you regain employment back at the store."

Laurel shook her head. "Why would I do that? I can handle my own affairs, thank you. For the record, I have a job. Thankfully I'll never have to be part of the Jamison operation ever again," Laurel shouted.

"Is everything okay, Laurel?" Andrea asked.

Christen inwardly seethed. She was the bad person once again. Maybe it was time she actually become that woman.

Laurel blushed. "Absolutely. Christen and I were just chewing the fat."

"Hey, that's great you two getting on so well. We were both worried." Andrea turned to her fiancé. "Right, David."

David gave a clown-like grin.

I'm going to kill him when we get out of here. Christen inwardly fumed.

"We were having a robust conversation, that's all," Christen replied.

"Great. See, darling, no problems," David said. He took Andrea's hand and placed it to his lips.

Christen mentally applauded her brother. "I'd love to try dessert," she said.

"Of course. You will love it. Laurel made it," Andrea said.

Christen gazed at Laurel. "Really? Homemade. How domestic." She had the satisfaction of watching Laurel's nostrils flare and her eyes narrow at her snide remark.

"Sure, I'll fetch it." Laurel stood.

Christen smirked as Laurel left the room.

Chapter Eight

Laurel walked into the glass-fronted Stephens and Associates law office. She glanced at the cream carpet and wondered if her shoes were clean enough to enter the building

There was a modest reception area dominated by a work of art on the wall. She had no idea who painted it but it was a darn sight better than any frieze Ronnie had ever created.

"Hello."

The cheery greeting had Laurel smiling. "Hi, I have an appointment with Carol Bannister. My name is…"

"Laurel Rogers." The receptionist grinned. "Please take a seat. Carol will be with you in a few shakes of a lamb's tail."

Laurel couldn't help but giggle at the words. "You're English, right?"

"Right. How did you guess? I've lived here ten years and still can't shake the accent."

Laurel grinned. "Oh, it's cute."

The receptionist chuckled. "One day I'm going to finally wish everyone a great day instead of a super day and say *hi* instead of *hello*."

Laurel shook her head. "Please never change, it's refreshing."

"I'll buzz Carol. I have that down pat."

"I'm sure you do." Laurel nodded before wandering over to sit on one of the pristine blue checked fabric couches.

Within five minutes, she saw Carol enter the reception area and stood.

Carol engulfed her in a hug. "How's it going, Laurel. We miss you at home. Although I must confess that my waistline doesn't." Carol touched her waist.

"I'm doing great. Well, it's actually early days yet. I miss you guys," Laurel said.

Carol stepped back and scrutinized Laurel. "Let's go to my office." Carol smiled and turned toward the direction she had entered.

"Great." Laurel followed and smiled at the receptionist as they left the area.

"Where did you get your receptionist?"

Carol turned and frowned. "Did she confuse you? I'm sorry. Lisa is English. She came with great credentials. I guess what they say about idiosyncrasies is right. Damned if I understand half of her terms at times. She's brilliant, though, with clients. Go figure."

"I can figure. She's lovely." Laurel giggled. "She said something about lamb's tails, not quite sure if I have it right but I think that means speedy."

Carol laughed. "Got it in one, Laurel."

Carol opened the door to one of the offices in the corridor. "This is my domain."

As they entered the plush office, Laurel was sure her jaw was on the floor. "Just how important are you?"

Carol laughed. "Don't be impressed, my friend. This is just for the clients. Things can be very deceptive. Trust me, it's all smoke and mirrors."

"Works for me." Laurel sat on one of the two sofas and sank into the luxurious chestnut leather.

"Right, what can I help you with?" Carol asked, sitting opposite her friend.

"Remember that conversation about compensation…"

†

Laurel grinned, satisfied her prized possession, her parents' wedding day photograph, was hung in just the right place. Taking a step back and folding her arms she allowed the good memories to flood her brain. "I miss you, Mom."

The softly spoken words splayed around the small area. She snuffled back tears as the burning image of her mother dying of cancer at forty-five surfaced. Laurel reached for her cell and pushed a speed dial number then pressed the iPhone snugly to her ear.

"Dad?" Laurel grinned. "Yeah right. Who else would it be... Dad, I'm having a few people over for dinner. It's my second dinner party…" Laurel frowned. "…I know you couldn't make the housewarming, Dad, and that was fine... Give me a day that you can make it and I will plan around that." Laurel grimaced and held the phone away from her ear and then sucked in a deep breath, exhaling slowly. "Dad, surely you must have some free time?" Laurel plonked on the sofa, listening intently. "Dad, really, it isn't an issue. If you can't find the time… Look, if you do find some free time call me… I love you." Laurel held the phone a few seconds before disengaging, hoping her dad would acknowledge the sentiment—he didn't.

She placed the phone in her pocket and gazed at the fading photo on the wall. “Why does he keep pushing me away? I miss you too, Mom. All that seems to matter to him is his work.” Laurel sighed. “One day something will make him change his mind. I just hope it won’t be too late.”

Laurel shuffled her bottom on the sofa and lifted her feet. Tears threatening to fall as she put the phone to her ear again to call Fiona.

“Hi. It’s Fe. Leave me a message if you are a hot woman. If you are an ex, isn’t that what it means? If you want my money, forget it, don’t have any.”

Laurel didn’t leave a reply and sniffed back more tears. With determination she dragged herself off the sofa and threw back her shoulders. “Right, if I have time on my hands they better not be idle.” She left the living area and went into her spare bedroom to unpack more boxes.

†

The market at Argyle was the only place to be for a bargain on a Saturday morning and thrived on its traditional reputation. Even during the gang years, the market had always been popular. However, once the market was over Argyle and Tenth were no-go areas for anyone but a member of the local brotherhood—no one was safe.

Six years previously a European tourist had accidentally ventured into the small market area just as it closed. Within an hour she had been divested of money, credit cards, and identity. Nothing out of the ordinary, even for a US citizen, except this was a twenty-something whose body was found raped, beaten, and disposed of in a Dumpster.

Something about that episode galvanized the local community and police force to work together to eradicate the brotherhood and anyone else who wanted to take over.

Today the area thrived with business people and couples with young families. This was definitely the place to be on a Saturday in Chester.

The community thrived and at the heart of it was the Saturday market.

Deciduous trees lined the street leading to Argyle Market. The leaves gone and only speckles of ice lingered from the night before providing a majestic impression. Christen smiled as she briskly walked along the street, following several others. People of all ages propelled themselves to the best market in town. Her apartment was two blocks away. She had moved into the area five years earlier after it had been cleaned up. It hadn't been that easy at first as the dregs of gangster mentality still turned up in the odd dark alley. She'd experienced that firsthand. A stolen wallet and a black eye hadn't deterred her. She had persevered much to the consternation of her brothers. Hank had been the most vocal on the subject. Well, he hadn't had to live in a one-bedroom apartment for years. It hadn't been that bad when Macy shared it with her. The confines had gotten to her when Macy upped and left for no apparent reason. Now she owned a three-bedroom apartment in a thriving community that was worth five times what she paid for it. It was about the only investment that had given her any real collateral.

Rounding the end of the street, she stopped and drank in the sights, sounds, and smells of the market. Vendors were touting their wares with some shouting so hard they drowned out the others on either side of them. Music blared and with a frown she attempted to decipher who the artist was—she didn't recognize the song or the singer.

Laughter and people talking loudly greeted her as she stepped into the throng. Sidestepping the kitchen gadget guy—there was no reason to look since she couldn't cook—her gaze tracked to the local artist stall and she headed there. It was always busy and today was no different as people jostled to look at the works on offer. Taking her time, she checked out the large prints for sale. Some she'd seen many times before and she thought it was time they were taken off sale or offered at a reduced price. Then her gaze caught a watercolor, in vibrant reds, greens, and yellows, faintly abstract but eye-catching. She moved closer.

"Do you like that?"

Christen turned to the seller. She was a grungy-looking, fresh-faced young woman with red cheeks, bright blue eyes, and a multicolored crocheted woolen hat with wisps of light brown hair trailing around her thin neck. "It's eye-catching."

"Absolutely is. The artist is a friend of mine," the seller gushed. She waved a fingerless gloved hand in the painting's direction. "She caught it perfectly, didn't she?"

Christen considered the remark. The painting depicted High Street on a typical warm summer day, prominently presenting their store flanked by the park. "Yes. At least it looked like that before all the renovations in that area ten years ago." Christen looked for the artist's name or initials. She scrutinized the corners but saw nothing. "Who painted this?"

The girl smiled. "Harley Jackson."

Christen scratched her head pondering the name. "Haven't heard of her before. She must be new."

"Be right back." The young woman dashed off to take payment for a small print.

Christen chewed on her bottom lip. She liked it. The artist captured what it was like before everything changed…

"She's kind of new. Been painting for years but never quite had the confidence to share publically, I'm glad she has. Kept telling her but she said the artist life wasn't for her."

"I can understand that. Putting yourself out there, especially with something as personal as a creative work, is hard, I'm sure. How much is she asking?" Christen asked.

"Oh." The young woman blushed.

"I assumed it's for sale as you have it in a prominent position?"

The woman laughed. "Well, yes, but, to be honest, she didn't think that it would sell…at least not this quick. We only put it out today. I'll call her, shall I?" The expectant blue eyes appeared to twinkle at Christen.

"Sure."

The woman smiled even wider and then pulled out her phone. "Give me a few minutes; she's going to be stoked."

Christen rolled her eyes. She hadn't said she was buying it. She was just making an inquiry. Still it was a damn fine picture and the artist was obviously talented.

A few minutes later the woman returned, her drooping lips told its own story.

"I'm sorry, she's not answering."

Christen shrugged and began to turn away before spinning back around. "I'll be here next week around this time. If you finally get hold of Ms. Jackson and find out the price, I'll drop by." Talk about a sudden shift in demeanor. A light turned on in the young woman's face and it made Christen smile at her.

"I will. I will. Thank you."

Christen nodded and headed off to her next destination—breakfast coffee and a bacon-filled bagel at the rattiest looking stall in the market. Her mouth watered. It was the best breakfast around.

Chapter Nine

David Jamison paced the green carpeted floor of Christen's assistant's office. It was becoming a regular occurrence of late.

"When is she due back, Barry?" David barked.

Barry raised perfectly straight eyebrows, wriggled them around before answering. "As I told you a few minutes ago, she's due back within half an hour. Christen is owed a break from this mausoleum, you know." Barry crossed his arms over his thin chest.

David scowled before depositing himself on the wooden chair opposite Barry. The chair wobbled precariously at the sudden weight. "I bet you don't say things like that to my brother," David petulantly replied.

Barry shrugged. "I would, except he doesn't speak to lowly assistants."

"Hmm. Chris always said you told it how it is, even if people didn't like it," David said before standing again.

The door opened at that moment and Helen Richardson from the women's department breezed in. "I want to speak with her immediately."

"Take a place in line." Barry pointed to David standing in the room.

David had the satisfaction of watching 'the bitch from hell' as everyone dubbed her, give him a shocked look.

"I'm sorry, Mr. Jamison, I wasn't aware that you were here."

The shamefaced way the woman spoke, made David smile for a second. "Is there a problem you haven't told me about, Helen?"

Helen, with her hand still on the doorknob, shuffled around. "No, not really."

"Doesn't sound that way to me. Can I help?" David leaned against a filing cabinet and watched the woman's squat nose wrinkle a few times. *Reminds me of Samantha in* Bewitched *or should that be her mother*. He almost laughed aloud but stopped himself in time.

Before Helen could answer, she was propelled further into the room as the door was pushed open and Christen walked in.

"Did I miss a meeting?" Christen frowned at Barry.

Barry rolled his eyes and shook his head. "No, though you are evidently in demand. David was first in line if that helps."

Christen gazed at David. Then turned to Helen, "Is it important, Helen, or can it wait until tomorrow?"

Helen sniffed the air and nodded.

"Barry, make an appointment for Helen tomorrow morning please."

Christen walked to her office door and opened it. "Come in, David."

The door shut behind them.

†

"Hmm you need a morning, how does ten sound? Oh, actually tomorrow is Saturday and Ms. Jamison doesn't work the morning shift. Let me recheck this and get back to you," Barry said.

Helen grimaced. "I hate working here," she grumbled. "It's all about them. They have no conception what protocol is. Let me tell you..."

Barry lifted a perfectly manicured finger to stop her further comments. "I don't want to know, Helen. Whatever beef you have with the management you need to deal with it silently or directly with them."

"You just wait for them to turn on you, then you might not be so protective," Helen sneered and flounced out the door.

"Wonderful, and I thought I was the only prima donna in this office." Barry chuckled and picked up his jacket from the back of the chair before flicking his phone to answering machine. "Now to find out all the juicy gossip from the canteen." He left the room moments after Helen with just enough time not to meet her at the elevator.

†

Christen sat at her desk twiddling her pen. "I'm waiting?"

David growled. "Look, Mom is due tomorrow afternoon and I want Andrea to be there. That bitch told her that she can't have the time off."

"Ah, so that's why you were both in my office." Christen nodded then gave David a long look. "This isn't my problem, David. I have no oversee duty regarding time off. You'll need to see Derek in personnel."

"Chris, you know I can't do that. It would look bad."

"In what way? That you are flouting all the rules for your girlfriend? Yes, I'm sure it would make you look bad. When has that ever bothered you before?" Christen leaned back in her chair and switched on her computer.

"This is different. Andrea doesn't want to be singled out."

Christen laughed. "Well, you can't have your cake and eat it too, can you, David? When you announced your engagement a couple of weeks ago, you didn't think it would simply be between the families, did you?"

David pulled at his lip, reminding Christen of her brother as a child when he was perplexed.

"Helen admires you, Christen. Can't you have a quiet word with her?"

"No."

David glared at her. "Why not? What harm will it do you? I would have thought you would want Andrea there since it will take some of the pressure off you when Mom arrives."

Christen abruptly stood. "That was below the belt, David. Besides, I have decided to tell her the truth. What the hell difference will it make? She isn't staying. She made that plain when she finally told us the date she was arriving. If she's upset with me then it will be only for a short time before she'll disappear off to France again to be with dear Frances."

"Oh that sounds bitter, sis, and we both know you aren't that type of person. Won't you reconsider for me? Please," David cajoled.

Christen closed her eyes for a second before waggling a finger at him. "This is the last time I bail you out, dear brother, and I mean it."

David rushed around the desk and hugged her before planting a wet kiss on her cheek. He grinned and jauntily left the room.

Christen grimaced as she wiped away the moisture from her cheek. “I hope he doesn’t kiss like that all the time, it’s like having a dog slobbering over you.” She entered her password and blankly stared at the screen. Then she pressed her intercom. “Barry?”

There was no answer and she flicked a glance at the clock on the wall. “Darn, he’s at lunch.” She walked around her desk and slid on her suit jacket that she’d only minutes before removed. “I guess I’ll go see Helen now.”

As the doors of the elevator opened on the fourth floor, Christen was greeted by a larger-than-life sign of a woman who, in her opinion, was suffering from bulimia. The model was dressed in a classic black A-line dress and pointing to a large champagne glass and the slogan—Jamison’s classic range, the only clothes to be seen in for any occasion.

“Yeah right,” she whispered, stepping out of the elevator and looking around the spacious floor. Two-thirds of it was dominated by women’s wear while the other third was given over to menswear. Twenty years ago, the guy’s section was a tiny area on the first floor next to the sporting goods. She smiled as she recalled David’s constant battle with Hank about increasing the floor space for men and adding it to the women’s area. It made great marketing sense. Lola, Hank’s third wife, might not be her favorite person but she had championed David’s ideas and Hank had given in. Profits increased in that area and Hank, as always, took the credit and applauded his wife's input. David wasn't even mentioned.

"Ms. Jamison, it's good to see you on the floor. Do you need any help?"

Christen looked at the woman who had asked her the question. "No," Christen snapped. She walked on down the floor but stole a glance at the counter assistant who looked devastated. "Crap," she mumbled. She made her way to the counter and gazed at the woman, who she deduced was barely a child or looked it. "Are you new," she looked at the nametag, "Sally?"

"Yes, I'm new. Well, about three months ago..."

Stroking a pink lacquered nail down her chin Christen nodded. "Well, Sally, what do you have on special offer this week?"

A bubble of laughter threatened to erupt as Sally grinned and began placing several colors of the same underwear brand in front of her. "It's a great offer. Two for one and the quality is wonderful. What style do you prefer?" Sally asked, gazing at Christen naively.

Christen couldn't believe she was standing there speaking to the woman about underwear. The girl was showing her Chinese knockoffs that a four to one offer wouldn't tempt her. Still she looked at the girl's wonderful green glowing eyes that reminded her of... *Wow, she's a baby, get a grip.* "Perhaps another time. Thank you, Sally."

"Well, you know where I am. If ever you need help in the lingerie area, I'm your girl," Sally gushed.

Biting her lip, Christen smiled. "I'll remember that." She turned away and quickly made her way to Helen Richardson's tiny office. She knocked and waited.

"I'm busy, come back in fifteen minutes," Helen shouted.

Christen opened the door and gave Helen her best glare.

"Ms. Jamison, I'm sorry. If you had only just come inside I wouldn't have tried to…" Helen didn't finish.

Christen closed the door behind her and took a seat in front of the woman. "That's perfectly okay, Helen. You wanted to see me."

Helen shuffled in her chair. "I did, yes. Thank you for taking the time…"

"You said it was important, Helen. I trust your judgment, therefore I decided tomorrow wasn't good enough. How can I help you?" Christen asked. She watched as Helen's face went from angry red to a pink hue.

"You know I don't complain often."

"Well actually, you don't belong to my staff so I'm not really sure…"

"It's your brother. He wants to take one of my staff out of her normal shift pattern."

Christen drew a slow breath. "Andrea I take it?" At Helen's nod, Christen continued. "Will it cause a major drama?"

Helen's eyes flew open. "With all that's going on, Ms. Jamison, of course it will. She will be getting special treatment when most of us are crossing our fingers we are not on the next firing list. It just isn't right," Helen ardently pleaded.

Christen frowned. "I'm puzzled, Helen. I haven't heard any such thing. The last firings were three months ago."

Helen shook her head vigorously. "I keep telling everyone no one is safe and the sales are sluggish this time of year. If you don't know that then perhaps you're not safe either," Helen said.

"I was talking to a new assistant on the floor that you employed three months ago, Sally…I don't know her last name. That doesn't indicate more layoffs to me, Helen. In fact, it tells me the reverse." Christen frowned.

Helen snorted, throwing her pen violently on the desk. "Exactly. We are being replaced by young untrained people. I've seen it for the last couple of years. This year was worse. We lost so much experience. It isn't right, Ms. Jamison, it isn't!"

"Helen, please calm down. Let me check into things and see what's going on. You care about Andrea right?"

"Oh, of course. She's one of my babies." Helen bit her lip and lowered her gaze. "I trained her for years. She's very good. I'm very happy for her and your brother, but she could take a lot of flak if things go pear shaped again. It isn't a happy company these days, Ms. Jamison. It's not like when your dad and mom ran the store," Helen said.

The defeated tones resonated in Christen's mind. It was pretty much how she felt these days. "I'm going to ask for a personal favor, Helen. Please allow Andrea to take tomorrow off. I promise if you ever need me to help you in any way I will…no matter the circumstances." Christen's heart thudded at her words.

Helen stared at her for several seconds. "I will and you don't owe me anything. Thank you for listening."

Christen saw tears welling in Helen's eyes and her own smarted in sympathy. She stood and smiled. "We older employees have to stick together, right?"

Helen smiled. "Yes. I knew you would understand. You are very much like your mother."

Knocked sideways by the remark, Christen left the room. In all her life she'd never been compared on the same parallel with her mother.

Chapter Ten

Andrea Forrester giggled as David tickled her sides. “Don’t, please David, you know how I hate it.”

“Laughing is good for the soul, Andrea, and after tonight you do become the official property of the Jamison clan. I can do anything I want.” David chuckled and continued to tickle Andrea.

Pulling away, Andrea glared at him. “We aren’t getting married, just having dinner with your family. I’m offended that you think you own me. Love isn’t like that. You don’t own me, no one does, no one ever will. Love is like life, it needs nourishment, love, and understanding. If you don’t do that it dies.”

David shrugged. “Andy, I was only…”

“No! You are saying you own me. You don’t.”

“I love you, doesn’t that count?” David asked.

Andrea closed her eyes for a few seconds. “If love means the same thing to you that it does to me, then yes. If it means ownership. No! I’m not a slave.” Andrea drew away.

“Oh come on, love, you are definitely not a slave…except to love me.” David laughed.

Andrea got out of bed and went to the window of her apartment. “What would you say to that if I said the same thing, David?”

"I just said, *I love you.* Now come back to bed," David said.

"No!" Andrea stomped around the bedroom and began picking up her clothes.

David climbed out of the bed and stood in front of her. "I'm sorry. Andy, I love you and want you to be happy. To tell the truth…I'm scared."

Andrea glared at him. "Don't try those little boy lost expressions on me. It doesn't work."

David dropped his gaze and moved out of her personal space. "It's the truth but if you want me to go I will. Are you still coming to dinner or shall I call to cancel?"

Andrea sucked in a deep breath. "Why are you scared?"

David shrugged. "I haven't seen Mom in nearly fourteen years. I love her, but deep down I think she let us down and I'm not sure I won't say that to her."

Andrea's heart went out to him for opening up and she drew David's head to her. "It will be just fine, David, trust me. You love your mom, she loves you, so everything will work out."

David's head snuggled into her body. "I love you, Andy. Don't leave me too."

The pathetic words resonated in Andrea as she kissed the top of his head. "Never."

†

Laurel gazed at her reflection in the mirror and smiled. Six months ago she was a dress size larger and, according to Fiona's hairdresser when her new lover had taken her to have an updated style, her hairstyle was from the nineties. Gone were the long tresses of auburn hair that she'd often scrunch up in a bun for work. Now her hair was in a bob that didn't quite reach her shoulders and it shone like never before. Threading her fingers through the hair at her temple she grinned as it bounced back into shape as soon as the hair was released.

She smoothed her hands down the black jeans that fit her snugly, but they did fit. She hadn't worn jeans in over a decade. Ronnie had always said she would look terrible in extra-size fit jeans. Well, Ronnie was wrong. Laurel wrinkled her nose at the obnoxious ex-partner she thought she'd loved.

"What a waste of six years of my time." Laurel turned to the plain black jacket on the bed and retrieved it. "I can't get those years back but I'm damned if I'm going to lose anymore to her or anyone who treats me badly, and that includes Fiona." As she left her bedroom she glanced at Minnie Mouse on her wrist—five thirty. "You'd better be there at Jane's this time, Fiona." She left her apartment.

A third cup of coffee later Laurel drummed her fingernails on the Formica table at Jane's Café. She drew in a shallow breath to calm her anger. "That's it. I deserve better." Laurel stood and turned before accidentally bumping into the person who was about to sit behind her.

"Sorry."

"Sorry."

Laurel's eyes widened. "Ms. Jamison?"

"Yes, and please call me Christen. We have had social interaction, therefore I think that's only fair. Otherwise I will have to call you Ms. Rogers. Unless that's what you want me to call you?"

It wasn't charming as such but Laurel had the distinct impression Christen wasn't being condescending. She was trying to be friendly. "Christen, it is then."

Christen smiled. “Thank you, Laurel. Were you leaving?”

“Yes, I’m all coffeed out. One is normally enough for me but having had three I’ll be up all night.” Laurel shrugged.

“So why did you…that is, have three?”

Laurel knew her cheeks went red. “I was waiting for someone who obviously couldn’t make it.” She began to walk away.

“That’s a shame. Look, if you’re going to be up all night anyway, want to join me for another coffee or tea, maybe water? Whatever?” Christen asked.

Laurel had a multitude of reasons why she didn’t want to but heard herself say, “Yes.”

“Wonderful want to change tables.”

“Hey, let’s be decadent shall we?” She pointed to a different table. “I’ve never sat there before,” Laurel said. She was amazed when Christen pulled out a chair for her before taking the one opposite.

“I’ve only tried half of them myself.” Christen chuckled.

Laurel liked the sound. It was happy and not contrived. Who would have thought the dragon could be…nice. “Obviously we come here at different times because I don’t recall you ever being here when I have. I’ve been coming here twice a week for the last few months.” Laurel stared at Christen.

“I’m a regular, especially at this time on a Friday. Jane, the owner, is an old college buddy. When I came to live in the neighborhood five years ago, we caught up again. It’s a small world I find.”

Laurel nodded. "It sure is. We've seen each other more times in the last few months than the fifteen years I worked for Jamison's."

A woman with short-cropped blond hair and several tattoos on her arms arrived at the table with a notebook poised to take an order. "What can I get you, Chris?"

Laurel frowned at the familiar tone. *How the hell hadn't she seen Christen here before?*

"Same as always, Sage. Laurel, what do you want?" Christen asked, turning to her.

For a few seconds Christen's pale blue eyes stared at her attentively. "Do you mind if I have a soda?"

"The lady wants a soda, Sage. Can you bring the menu over, please?"

"Absolutely." Sage sashayed to another table. Then a few minutes later deposited two menus on the table.

"You eat here too?" Laurel asked.

Christen shrugged. "I'm not sure I want to admit this but I don't cook. At least nothing beyond eggs and toast."

Laurel shook her head and laughed.

"I know it's terrible. My mother wasn't the domesticated kind and there was always a cook so…" Christen lifted her hands in the air.

"There is a downside to having a cook then," Laurel said and grinned.

"Hmm. Anyway, an accomplishment that is definitely in your repertoire. The dessert at Andrea's was the best chocolate truffle tort I've ever had and believe me I've had a lot. It's my favorite."

Laurel blushed. "Thank you."

"If you have that kind of skill, why work at Jamison's for so long? For sure, the department you used to work in isn't exactly in that league." Christen smiled.

"I didn't have that skill when I started at Jamison's. I developed it over the years. Look at me…I don't go hungry." Laurel closed her eyes, wishing she hadn't said what she did as her hands settled unconsciously on her less than flat stomach.

Christen stared at her. "You look good to me. Though I suspect the last few months haven't exactly been easy for you. You lost your job, your partner, and your home in the space of a week. Stressful times."

"How do you know about my partner and home?" Laurel pouted.

"You told us at the meeting when we terminated your employment. Very emotionally, as it happens," Christen quietly said.

Laurel dredged up the memories of that event and closed her eyes as she recalled it vividly. "I did, didn't I?" She could feel the heat on her face.

"Afraid so. Hi, Sage, thank you."

"No problem, the special tonight is the kale and pumpkin quiche." Christen scrunched up her face and Laurel laughed. "I know, but I have to tell you." Sage giggled. "Jane said she saved a T-bone which has your name on it."

Christen chuckled. "I guess you know my answer, Sage. Medium to rare and I'll have the fries tonight."

"And?" Sage turned to Laurel and she frowned.

"I'm sorry I haven't looked at the menu in fact…"

"Sage, she just wants soda."

"Okay." Sage turned away.

"Actually can you make that two T-bones, same order?" Laurel grinned.

"For a friend of Christen's, sure thing. It is so rare…I mean like never. Jane is going to flip," she said and left to place the order.

Laurel shrugged. "Do you mind me joining you for dinner?"

"No. No, it will be a pleasure. I usually eat alone," Christen replied and looked around the busy café.

"Thanks. Do you live around here? What do you think of the Argyle Market?" Laurel rapidly spoke and saw Christen's face change dramatically. "Sorry, too many questions."

"Don't worry and yes, I live two blocks away. I love Argyle Market. It's my go-to place every Saturday morning. There is nothing better than a walk around the market filled with people haggling over just about everything under the sun. And I love having a greasy bacon and sausage roll at Gina's. Do you know it?"

"Actually, not that I recall. I haven't been there for years, used to go with my parents when I was a kid but don't recall that much about it." Laurel frowned.

Christen nodded. "Hasn't changed any. I suspect even the music is the same?"

Laurel chuckled. "I remember the music, eighties, right. Is it still the same?"

Christen laughed and nodded.

As their drinks were placed on the table Laurel's eyebrows rose when Christen stood and embraced the waif-like woman who had served them. She looked like she needed a few square meals since her flesh hung from her body.

"Jane, you didn't have to bring this out yourself," Christen said, hugging her friend.

"Of course I do. Sage was right, you do have company. I'm so glad, Christen."

Laurel pursed her lips sure that Christen wouldn't want her to hear that remark. Nonetheless, she had. Didn't Christen Jamison have any friends to socialize with?

"Jane, this is Laurel." Christen released the hug and both turned to Laurel.

"Pleased to meet you, Jane."

"It's a pleasure, Laurel. So how did you two meet?"

Laurel blinked rapidly. "At work, I guess."

Christen frowned and returned to her seat.

Jane raised her eyebrows. "I'm surprised you still speak to her then, never mind have dinner together. Jamison's is one of the worst companies to work for these days."

"Please, Jane, it isn't that bad," Christen replied.

Jane looked at Christen then turned to Laurel and smiled. "I guess not if Laurel is here with you after hours."

"Well actually, I don't work there anymore. In fact, I was let go months ago," Laurel said.

"Oh. Well, that makes sense then. Good call on you to see behind the cold front she gives at work, Laurel. Not many, if any, do and you'll find it's worth it."

"Jane." Christen glared at her friend.

Jane chuckled and grinned at Christen. "You know it's true, if it wasn't for you…"

"Enough, Jane. Shouldn't you be in the kitchen supervising cooking our steaks?" Christen pleaded.

Laurel chuckled and Jane smiled.

"I'm going. Good to see you, Laurel. I hope this isn't the last. See you Sunday, Christen." Jane tottered off in the direction of the counter.

"So you aren't totally bereft of friends." Laurel smiled.

Christen shrugged, "No, but they are few and mean a great deal to me. I can count on one hand the closest friends I have. I guess that's not the case with you."

"Oh, I might have a tad more." Laurel sipped her soda. "Do you mind if I ask a personal question?"

"Go ahead," Christen said.

"Andrea is my best friend and I love her dearly. Is your brother really serious about her? He does have a reputation as a womanizer. I don't want her to be just a fad. It would break her heart." Laurel sighed as she concluded speaking and watched several reactions flit across Christen's features, none of which she could decipher. She had no point of reference for the woman.

"I believe him to be genuine in his affections."

"That's it?" Laurel frowned.

"My father was a womanizer. I'm sure that's not news to you. It was a joke I believe, in the store. I'm surprised no one contested his will, he's sure to have other children by liaisons. They did not and have not come forth so perhaps my father was careful for the only time in his life," Christen quietly said, then sipped her coffee.

"Look, I shouldn't have…"

"No, I'm trying to explain David. He has many traits of my father…who doesn't of their parents? Right? In defense of my brother he has loved many women but until now has never gone to such lengths as he has to make his relationship with Andrea work. Never to my knowledge, and believe me I'd know, had he ever asked anyone to marry him." Christen took another sip of her drink.

Laurel was fascinated by this open dialogue and she actually believed Christen.

"David loves Andrea—she's the one for him," Christen said.

Laurel was at a loss for words and was thankful when Sage turned up with their meal.

"Enjoy, ladies." Sage grinned and left.

Laurel looked at the enormous steak that filled the plate. Moments later, Sage returned with the fries and salad and Laurel's eyes widened. "I'm going to be here all night eating this." Picking up her utensils she began to devour the delicious-smelling meal with the sound of Christen's gentle laughter filling her ears.

After the meal, which Laurel felt had been made for two people not one, she sank back in the chair and grinned. "That was excellent. Wow. Now I know why you eat here on a Friday evening. Who wouldn't? It's definitely on my list now."

Christen chuckled as she wiped a napkin over her lips and settled back in her chair. "Jane has a chef now but if you thought that was good you should have tried her Lamb racks." Christen lifted two fingers together and kissed them.

Laurel grinned and sighed. "I hope you don't mind but Jane doesn't look well."

Christen glanced toward the kitchen area and pursed her lips then nodded. "Two years ago she was diagnosed with breast cancer. She's had the operation and now we are hopeful for a full recovery."

Laurel heard the matter-of-fact words and didn't buy it.

"There's something more, look if I'm prying…"

"It's okay, Laurel." Christen bent forward and sipped her water. "She was in a long-term relationship at the time. He left her once she'd been diagnosed. It took its toll more than the cancer. As I said, we are hopeful. She needs to know people care about her."

Laurel heard the quietly spoken words and there was something more. A tenderness that she would never have expected. "It's good to have friends who care, helps us get through the hard times. Sometimes we don't really appreciate them until the last minute. Believe me I know."

Christen hung her head.

"Hey, look. I wasn't talking about you or being sacked from Jamison's. In fact, you did me a huge favor. I love where I work now. It's more in keeping with my talents…some of them at least," Laurel said and reached across to take Christen's hand.

Christen looked up and gave a tight smile.

"Okay, where in Chester do you love the most?" Laurel asked.

"Argyle Street Market on a Saturday morning. You can't beat it," Christen said.

"Maybe I need to revisit Argyle Market."

"Come with me tomorrow. I'll show you what you've forgotten and then some." Christen grinned.

Laurel chewed on that and as she gazed at Christen's expression she knew the answer immediately. "Sounds like a plan, what time?"

†

Christen placed her door keys on the wooden key hanger her grandmother had given her as a five-year-old. Not that she could remember but everyone else in the family did. That Christmas, apparently, everyone had received an heirloom. They mentioned it every Christmas until she had gone to college. Hers had been a key hanger, wooden with faded flowers embellished on each side and golden hooks, inexpensive, and definitely throwaway. Yet of all the possessions she had ever gained in her life this trinket came with her everywhere. It was important and useful. *I wonder if the others have their heirlooms from Grams.*

Walking into the living area, she sat on the pristine red sofa. "I had a great time. I hope I see her tomorrow at the market. We said Gina's at ten." As the words resonated in the white-walled room she shook her head and smiled. "I'm going crazy, talking to myself." Christen picked up the TV remote and flicked a switch. She didn't want to watch the ten o'clock news. It was way too depressing. What she wanted was to continue enjoying the night. It had been a long time since she enjoyed another woman's company who wasn't a really old friend. She scrambled over to her DVD collection and took out one of her favorite movies, *The Birdcage*.

†

Laurel was awakened out of a wonderful dream by the insistent buzzing of the intercom. Scrunching her eyes she looked at her bedside clock—three forty-five. She pulled her pillow over her head and attempted to shut out the noise but it continued along with a loud rendition of her name.

"Damn you, Fiona!"

She dragged one leg after another and placed her feet in fluffy slippers. Then half-asleep she switched on the light in her bedroom and groaned as the brightness taunted her sensitive eyes. "I hate you, Fiona."

Reaching the intercom, she pressed the button. "What? It's late…no early."

"Oh come on, Lau, it's early. Let's have some fun."

"No, you stood me up," Laurel shouted.

"Come on, it was Friday night and things turn up. I had an unexpected gig. You know I need the money. Don't be a crab apple."

"Go away, Fiona, I'm done with you using me. Been through that, worn the T-shirt, and hated every minute."

There was silence for a few moments and Laurel was about to release the intercom button.

"Please let me in and I'll explain. I'll just stay for coffee, nothing more. And if you want me to leave after that I will," Fiona pleaded.

It was the little girl lost voice Fiona used, very well to her advantage, that had Laurel pressing the button for her to come up to the apartment. *At least she wants me, if only for sex, and it's better than being alone.*

As Laurel let Fiona through the door she narrowed her eyes, looking her lover over. Disheveled, sweaty, and giving her that damned alluring smile that made everything okay.

Fiona wrapped Laurel in a bear hug and kissed her neck slowly. Laurel's heart pounded at the sensual touch. Closing her eyes she allowed the burning river of blood to flood her body, her excitement increasing as Fiona's tongue trailed to the V of the T-shirt she had thrown on to answer the door.

Practiced hands wandered over her breasts. Laurel dragged her gaze to the tousled head of hair that nuzzled her and she threw back her head as teeth grazed her left nipple. "You said coffee," Laurel ground out as Fiona sucked in a nipple. "Don't be so rough, Fiona."

"You love it, Lau. Come on, let's get to bed. I want to make love to you until lunch." Fiona, her mouth sucking Laurel's breast, lifted her up and carried Laurel to bed.

In the recesses of her mind, Laurel knew she wanted more out of a relationship than just sex but her body betrayed her and she gave in to its demands. A fleeting memory of Christen surfaced only to be drowned out by the insistent ministrations of Fiona.

†

Gina Edwards grinned as Christen sat on one of the three benches next to an overextended wooden table. “Hey, Christen, same as usual?” Gina asked, waving a spatula in the air from the stall.

Christen smiled. “Can it wait? I’m expecting someone.” Christen glanced at her watch, “Should be here anytime. I’ll have coffee though.”

“Sure thing.” Gina turned her attention to the grill filled with bacon and sausage, sizzling away.

Christen crossed her ankles and leaned back breathing in the cold breeze and the delicious aroma of her favorite breakfast treat. She’d go to the art stall after breakfast. She smiled thinking that maybe Laurel would want to go with her and see what she was interested in and give her a verdict.

After she drank her coffee she glanced at her watch. It was fifteen after ten. Could she be late or just not coming? How would I know if she was genuine when she said she would? An angel in her mind said ‘have faith’ and she would try.

Gina smiled at her not for the first time since she’d taken a seat, only this time Christen was sure it was sympathetic. Obviously she’s seen the stood-up person more times than not.

Resigned, Christen walked over to Gina. “I guess my friend has been delayed. Look, I need to see another stall owner for a few minutes then I’ll have a takeout roll.”

“Maybe she was delayed. It will be ready whenever you get back. Take your time.” Gina smiled.

“Thanks, Gina.” Christen strode off in the direction of the art stall.

As she came close, the young woman from the previous week was not there. Instead a gnarled featured man she decided was in his sixties gave her a dismissive look. He definitely wasn't good for business. Christen pointed to the painting she liked. "I came by last week and was interested to know the price. The young woman said she'd find out for me if I came back this week."

The old man stared at her unblinking.

Did I speak in a foreign language? Christen moved closer to the painting. "It didn't have a price?"

"Oh, Harley's work. Sasha never mentioned it to me but the young never think to write anything down these days. It's all on them there phone things they carry everywhere." He shuffled to the table and pulled out a ledger-style book. "Naw nothin' here. My granddaughter is sick. Caught the flu bug that's going around."

Christen frowned. "I guess that means no price then?"

The old man pulled on a sharp chin and narrowed his eyes at her. "What do you think is a fair price?"

Taken off guard by the question Christen simply stood there speechless.

"It's a good watercolor I have to say. She's talented, Harley is, especially with her parentage. Pity it's taken so long for her to release any work," the old man said.

"Can you try calling the artist? I think it's a bit unfair we just make up a price?" Christen pursed her lips.

"I'll try. Got to go over to the bar across the street though to use the phone. Want to come back in a few minutes." He shrugged.

"You could use my phone." Christen retrieved her iPhone from her jeans pocket and handed it to him. She almost laughed as his face dropped at the offer. "Look, give me the number and I'll call it, then you can do all the talking," Christen said.

Seconds later she dialed the number the man gave her and she heard the phone begin to ring.

"Hi?" The voice sounded deep, husky, and sleepy. She passed it over to the old man and walked a few paces away.

A few minutes later the man tapped her on the back and gave her the phone. "Five hundred dollars," he said.

Christen blinked rapidly. "Wow, that's high for a new artist."

"Sorry, she wouldn't budge on the price."

"Thanks. It's a bit steep for my budget."

Christen walked away, back toward Gina's stall. The morning wasn't turning out anything like she had expected when she woke up. Deflated was the best description she could come up with. "I'll have that roll now, Gina," Christen said.

"Not a good day, Christen?" Gina said.

"A couple of disappointments. Nothing that hasn't happened before and will probably happen again." Christen winked. "Still you'll make up for it with this."

Gina handed her the bacon and sausage roll.

"That's the spirit. Chin up. My dad used to say there is always something good just around the corner." Gina grinned. "He was always right too. Have a great week, Christen."

"Thanks, Gina, you too. See you next week, God willing."

Christen walked away, salivating at the smell of the food in her hand. She unpeeled the wrapping and tucked into the roll, ignoring the greasy fluid dribbling down her chin.

Chapter Eleven

Samantha Jamison drew in a ragged breath and tried to settle the nerves in her stomach. After all, these were her children. Her hand clutched the ivory cane, her fingers slipping around the silver bird handle. She gazed at the delicate work a jeweler had painstakingly undertaken for her three months ago, when she had broken her ankle and was given a cane for rehabilitation. It had meant a delay to her plans to visit her family, and her aide Isabella had been unable to make the journey as she had gone back to University. Frances had volunteered to go but she had declined her eldest daughter's offer. This had to be about her other children and having Frances here would have made matters even more awkward. She smiled as she scrutinized the bird on the handle—a Phoenix—fitting in the circumstances.

There was a knock at the hotel door. She stood and gingerly walked over, pursing her lips in trepidation before masking it with a smile as she opened the door. "Hank, how lovely…you are the first." Samantha reached up and drew him into a gentle hug and kissed his stubbly cheek.

Hank withdrew from the hold and dwarfed her. He shrugged and moved further into the room. "Why did you stay here instead of the Hilton; it's premier?" Hank gruffly asked.

Samantha turned and walked over to the chintz styled sofa and sat down. "Actually this is more expensive than the Hilton and I loved the sound of it as soon as I heard its name. Did you ever see *The Best Exotic Marigold Hotel*?" Samantha saw Hank's bushy eyebrows furrow. "No. No of course not. Well, it might not be the same place as the movie but it's excellent. Where are your siblings?"

Hank placed his hands in his trouser pockets. "God knows. I told them one thirty sharp."

"I'm sure they will be here soon. Now, how have you been and your new wife. Lola, isn't it? I'm looking forward to meeting her," Samantha said.

Hank gave a grumpy clearing of his throat. "She's not that new. We've been married six years. She's as well as you'd expect. What about Frances and the diplomat."

Samantha sucked in a breath to soothe her anger. "Your sister is very well and Daniel may be moving up the ranks again. The twins will be twenty-one in a few months."

"Great." Hank glanced at his watch. "Where the hell are they?"

No sooner had he made the statement there was another knock on the door.

"I'll get it." Hank strode off to the door and flung it open. "About time. What's she doing here?"

David entered the room. "Good to see you too, brother. This is my future wife, so be polite for a change."

Samantha smiled as she heard the exchange between the brothers. They had never seen eye to eye—ever. "David." Samantha stood as he approached the sofa and she embraced her youngest son.

"Mother, it's been way too long." He kissed her cheek then drew her away a little and grinned. "You don't look any older than the last time I saw you."

Samantha laughed. "As always, so very flattering. Now did I hear something about a fiancée?"

David nodded and his smile widened even more. "Andrea, come on, sweetie, meet my mother Samantha."

Andrea hesitantly walked forward and held out her hand.

Samantha dismissed the polite gesture and hugged her as tight as her frail body allowed. "You are going to be family, Andrea, a handshake is for a business deal."

"Well, if I thought this was going to be one big family get-together I'd have brought Lola," Hank sneered.

"Is Christen coming, David?" Samantha whispered.

David nodded. Hugging his mother close again and returned the whisper, "Chris volunteered to drive us here. Valet parking isn't an option for her."

Samantha nodded slowly. "Your sister hates anyone driving her car."

"Yes, that's Chris. She hasn't changed a bit," David said.

"Please take a seat, my dears, I'm looking forward to hearing about your romance."

The third knock on the door had Hank opening the door again. "Good, at least you didn't bring a tagalong. Not that you have one."

"Interesting," Samantha softly said as she heard the sibling's exchange.

Christen entered the room and simply stared at her mother.

Samantha understood completely the stance, allowing her youngest child to decide what was best for her. She was as beautiful, if not more so, than the last time they had seen each other physically—the day she left for France a decade and a half ago.

"Mother," Christen finally said. She walked up to her mother and gave her a brief hug and peck on the cheek. It was over so fast you would barely know it happened.

"You look wonderful, darling."

"Thanks." Christen moved away and went to stand near the sliding patio door leading to the balcony that overlooked Lancaster Park.

Silence descended on the room.

"Well, I don't know about the rest of you, but I'm famished. Plus this place is unbelievably hard to get a reservation any time of the day. You did book, right Mother?" David asked.

Samantha chuckled. "Yes, David. Shall we go? I'm now fascinated to see if it's as good as people claim." She stood and her ankle let her down for a few seconds as she tottered on her cane.

"Did you bring a wheelchair?" Hank asked.

"I did not," Samantha bristled. "I'm quite capable of using my cane to get around."

David chuckled and winked at his mother then at his fiancée. "Let's have lunch then, shall we?"

They left the room and Samantha breathed a sigh of relief. *That's the hard part and it's over. I hope.*

†

Christen pressed her head against the glass mirror in the restroom of the restaurant. Her mother looked old and frail. How could she possibly have been afraid to see her?

The door to the restroom opened and she pulled away guiltily.

"Hey, are you okay? You left the table suddenly and I was worried," Andrea said.

Christen glared at Andrea. Then softened her gaze as she saw genuine concern in the woman's eyes. "It's a bit overwhelming," Christen admitted. "What about you?"

Andrea shrugged. "Your mother is a very gracious and warm woman. I knew David got those traits from one of your parents."

"Yeah and he got the rest from the other," Christen said. As soon as the words left her mouth regretted it. "Sorry. David has changed."

"I know about your dad. David told me the hard facts. He is nothing like that man, trust me," Andrea softly said.

Christen concentrated on Andrea, her eyes reflected the conviction in her voice. "I bet your family isn't as fragmented as ours?"

Andrea shrugged and fluffed the bangs of her hair as she peered into the mirror. "Not in the same way, but everyone has skeletons in their cupboard."

"What's yours?" Christen asked.

"My dad's eldest brother is a scumbag of the worst order. He strangled his wife and left the five kids to fend for themselves in Death Valley."

Christen's mouth dropped. "Did they survive?"

Andrea smiled. "You know, we might see tourists as a necessary evil but it was an English couple that got lost and amazingly found the kids as they searched for a route out. Lucky kids." Andrea affixed more lipstick.

Christen was stunned at the confession. She wondered if the woman was really telling her the truth. "What happened to the children?"

Andrea beamed. “The English couple wanted to adopt the kids and went to great lengths to do so. They even gave up their English citizenship.”

“Did they succeed” What about the parental family links…your dad and grandparents? You know what I mean?” Christen could not believe what she was hearing and allowed herself to be pulled into the quirky story.

“Auntie Kate and Uncle Dave are as much a part of the family as if they were born to it. The eldest child even went to Oxford.”

Christen was speechless for lots of reasons. “The best I can say that I’ve done is support UNICEF.”

“Hey, you’ll meet them at the wedding. I thought you might laugh at their accent. Even after thirty years they have a cute way of saying things.” Andrea grinned. “I guess we should go back or we’ll have David hammering at the door. Your mom might be great but Hank…”

Christen knew she looked perplexed and nodded. “Yes. Yes we should. Thank you, Andrea.”

Andrea smiled. “Anytime.”

Did that mean she could ask Andrea for Laurel’s number? *No. It’s too early and stupid for me to even think about.* The woman had, after all, stood her up. She followed Andrea out of the room.

†

Samantha fingered the phoenix on her cane as she stared at her youngest child. Christen had always been the most sensitive and yet the strongest of her children. She never allowed people to see how others’ actions—even her siblings—hurt her. She would bring that determined stare into focus and scare the best of them. Yet deep down her hurt was palpable. A mother always knew. A mother knew even now. "You have barely spoken, Christen."

Christen shrugged. "Hank and David had a lot to say."

"And you don't?" Samantha caught her daughter's gaze. It had that frightened yet determined look she remembered.

Christen looked at the others in the room.

Samantha reached across and took Christen's hand. It tensed. "I'm sorry."

Christen removed her hand. "For what?"

"It may not make sense to you but I had to leave and not come back until the time was right," Samantha said.

Christen shook her head. "Frances needed you. Right?"

Samantha heard the bitterness in the retort. It was understandable. "She didn't. In fact, I was a burden to her and Daniel. I needed to leave and try to understand my life," her frail shoulders lifted slightly, "whatever that life was to be. I can't expect you to understand. I can't expect you to…"

"I understand," Christen said.

Samantha gave Christen a frown.

"Let's get this out in the open finally." Christen waved over David. "We know, even ox head Hank knows. Dad was a reprobate, womanizer for you, big brother. Dad was only good for one thing…the store. We don't hate you, Mother. We love you in our own ways. The thing I don't like…"

"Christen don't," David said.

"Don't? It's been fourteen years. It's time. Why did you leave us? We had to take the fallout from Father's affairs. Hank…well Hank in the early days made it work for all of us."

Samantha looked at the expression on her eldest son's face. It was the closest to pride she had ever seen from him. Christen was on a roll.

"Mother, why are you here?" Christen asked.

There it was. That forthright tilt of the head and jut of chin, indicating an imminently dangerous situation if you didn't know it was coming. "I'm writing my memoirs and have a publisher. I felt it wise to tell you in person."

Hank gave a belly laugh.

"You find it funny, Hank?" Samantha stared at her son.

Hank shrugged and grunted something unintelligible.

"That's why you are here?" Pencil-thin eyebrows rose as Christen spoke.

Samantha gave Christen a small smile. She knew what she said next could have her alienating her daughter for good. "No. Not the only reason. Believe it or not if you will, but I've missed you and want to connect again if you will all allow me. Cards, presents, and the odd phone call don't quite help me picture if you are all happy. I know you say you are."

David leaned forward and kissed his mother. "Great news on the book and I'm glad you're back." He turned to Andrea. "We both are. Aren't we, darling?"

Andrea turned beet red and nodded.

Samantha figured the young woman was completely out of her depth and she knew exactly what that felt like. She herself was virtually a stranger to her own children.

"Well, I have a meeting before dinner tonight so I have to go," Hank said. He sidled up to Samantha and kissed her cheek. "Lola is dying to meet you. I made reservations at Casters. I figured you'd had enough Froggy food and could do with some plain old American chow." Hank dismissed the rest of the people in the room with a quick nod and left the room.

David shrugged. "Andrea and I have to talk to Francois in the restaurant. He has made a special time for us since we've decided to have our wedding feast here." He turned to Christen. "See you in the foyer in half an hour?"

Christen opened her mouth, but didn't speak.

Samantha wondered if her daughter had ever been lost for words before. David gave her a warm hug and kiss and Andrea shyly smiled, and she watched as they left. Afterward, if she had a knife she could cut the atmosphere with it.

"I know you didn't approve of my decision to move away, Christen, and I'm sorry. However, you were happy and so in love with Macy that I didn't think you'd hurt as much as you obviously have." Christen spun around and Samantha flinched at the power of the gaze turned on her.

"I don't. Hurt that is," Christen said through clenched teeth before sitting down on the chair nearest to her.

Samantha twiddled with the handle of her cane and then stared at her daughter. "Tell me what's really wrong, darling. Because as much as you might be angry that I've been away so long you have never held a grudge and always move on. I have been extremely proud and envious of that personal trait of yours."

"Envious of me?" Christen frowned.

"Yes. I wish I was as strong as you. Perhaps my life would have been different," Samantha softly spoke.

Christen clasped her hands in front of her. Then looking directly at Samantha said, "Do you regret having us with Dad?"

Samantha's blood drained and her heart stopped. She paused for a moment before speaking, her fingers clutching the cane. "Christen, I have many regrets in my life, that is true. Some I could have prevented, and didn't, others blindsided me. One thing I know is that each and every one of my children came into this world with love from both parents. I loved your father for many years and he loved me in his own way. What I didn't realize was that we all have options in life. He opted to take adultery as his. I was left behind with foolish pride on what marriage should be. I thought it was forever."

"Well, Hank at least divorces one wife before he takes another lover," Christen sneered.

"And you? Are you and Macy still as happy as when you met?" Samantha asked. She watched Christen shift nervously on the sofa.

"No. We split up a year after you left," Christen declared.

"But you have always written…" Samantha stopped. "You didn't want me to worry?"

Christen shrugged.

Samantha's tears built like a dam behind her eyelids. "You could have told me, darling."

"Yeah right. You were running away from your own demons. We knew that," Christen said and dropped her gaze.

"Fourteen years later?"

"Thirteen, to be exact, and I always thought you'd be coming home so I could you tell you in person. Each year you stayed away the pretense continued," Christen said.

"I'm sorry, my darling, for not being here when you needed me." Samantha allowed the tears welling up to release.

"Don't cry, Mother. It doesn't matter," Christen said before standing. "I'd better go and see if the lovebirds are ready."

"I'm truly sorry, Christen, for not being here for you. If I had known…" Samantha wiped away her tears. When she did she saw only an ice-cold expression from her youngest child.

"You are coming to dinner tonight, though, aren't you, Christen?"

"Wouldn't miss it. Hank and Lola, David and Andrea…yep, the happy couples and just little old me." Christen moved to the door.

Samantha stood, her body shaking. "You don't have anyone in your life right now?"

"Don't try fishing, Mother. It's been too long. I'll see you later." Christen gave her mother a chaste kiss before leaving the room.

Samantha stood and looked around her. It was a room with lovely things but not a home. Her home. What she wouldn't give to have Frances open the door and drop into the chair and tell her about her day. She sighed and drew out a handkerchief to blow her nose.

Chapter Twelve

Laurel entered Maisey's bakery and drummed up a smile for her boss.

"Harley, you're early and you look as if you haven't slept all weekend. Don't tell me you've been burning the midnight oil on your days off," Maisey said, giving her a saucy wink.

Groaning, Laurel went around the counter, past Maisey, and into the back room. After pulling on a clean apron she returned to the front of the shop.

"It was a pretty hectic Saturday. Fiona wanted to take a bike ride to Lake Wren on Sunday and we didn't get back to my place until seven. I had to play catch-up doing the laundry and cleaning up my place so I didn't get much sleep. I'm not complaining…well, not really." Laurel managed a chuckle.

Maisey laughed. "I wish I had that kind of weekend. Still, I've had them in my time, now I'm more of a stay-at-home watching-movies kinda gal."

Laurel looked at the half-filled shelves. No matter how bad she felt she loved working here. It was worth getting up for…not like at Jamison's. "Shit," she mumbled.

"What was that?" Maisey asked. "You look like you just lost your best friend. Was it something I said?" Maisey inquired.

"No. No, it's something I did. Oh no, she'll think I'm a liar," Laurel said, placing a hand to her mouth.

"Fiona?"

"Not Fiona. Christen," Laurel softly said.

"Oh. Who's Christen?"

"Someone I was supposed to meet Saturday morning."

Maisey frowned. "Oh. I'll put the coffeepot on and we can have a caffeine fix before we get started on the morning bake."

"Sounds good." Laurel closed her eyes. She'd totally forgotten about meeting Christen at the market. "How could I forget such a thing. She was so nice to me and we had a great time Friday over dinner."

A few minutes later, coffee mug in hand Laurel sighed as she caught Maisey's inquiring glance. "I met up with someone from Jamison's…in fact it was a Jamison," Laurel said, contemplating the dark liquid in front of her.

"I didn't know you were so well connected. It must have been Friday. Right?"

"How did you know?" Laurel frowned.

"I might be getting old but I'm not senile. From what you told me you were with Fiona Saturday and Sunday."

Laurel's eyebrows knotted together. "Yes. Sorry. Fiona stood me up on Friday evening at Jane's Café…"

"Not again, Laurel. You deserve so much better. But what a lovely place. Did you meet Jane? Such a tragedy."

Laurel nodded. "Yep, Christen told me the story. What a stinker of a husband."

"At least she's in remission and can begin to look forward to life again. So this Christen?" Maisey asked.

"Christen was just arriving as I was about to leave. There is only so much coffee I could consume in a session."

"So you met up with this old boss of yours and..." Maisey said, hugging her own cup closer.

The transfixed gaze she received from Maisey had Laurel chuckling. "You know, if what I'd done wasn't so bad, this would be funny."

"Well, let me be the judge of that, Harley. I've had lots of experience believe me." Maisey grinned.

"I can't remember how it happened but I accepted her invitation for a drink. I ordered a soda. After a while she was going to order food and I decided to join her. I figured what the hell; Fiona had stood me up and why should I eat alone. Right?"

"Laurel dear, after Ronnie don't you think that how Fiona is treating you isn't right? If you care about someone you don't do dirty tricks like standing them up. And we both know this isn't the first time. "Maisey pursed her lips.

"Fiona is Fiona. I understand what she wants and what I want. Don't worry, Maisey."

Maisey nodded. "Oh, so you were using this Christen person?"

"No, I don't use people." Laurel scrunched her face. "Maybe. Generally it's the reverse for me. Anyway, we had a nice chat. I'm sure I told you that I'd met her at Andrea's." She saw Maisey nod. "She's David's sister." Laurel knew her explanation was all over the place.

Maisey laughed and shook her head. "And?"

"Well, I said I'd meet her at the Argyle Market Saturday morning for breakfast."

"Obviously you never made it. In fact, you said you forgot. So why does it matter?" Maisey asked.

Laurel tried and failed to unscramble her troubled brain. "I don't know, but it does."

"Well, if everything they say about the Jamison clan is correct it shouldn't worry you. Besides, call it payback for laying you off. I have found the circle eventually turns. Although this Christen doesn't sound like such a bad person or you wouldn't have wanted to share a meal with her or meet her the next day."

"She isn't. She was really nice," Laurel softly said.

Maisey smiled. "Good to know that not every reputation, however well earned, transmits beyond the workplace. Call her and apologize. That's my advice."

Laurel balled her fingers. "I don't have her number."

Maisey glanced at the clock. "Right, young whippersnapper, it's time to get those ovens working."

Laurel grinned and then hugged Maisey. "I love you, Maisey, and best yet I love working for you. Thank you."

Maisey hugged Laurel back. "You are the daughter I wish I'd had. Come on now, no sentiment. We old women are susceptible."

Laurel laughed. "Yeah right."

†

"Hey Laurel, what can I do for you?" Andrea grinned as she faced her friend.

Laurel picked up a coral lipstick on the counter and looked at it. Then focused her gaze on Andrea.

"Andy, I need to contact Ms. Jamison, do you have her number?"

Andrea smirked. "Sure, press twenty-one on the phone pad and you're there in the inner sanctum. Well, close, it's her assistant."

"I can't do that, I don't work here," Laurel said.

Andrea giggled. "You are so…never mind. Why don't you come over for dinner tonight, just you and me, and I'll try to get that number for you," Andrea said. "Is it a date?"

"I'm not sure. Fiona might…"

"Forget Fiona. This is about you, not her. No one should dictate what someone should do. You do it because it's the best thing for you. Have you made plans with Fiona?" Andrea asked.

"No. Well, not really. It's more like she just turns up."

"You deserve better. For God's sake, after what Ronnie put you through I'd think you'd learn, Laurel. Why is it that you are so nice but pick the worst possible people to be with?" Andrea said to take away the sting of her words.

Laurel scrunched her face. "Must have a sign above my head that says sucker. Sounds great about tonight. Is seven okay?"

"Perfect."

Laurel grinned. "Okay, I'll see you then." She waved at her friend before walking away.

Andrea watched Laurel go and pursed her lips. "Hmm, that's intriguing. I can't wait to find out more."

†

Christen tapped her fingers against the keyboard on her desk and then as a spreadsheet appeared she forcibly struck the keys. There was a sharp knock on the door before Barry's head appeared around the door. She flashed him a severe look.

"I didn't say enter," Christen growled.

Barry entered and closed the door behind him before placing his hands on his hips.

"Well, let me say, thank God I didn't wait or my head would have been severed at the neck, if the pummeling of your keyboard is anything to go by."

Christen curled her upper lip. "What do you want?"

"I want to know what you want for lunch. Are you are having a normal lunch or visiting with your mom?"

Christen drew a deep breath. *My mother again.* "She's having lunch with Hank and the board today. I'm having my usual lunch."

"It's raining, Christen. Are you staying in or going to the park?"

Christen turned to stare blindly out the window. She saw raindrops cascading down the glass, evidence that it was raining heavily. "I guess I'm inside today."

Barry moved forward. "Look, I know you don't normally sit with the lower classes but would you like to have lunch with me in the canteen today?"

Christen frowned. "What a crock of shit. We have lunch together lots of times, and don't call yourself lower classes. You know that's not what I think of you or anyone else who works here. We all have a job to do."

"Sorry. I know you're not like the rest of them. I sometimes wonder why you do what you do. You would be better suited as a nurse or something like that." He smiled at her. "Want to come with me?"

"Why would I do that?"

"Maybe because you need someone to talk to today and I'm the only person here who knows you well enough to just listen and not judge. Well, except for David. He's away…I checked. Besides, the canteen is so colorful." Barry grinned.

"What did I ever do to deserve you in my life, Barry?" Christen shook her head and smiled. "Thanks, but I'd prefer lunch here if that's okay. I don't want anyone listening in."

"Then, my dear friend, it shall be so." He turned to leave then looked back. "I've often wondered the same thing."

"What?" Christen asked.

"What I did to deserve you in my life. Greg Campion is champing at the bit, by the way, to have his weekly audience with you."

Christen laughed. "Send him in. I'm all agog for information on the financial results of the sports department."

Barry grinned and left the room.

The door burst open and Greg, complete with dyed blond hair, muscular body fit for a football linebacker, and standing six foot five, entered her office. "We had a cracking week, Chris. Now how about that update of my area that I wanted."

Under her breath, Christen said, "I'm sure you did and I'm sure you have, but only according to your interpretation not mine."

Chapter Thirteen

Samantha sat in the chair next to Hank and surveyed the others in the room. Everyone was a stranger. Except her son, there wasn't a familiar face. She let out a small sigh. *Life does move on. Perhaps this isn't where I should be.*

"Gentlemen, my mother Samantha Jamison, who is the fifty-one percent shareholder of Jamison's."

Everyone around the room stood up and applauded then regained their seat.

Hank remained standing and used a laser pointer to indicate the items on the screen that appeared. "Mother, I'm sure you will approve of the changes we have made and the profit projections for the next year."

Samantha gave her son a small smile before he began his presentation. For the next hour she listened to projections and options and made no comment though the board enthused over several points.

When Hank finished his presentation, he looked at his mother. "Any questions?"

Samantha considered what she had heard…

"Great, that means we can go on with our plans," Hank said.

Samantha stood and steadied herself on her cane. "I have questions, in fact really only one question. How does this impact our staff?"

Hank frowned and puffed out his chest. "Mother, that's irrelevant."

"This business is people, Hank. People who serve and people who buy. When you disengage one from the other it becomes merely a supermarket. Are we now a supermarket?" Samantha asked.

"No. Hell no. We have a prestigious clientele."

"So, what do prestigious clientele expect? No one they know? A new person every time they shop? To me that is just like a big box store. Give me the profits of K-mart and I might agree to your proposals. Otherwise, consider who you are selling to and to the staff—long-time staff—our store requires." Samantha clenched her hands tightly around the phoenix head of her cane.

Hank's cheeks diffused red as he glanced around the room.

Samantha knew in that moment that her son was not running the company. The so-called board members were. "I will be back in two days' time. Come up with another strategy that makes me happy or I shall personally sack the whole board," Samantha softly said before moving toward the door.

"We are having lunch, Mother," Hank cried.

Samantha looked around the room. "Not with me." She left the room.

†

Christen opened the sandwich packet Barry had deposited in front of her. She smiled as the aroma of her favorite chicken mayo wrap assailed her nostrils. "Perfect."

Barry grinned and sat next to her. He had a large brown paper bag and ripped it open. Inside was the largest BLT sandwich she had ever seen. It must have had at least four layers.

"Wow, that's humongous." Christen shook her head. "How do you keep your figure eating a thing like that?"

Barry winked. "Probably the same as you. It's in the genes. Malcolm would have a hissy fit if he saw what I eat here at lunch each day. If he looks at a doughnut there goes the waistline."

"How is Malcolm?" Christen asked as she bit into her wrap.

"Busy as always but he loves the work. Not my kind of profession being a social service worker," Barry shuddered. "All that angst." He bit down and took a chunk out of his sandwich.

Christen chewed her food and then took a sip of the orange juice Barry brought for her. "I know, but he loves kids and wants the best for them and their families. Do you remember at Jane's last year? He had her nieces and nephew in stitches. Got to say, me too. Have you ever thought…?"

Barry held up his hand. "Don't go there. It's not up for discussion. I love the man and all he is and does but bringing it home twenty-four seven nope. Anyway, I always hoped that you'd get fixed up long term and want a surrogate father. Malcolm is your man."

Christen spit out some of the lettuce of her lunch at the statement. "Me? I haven't had a girlfriend since…well since Macy left and that's thirteen years now." Christen scratched the back of her neck. "Hell where has the time gone."

Barry gazed at Christen and she gave him a concentrated look in return. "Beats me. So what's the matter with my best friend that she is taking it out on the keyboard?"

Christen sighed and put down her wrap and then drew her eyes to the pristine white ceiling of the office. "What if I said that I was interested in someone but didn't think I had a chance?"

Barry softly whistled before he grinned, displaying his gleaming white teeth.

"Tell me all. Who is it? Do I know her? Where did you meet? And why do you think that?"

Christen moved back in her chair at the barrage of questions. Then laughed. "I don't think you will know her. We met at a mutual friend's and it's a long story."

Barry laughed, steepling his fingers and tapping them together. "Now how many times have I heard that in my lifetime? Isn't that a stock and trade remark for our community. Darling, everything is a long story, which is why we spend so much time pondering what is and isn't wonderful." He giggled and took another huge bite of his sandwich.

"Well, we did arrange to meet at Argyle Market for breakfast but she never turned up. You know, I thought she would because she seemed genuine when she accepted the invite." Christen recalled Laurel's seemingly enthusiastic agreement to meet for breakfast.

"Does she know who you are?" Barry asked.

"Yes, but she isn't impressed. Quite the reverse. That's one part of the long story."

"Christen, she didn't work here did she?" Barry's eyes widened.

There was a tap on the door and it opened. The click of a cane was the first noise they heard, then her mother entered the room. "I'm sorry, Christen. I wasn't sure if you were in or…"

Barry shot out of his chair and ran over to hug Samantha. "Sammy, it's so wonderful to see you, now you are a sight for sore eyes."

Christen watched as Barry held her mother gently away and looked at her. "My, the French are looking after you, that's for sure. I don't think you look a day older than the last time I saw you." Barry planted a kiss on her mother's cheek.

Samantha chuckled, her cheeks stained red. "Barry, you have made me the most welcome in this short time than anyone in the days since I've been back. Thank you."

Christen heard the simple reaction and saw tears running down her mother's cheeks. She bit her lip at the gut reaction she had. They hadn't been very welcoming, not even enough to pick her up from the airport.

Christen stood.

"Christen, you didn't tell me Sammy was invited for lunch." Barry turned to her and winked.

Christen shrugged. "Sorry." She wasn't going to admit that she didn't know either—even if Barry was her best friend.

Barry smiled and turned back to her mother. "Sammy, now if I remember correctly your favorite is ham on rye with pickle right?"

"How did you…yes. Thank you that will be wonderful. Do you still go to the bakery on Essex Street?"

"Of course, it's the only place for proper fast food. Be back in a jiffy." Barry bustled out of the room.

"I'm sorry I didn't want to interrupt if it was a business lunch," Samantha said.

Christen shrugged. "You didn't. We were having a friendly lunch. That doesn't occur often, it just worked out today. I thought you were having lunch with the board. Did something come up?"

"I was, and yes something came up."

"Oh. If it isn't a Hank state secret, dare I ask?" Christen waved to a seat and her mother sat down.

"Someone should have told me," Samantha quietly replied.

"Told you what exactly?" Christen sat opposite her mother.

Samantha looked at the half-eaten lunches and smiled. "I remember when you and Barry came home from college that first year and you took over the summerhouse in Raven. There were pizza cartons and take-out trays a mile deep. Not to mention all those beer bottles."

"There was not." Christen recalled the time and smiled. "Maybe half a mile."

Samantha chuckled. "Your father told you never to bring Barry home again. As usual you ignored that and brought him for Thanksgiving that year. He charmed everyone except your father. I remember the first time he called me *Sammy*. That brought such memories of my childhood back to me."

Christen saw tears drip slowly down her mother's cheeks and her heart thawed at the memories. What was the point in being bitter? Her mother was here now and the past was the past. How simple that sounded and in reality it was as simple as forgiving and moving forward.

"He's a good guy. I recall you threw an oven glove at him the first time he called you Sammy. Barry loves people and he liked our family—well maybe not Dad and Hank, but the three of us had good times at vacation time."

"Is he still with…now let me think, Malcolm? He met him just before your father died, if I recall."

Christen was amazed at her mother's retention of detail. "Yep. In a few months they have a wedding ceremony planned. I thought they should do it immediately in case, somehow, the ruling gets overturned."

"Christen, how cynical. I doubt it will change, and even if it does change love is a powerful force and it doesn't need to be acknowledged by anyone at the end of the day except for the two people who love each other," Samantha said.

Christen mused that over and sighed.

"You don't agree?"

"For some people perhaps," Christen replied. "You mentioned that we should have told you something important?"

Samantha nodded. "The company is making reasonable profits, but at what cost? I found out today our staff takes the brunt of the burden. For all your father's faults, that was not something he would condone. I do not either. Do you?" Samantha asked. She fixed her gaze directly on Christen.

"No," Christen declared.

"Why haven't you told me this? Does David agree with you?"

"Yes, he does. We have no voice on the board. We are just workers. Hell, the ax could fall on either of us at any time. I suppose the only reason it doesn't is that we are family." Christen shook her head. "It's a cutthroat business now. Hank is doing…well, what he thinks is right."

"You obviously do not agree," Samantha said.

"What do you want me to say? That my brother is incompetent? I won't. He's just been led astray by the board." Christen shook her head.

"How have these board members taken control?"

"Because you gave Hank autonomy over your vote and he thinks they know better than anyone. He's a puppet," Christen said.

"Then it's time I took back control. Will you help me?" Samantha asked.

Christen sighed. "What about Hank? As much as I loathe what he's doing now, for years he did a fine job. I think he deserves a chance to change direction."

Samantha moved her cane and it clunked against one of the conference table's legs. Then she chuckled. "Thank you, Christen."

"For what?" Christen frowned.

"Supporting the family no matter how easy it would be to feed Hank to the wolves. You have not changed, my darling. For what it's worth, of all my children I have always been confident that you will always do the right thing."

Christen was taken aback at the statement but more so by the pride she heard in her mother's voice. "It is the right thing to do. Not everyone gets it right first time around or even the second. I might balk to help at the third." Christen shrugged and smiled.

"Are you willing to help me remove this board and see if we can salvage Jamison's image with its staff and I'm sure the customers?"

"I will," Christen said.

Barry entered the room. "Have I missed anything exciting?" He placed a brown bag next to Samantha and winked.

"Not really, just in time for a strategy meeting," Samantha said.

Barry frowned and turned to Christen.

"We are going to take back the company."

Barry threw up his arms and squealed. "At last sense has come to the table."

†

David Jamison parked his red Ferrari in his personal parking spot behind the store and ambled around the building to the staff entrance. He grinned at Delia, who was mopping the floor, and gave her a wink. As usual, the sexagenarian blushed and giggled.

He took the elevator to the fifth floor and arrived at his sister's office with a minute to spare. She had been adamant he arrive no later than three, threatening that he would be in big trouble if he was late. Sweeping into the outer office he was surprised to see Barry's chair empty and wandered to Christen's office door. Rapping on the windowpane twice, he entered.

"You requested my company at three sharp and here I am," David said. He gazed at the conference table and was amazed to see Barry and his mother.

"Mother?" He raised his eyebrows and then frowned. "Okay, what have I done now?"

"Get over yourself, David. It isn't all about you. Mom has come to a decision and I've decided to help. We want to ask if you are on board too," Christen said and pointed to a seat next to their mother.

David walked toward the seat, smiled at his mother and pecked her on the cheek. "Good to see you, Mom. I thought Hank had you all to himself today?"

"He perhaps thought that too. I, on the other hand, decided otherwise."

David sat and glanced at Barry, who gave him a huge grin. *Well he's happy.* "Okay, what's going on and how can I help?"

Christen nodded to their mother.

"David, I do not like what is happening to the store and I intend to remove the board and start again. That may mean removing Hank too," Samantha said. She lifted her chin and eyed him directly.

David opened his mouth then shut it before frowning and scratching the side of his neck and pursing his lips. "That's impossible. Hank wouldn't let you do that. Besides, if you do, who will run it in the interim?"

Samantha smiled. She glanced at Christen and then back to him.

"Oh no, I can't. I have a wedding to plan and I'm not cut out for the top job. Trust me on that one." David glared at Christen, who appeared to ignore him.

"Christen is better suited to take the helm for a period of time. You can be her second in command. When we find the right candidates who have the vision we do then things can be changed," Samantha forthrightly announced.

David shook his head, wondering if he was dreaming and would wake any moment. He didn't. "I think this is madness. Hank wasn't always this stupid. Aren't we going to give him a chance to redeem himself?"

"Yes, of course. He deserves to run the company but only if he will agree to my terms," Samantha said.

David heard the steel in the reply. Some might have thought their mother merely a pawn in the store hierarchy but she had major influence, even when his father was alive.

"Does that mean you will not be helping?" Christen asked.

"I need this job, Christen. If Hank doesn't like what we are doing and manages to take control after we try a coup we will be out on the street," David groaned.

"That's why we have to keep it under wraps until Mom meets with her lawyer in an hour to rescind the power of attorney over her assets here. Then we can go forward." Christen passed over a thin manila file to him.

"What's this?" David glanced inside at the names of several people who once worked at the company.

"Read that, including my notes at the end, and then decide whose side you are on." Christen stood. "I have a meeting with the managers of the second floor now, so we will catch up in the morning. I figure breakfast with Mother will be ideal. Shall we say seven thirty?"

"Seven thirty? Wow, Christen, you certainly don't waste time do you." He shook his head. "I'll be there." David glanced at the file and fingered a few of the sheets. "I'll take Mom back to her hotel if she's done here or to her lawyer. Whichever."

"Thank you, darling, that will be delightful. Perhaps we can have a coffee whilst I wait for my lawyer." Samantha rose.

"Sure thing, Mom." David rolled his eyes.

"Thank you, Christen." Samantha smiled.

Christen stood too and went around the table and hugged Samantha.

David watched in fascination. He hadn't expected to see that. Things were happening fast around here.

Christen hugged Barry and they all left the room.

Chapter Fourteen

Laurel rang Andrea's doorbell and waited. She didn't have to wait long as the door was swung open.

"Lau, you are not going to believe what's happening at Jamison's," Andrea gushed as she pulled Laurel inside and closed the door.

The smell of chili greeted Laurel. It was one of Andrea's favorite dishes, probably because it was one of the few she didn't burn. "Dinner smells great. I brought wine." Laurel thrust a bottle of rosé at her friend.

"Excellent, it will work well with the meal. Just like David, you always know these things." Andrea went into the kitchen and Laurel followed, removing her coat and placing it on the coat hook near the door.

"So what's the score at Jamison's?" Laurel climbed onto the barstool opposite Andrea.

"I called David to find out Christen's private number."

"Oh." Laurel bit her lip.

Waving a red-stained wooden spoon around, Andrea grinned. "Don't worry. I said it was for me. I wanted to have a chat with her."

"Great, thanks for that." Laurel's heart skipped a beat at the prospect of calling Christen.

"Well, there's going to be eruptions at Jamison's in the next few days. You know I told you David's mother arrived last weekend."

"No, but then…"

"Yeah, yeah. Well, she's not happy with the way the store is being run and wants to take it away from Hank…well, mainly the board I think. Can you believe that after all these years something like that would happen?" Andrea said. She turned her back and stirred the chili pot.

Laurel blinked rapidly. "Andrea, I think David told you that in private. I'm sure it isn't something that he expected you to broadcast," Laurel said. She reached for the wine bottle, opened it, took the two glasses from the corner of the counter, and began to pour the liquid liberally.

"Oh, I'm not broadcasting it. Whom are you going to tell? Besides, if I can't tell my best friend, who can I tell," Andrea said.

"No one probably. But that isn't the point," Laurel whispered not loud enough for Andrea to hear.

"Laurel, maybe you will get your job back. Wouldn't that be cool? We'd see each other every day again. I miss you at work." Andrea removed the pot from the stove and began to ladle the meal into two red earthenware bowls. "I have that crusty bread you love, and yes it's Maisey's special bake."

Laurel laughed. "And how did you shop at my workplace and I didn't see you?"

"Because I sent Rita. She wanted a special cake for her mother's birthday so I asked her to pick me up a loaf of bread." Andrea winked, passing a steaming bowl along the counter before sitting opposite Laurel. "Tuck in."

"Where's the bread?"

"Oops, silly me." Andrea spun around and seconds later placed a warm loaf of bread between them. They began to eat with gusto.

†

Laurel smacked her lips. "As always, Andrea, your chili was outstanding."

Andrea smiled. "Thank you. Shall we take our wine and adjourn to the family room?"

Once in the room they both sank on the sofa before turning to put their feet up and facing each other.

"Thanks for tonight, Andrea. I miss not seeing you too. Just so you know I will never go back to Jamison's. That's in the past, like Ronnie."

Andrea nodded. "Have you heard from Ronnie?"

Laurel considered her reply for a few moments.

"Look, if you don't want to talk about it…"

"No. No, it's okay. She sent me a bill for a thousand bucks. She said I owed the rent on the apartment."

"She did what?" Andrea screamed.

Laurel lifted a hand. "I know! She threw me out right. Seems her trip to Europe wasn't as financially successful as she'd assumed. Now she's trying to make me pay for the rent in arrears while she's been gone."

"I'm speechless." Andrea placed a hand to her mouth. "Oh, Laurel, what are you going to do?"

Laurel laughed and it sounded harsh to her ears. "Carol's working on it. In fact, by the time she's finished, Carol said Ronnie will have nothing left and she'll owe me the next ten years' earnings in her paintings."

"Whoa. Are you okay with that? I know you must hate Ronnie, but you've never been vindictive." Andrea sipped her wine. "Great rosé, by the way. I'm glad you put me onto this. It's so much lighter to the palate than red."

"Yeah. Red gives me a headache." She let out a sigh. "I think Carol will just use a few frightening tactics so Ronnie doesn't keep coming back. Thank God she insisted the lease stay in her name when we moved in together or I'd be screwed." Laurel clenched her teeth.

Andrea laughed. "Yeah, it makes you wonder, doesn't it, what you should do with your assets if you live with someone. I don't have anything much to speak of, but at least my mortgage on this place is almost finished. There's no way I am going to lose everything if David and I split." Andrea frowned.

Laurel reached across and touched her friend's hand. "I hardly think that he'll take your home from you. He must have more money than the both of us combined."

"His apartment is nice. It has three bedrooms with a view to the mountain range but he's mortgaged to the hilt. There is the car that I know is worth a year of my salary. I swear he loves that more than me."

Laurel chuckled. "A bit cold to snuggle up to on a night though. Right?"

Andrea laughed. "Hmm. Anyway, enough of me. Please tell me what's the interest with Christen? I would have thought she'd be the last person besides Ronnie you ever wanted to speak to again."

"You could be right. I met her by accident at Jane's Café. She was alone and I was waiting for Fiona." Laurel mused over the evening.

"Fiona didn't turn up again, did she? Oh, don't tell me. She's always got an excuse. Lau, you deserve so much more. Carry on. I'm sorry for interrupting." Andrea shrugged.

Laurel eyed her friend. Andrea and Fiona had never really hit it off. She thought at first it was because of their differing lifestyles but that wasn't the case. "Andrea, it's okay. I know you're looking out for me and I love you for it. Going back to the story…I joined Christen for dinner. I had a good time. She was nothing like what I actually thought she was. In fact, I'd swear she's quite shy in some ways." Laurel grinned. "It was endearing."

"Endearing?" Andrea leaned a hand under her chin and smirked. "Really."

Laurel narrowed her eyes and smiled. "Yes, really. Bottom line, she asked if I wanted to meet her for a late breakfast at Argyle Market. Apparently she goes every Saturday if she can. I said I would."

"Good for you," Andrea said.

Laurel swiped a hand against her lips that had suddenly gone dry. "I didn't go. In fact, until yesterday, I'd totally forgotten her. Now I feel so guilty and need to apologize."

"Oh no. There was me thinking we could double date. Bummer."

"Andrea, please, I'm serious here."

"Okay, so what happened?" She held up her hand. "Wait, don't tell me, I know. Fiona stood you up and then turned up with a sob story for letting you down and all was forgiven?" Andrea shook her head. "Am I right?"

Laurel pulled in a silent breath. "You make it sound like I am being taken for a sucker again. Maybe I am. I like being with Fiona, she makes me feel alive. Right now it works for both of us." She shook her head. "You wouldn't understand. You've got the perfect partner." Her eyes captured Andrea's. "Can I have the number?"

Andrea stared at Laurel and nodded. "I'll text it to you."

"Thank you. Look, I know you are just looking out for me, but Fiona…"

"It's okay, Laurel. If Fiona makes you happy then I'm happy for you. Just don't ask me on a double date."

"What do you mean? Is it because you don't like her?"

"No. Because she might make a play for David and I'd have to hit her."

Laurel laughed so hard she was crying and looked at Andrea, who was also giggling uncontrollably. "Fiona likes women not men, Andrea. Sometimes I wonder at your intellect."

"You shouldn't, it's the same as yours and for the record, when have you known David Jamison not to charm anyone."

Laurel laughed. "Yeah, but charming them and getting into their pants is a different thing altogether."

"Really? Do you remember Christo Landros that night we both got a job at Jamison's?"

Laurel dredged her memory then blushed. "Andrea, that is one story that is never spoken of except between us in private and definitely not with David."

"You have to be kidding me." Andrea grinned. "Come on let's finish the bottle and you can stay tonight if you want."

Laurel grinned. "Okay, but on one condition."

"Name it?"

"I'm not sharing David's toothbrush."

Andrea cracked up again and when she stopped laughing, she shook her head. "That's a gross image."

Laurel laughed. "I'll get us more wine."

†

Christen checked the clock on the wall. It was nine. Looking out of the window below the lights outside showed random figures walking by the store.

Her eyes smarted at the information she'd pored over for hours. Much of it was like a puzzle without all the pieces and it defeated her. "I'm missing something, or maybe I'm just not capable of seeing the whole picture." She didn't understand why she readily agreed to shake the core of Jamison's. Maybe Hank hadn't done great, but the store was still there. She had hated her mother for so long that she was surprised they were now allies. "What does that make me? Any more of a puppet than Hank is?"

Her cell rang. She picked up the phone and looked at the caller ID. It was unknown to her. "Damn, I'm not in the mood for a cold caller." Her finger hovered over Accept but she pressed End, or so she thought. A voice echoed near to her ear. *Damn, I pressed the wrong button.* "Christen Jamison."

"Hi. Look, I'm sorry."

"Who are you?" Christen bit her lip.

"Laurel Rogers, Andrea's friend. We shared dinner together Friday night. Do you remember?"

Christen clenched a fist. "Vaguely."

"Right, of course. Anyway it was nice. Perhaps we can…well, anyway I just wanted to thank you."

There was a few seconds of silence.

"You never turned up at the market. I assumed you had forgotten, or, your friend had returned." Christen sucked in a silent breath.

"I'm sorry for leading you on to think that. Can we have coffee one day, maybe? My treat?"

Christen dropped her gaze to the number on her phone, frowning when it said it was a number she had previously called.

"Thanks, but I'm not into being a third-party castaway. Enjoy your life, Laurel." Christen ended the call.

"I need to find a life. A safe one where no can hurt me. I'm too old for trying to find romance." She dropped the phone and picked up a file in front of her.

†

Samantha snuggled on the couch with her phone on speaker as she waited for the call to connect.

"Hello, the Roche residence."

"Always the polite response. How I miss you, my darling, Frances. It's Mom." Samantha smiled as she heard the chuckle at the end of the line.

"Mom, I almost called you…several times actually, but Danny said it was your time and we had to wait. How is it?"

Samantha grinned. She could see her daughter in the hall of the grande mansion, as they called it in France, kicking off her shoes as she leaned against the purple painted wall. "It's going reasonably well."

"Mom, are they giving you a hard time? I can come over. It's only twelve hours with stopovers."

"Darling, no. What I have to do is better left to me. I just wanted to hear your voice and find out what you and the family have been up to." Samantha pictured herself back home.

"Oh, Mom, just the same. The twins want all the new gadgets and we said they have to earn it but," Frances chuckled, "I said no. Danny was the weak link and he gave in. Now we have twins rampaging through the streets of Paris. God help us."

"I wish I were there." Samantha closed her eyes and imagined for this short time she was back home.

"I do too. The twins hang on your every word. So how are my siblings?"

"David is engaged, she's a lovely young woman and I do actually believe he loves her."

"Wow. David is a worse cad than…I'm glad, kind of."

"I know, darling, but he's different. Love does that to you."

"What about Christen? Is she still with her friend?"

Samantha heard the undertones and chose at that moment to ignore it. "It was her partner, darling, and no, they split soon after I came to France. She's alone."

"Probably best."

"Frances, I love you very much, but love forgives and heals lots of chasms. I know you disapprove of Christen's choices of a partner but she is your sister."

"Yeah right. Doesn't mean I have to approve of her being a lesbian. Can you imagine what that might do if Danny goes for office?"

"Actually, I suspect he would gain a lot of votes these days."

"Mom!"

Samantha laughed, picturing Frances's outraged expression. "You are so conservative, my darling."

"Is Hank being as aloof and sober as usual?"

Samantha pulled at her lower lip and nodded. "Yes. He hasn't changed at all. If he has, it certainly is not for the good of the company."

"Mom, are you sure you don't need me to come over? I will. Danny and the kids will understand."

"I love you, darling, but your battles are at home and mine for the moment are here. How is Miss Pompadour?" Samantha smiled, picturing the Pomeranian pooch brought home by Danny one afternoon after completing his daily run.

"Hmm. You mean the spoiled rotten stray who I swear lost all of its tags just so Danny would bring her home," Frances regaled.

"And that part about spoiled doesn't have anything to do with the fact that you more than anyone else would be devastated if an owner turned up to claim her." Samantha's heart warmed as the beige-haired dog with drooling eyes came vividly to mind. She heard Frances chuckle.

"She misses you. Especially for her afternoon nap. She trots around your studio looking for you."

"Does she really look for me?" Samantha asked, tears welling in her eyes.

"We all do, and yes that means Danny too. He misses your sharp intellect because we both know I'm not up to your speed. I don't know how you do it, Mom."

Samantha settled back with a beaming smile.

"That's because I have a lot more years under my belt, darling."

Chapter Fifteen

Laurel had watched a man come to the shop every Monday through Friday since she began working at Maisey's bakery. He looked familiar but she couldn't quite place him. In the last couple of weeks when she served him, she'd been tempted to ask if they knew each other but didn't want him to get the wrong idea. She hadn't even asked Maisey if she knew who he was as it had always slipped her mind.

Now, as she enclosed the chicken mayo wrap in film she wondered if today she might find out.

"I'll have a chocolate muffin too. Thanks."

Laurel stopped her musing and nodded at him with a smile.

"My boss has a sweet tooth and she's been grouchy today so I thought she might need the sugar rush."

Laurel chuckled. "You must have one great boss if you think enough of her to consider her this way." *Lame, Laurel, lame, but it's an opening.*

The man pierced her with watery gray eyes. "She is much maligned but underneath she's the best. I wouldn't want to work for anyone else."

"You work close by?" Laurel asked, placing the muffin in a brown paper bag.

"Yep, the Jamison's Store. I've been there…arg forever, as my partner would say. Almost married to the place." He picked up the packages on the counter.

So that's where I know him from, but who is he? She'd ask Andrea. "Enjoy the lunch and I hope your boss is less grumpy."

"Me too, and she will be." The man winked and left the shop.

Several customers later, Laurel sat down for a breather. Lunchtime was always hectic and that made her happy as there would be no business without the lunch crowd.

"Slacking hmm…I'd better dock your pay."

Laurel smiled and stood up as Maisey entered the shop with a carton full of supplies.

"Yeah, and who would help you with the provisions? And I told you never to carry anything heavy." Laurel rushed forward and took the package. "Yep, way too heavy. I'll collect the stuff in the van while you serve the customers." Laurel went to the back room and deposited the carton then left by the side entrance to unload the rest of the provisions.

†

Christen paced her office for the hundredth time. She still hadn't solved the problem. She wanted to see Laurel Rogers again and stupidly she had blown her off the night before. *But who wouldn't have after being stood up?*

There was a knock on the door and Barry entered. "Lunch. Are you in a better mood?"

Christen sneered. "I'm in as good a mood as I want to be."

"Okay, is it waiting for Sammy's next chess move or something else?" Barry asked and placed the sacks on the table. "People are going to start talking you know. I haven't been to the canteen two days in succession and that is unheard of."

Christen snorted and sank down in a chair next to the food. "Do you ever feel that life moves on and you're two paces behind?" She blew out a breath. "I do. Especially today."

Barry sat next to her and passed over her wrap. She took it absently, unwrapping the familiar package. Taking out the chicken roll she bit into the contents.

"Every day. Hell, Christen, who doesn't? Please don't tell me this is the first time," Barry squealed.

"No…yes…well, it's different." Christen clenched her fists and wished she had not as the chicken oozed out of the wrap.

"Different, girlfriend? Please tell me more." Barry leaned his chin on the palms of his hands and gazed at her intently.

"This isn't funny, Barry."

Barry's eyes flared. "Did I say it was? It's the woman who used to work here, right?"

Christen glared at him.

Barry chuckled. "No worries. I have the perfect solution to your problems."

Christen frowned.

Barry slipped a brown bag to her and she gingerly opened it and a slow grin curved her lips. She turned and hugged Barry. "I love you. You idiot friend who puts up with me. Thank you."

"You have done the same for me more times than I can count on ten fingers. When you need me, I will be there, no matter what."

Christen withdrew from the hug and smiled. "That's what best friends do. No matter what. Chocolate chip muffin…hmm…did they have blueberry?"

"You are so demanding." Barry laughed.

Christen's mood improved and they ate their lunch with gusto.

†

"Are we ready?" Samantha turned to her entourage.

Christen, David, and Barry nodded.

"Then I suggest we don't keep Hank and the board waiting."

As they reached Hank's office area, there was no one around.

David moved ahead of them and without knocking gallantly held the door of the main conference room open for her and the rest to follow through.

"Thank you, David." Samantha smiled at her son.

He grinned.

Entering, Samantha noted Hank's twisted lips as he screwed up his eyes, gazing at them. He was just like his father, trying to intimidate with a stare. These days it didn't have any effect on her.

"Hank, thank you for arranging for the board to be here on such short notice." There was a murmur from several of the members but not loud enough to hear what was said.

"I thought it was just you, Mother. Why are *they* here?" He pointed at Christen, David, and Barry.

Samantha moved to the head of the table. "All in good time, Hank. It seems that we need more seats." Her eyes moved to Hank, who sneered.

"I'll get them," David said. He moved to the back of the room to collect four chairs from a stack there.

"Look, Mother, time is money. What's the problem?" Hank asked and sat down heavily in his chair at the head of the table.

"The first problem, my dear, is that you are sitting in my chair," Samantha softly said.

Hank's face went beet red. He stood and walked over to the nearest window and leaned against the ledge.

Samantha took the chair and guardedly looked at the men around the table. In this day and age she would have thought there would be at least one woman among them. *Why isn't Christen? David, I can understand; he wouldn't want the hassle. Interesting.*

When everyone was seated, except for Hank, Samantha drew in a deep breath to settle her nerves. If anyone looked under the table they would see her knees knocking. "Last night I saw my lawyer and addressed the matter of my power of attorney over my shareholding in the store." There was a series of shuffles and murmurs of disquiet from the board and she looked directly at Hank. "As of nine a.m. this morning I have rescinded that power handed to my son and it is now vested in me again."

"Mother, why?" Hank yelled.

Samantha remained calm. She never wanted to hurt any of her children but this had to be done. "Hank, your plans and obviously that of the board are in total contrast to what I want and I believe your father would have wanted. You treat our staff as if they are meaningless and *they*, my son, are the backbone of a store like Jamison's. I have contracted for an independent audit of the accounts. Christen," Samantha turned and smiled at her daughter, "has given me the basics, but she does not have access to the details of the formal accounts. I believe you use someone or a company called James Stanley."

Samantha shifted her gaze to a man two seats away from her. He looked uncomfortable and his chubby face now had bulging eyes. "Are you James Stanley?"

"Yes. It's my firm."

Samantha nodded. "Then will you please coordinate with Christen after the meeting so that she has access to all the records for our audit team."

"Hold on, Mother, you can't just breeze in here and say this stuff and demand things. What do you know about our business today? You've been away fourteen years," Hank harshly spat.

David stood.

Samantha smiled at her younger son and waved at him to sit. "No, David. Hank is right about one thing and one thing only. The time I've been away."

Samantha stood and rested on her cane.

"I have forgotten more about this business than you have ever learned in the time you have been running the store, Hank. Your father was the front man but trust me, son, the brains behind the success came from me."

Hank went pale and glanced around the room.

"These people who you have trusted with our future are not right for Jamison's and from today each one of you are served notice that at the end of the business day you are no longer on the board. This is a family business and it will revert to that. Hank, do you want to remain here?" Samantha heard the steel in her voice and a rush of pride ran through her veins. *There is life in the old dog yet.*

"You can't do this, Mother. We need these people." Hank waved his hand around the room.

"You need these people, Hank. Jamison's does not. If you want to leave with the others that is your choice. Let me know by the end of the day. I will be in Christen's office," Samantha said. She turned to her comrades. "Our business here is done. Let's find a decent cup of coffee."

They all marched out with Samantha at the helm.

†

Christen settled back in her chair and surveyed her empty office.

"What a hell of a day."

She placed her hands and stretched the skin back around her eyes. The phone rang and she absently answered it.

"Christen."

"Hi, Christen, it's Andrea. Is it a good time to talk?"

"Andrea, sure. What can I do for you?" Christen asked before frowning.

"David and I are going to celebrate tonight with your mom…you know about today. I figured you should be there, if you are free?"

Musing over the invitation Christen closed her eyes. *Too much family drama.* "Sorry, Andrea, I have plans. Perhaps another time."

"Yeah. Another time. I just thought…"

"Okay, is that all?" Christen bit out.

"I was just wondering…well, it's not my business, of course, but my friend Laurel asked for your number and I gave it to her. Was that okay?"

Christen bit her lip. "Yes, she called me."

"Oh, good. She was worried you might not understand."

"You know?" Christen barked.

There was silence at the other end for a while then a timid voice replied. "Yes, but she's my best friend. She was sorry. Look, I'm sorry to have bothered you, Christen."

"Yes, sorry. It's going around. Have a good evening, Andrea."

"Same to you. If you decide later to change your mind we will be at Samantha's hotel. Dinner is booked for eight."

"Bye." Christen finished the call. "Damn, does everyone know my business?"

She picked up her cell and looked at the last numbers received before selecting one.

Chapter Sixteen

Laurel watched Fiona pace her apartment, walking over to the coffee table, and flick through a magazine.

"Fiona, tell me what's going on, please? You've been like a cat on hot bricks since you arrived."

Fiona dropped the magazine and stared at Laurel. "You know that this is only casual, right?"

Laurel's heart raced at the statement. "Yes, for both of us. Do you want to end it?"

Fiona sank down on the sofa. "I like you, Laurel. I really do but…"

Laurel blanched at the use of her full name. *This is serious.* She heard the word *but* and knew what to expect. It happened every time. "But?"

Fiona stood pretty much in sync with how she had been behaving. "I met someone three weeks ago. She's married to a man and is driving me crazy. I don't know what to do."

Laurel raised her eyebrows and shook her head. "You're asking me?"

Fiona nodded. "Sorry, but I trust you. You are one of the nicest people I've ever met. Damn, I wish I felt this way for you."

"What does that make me? The safe bet," Laurel scoffed.

Fiona moved across the few feet that separated them and reached out, touching Laurel's forehead with her finger.

Laurel flinched at the touch. "Let's call it a day, Fiona. We won't hurt each other with lies. Trust me, it doesn't work."

"Can we still be friends?"

Fiona gave Laurel a hurt look she'd seen on a few occasions when Fiona wanted her own way. "Sure, we had a good time. If I'm honest, you helped me through a hard time," Laurel said. She stood and hugged Fiona. "Married is not good. Especially to a man."

Fiona frowned. "I know, but what can you do when the right person hits you head-on and you have no idea what to do."

"Be yourself, Fiona. Maybe it will work out and if it doesn't, pick yourself up and go forward," Laurel said softly.

"It's what you did, right?"

"Exactly what I did." Laurel reached up and kissed Fiona's cheek. "Go for it. Give it your best. I'll be here for you if you need someone to talk to." She shook her head. "But we will never be lovers again."

"You really are the best, Lau." Fiona headed for the door.

"Oh, when and if you want to talk, make it a reasonable hour, please. I do get up early for work."

Fiona grinned and waved as she closed the apartment door behind her.

Laurel sat down and sighed. "Well that's a relief. I feel like a boulder has been taken off my back." She chuckled and reached for the remote just as the phone rang.

†

Christen nervously smoothed the invisible creases on the beige A-line skirt she wore, complementing her tan silk blouse, and wheat-colored cotton jacket. She glanced at her watch. It was seven forty-five and the hotel lobby was packed. It certainly maintained its clientele. She'd been waiting the last ten minutes and the place was streaming with people. Albeit there were two conferences and a wedding party, but on a Wednesday that was great marketing.

Christen pulled out her cell and contemplated calling to see if there was a problem. Then she put it back in her pocket. *She'll think I'm stupid.*

"Christen."

Christen was surprised at the person standing in front of her.

"Helen."

Helen Richardson grinned as they came within a foot of each other. "It's hectic here tonight. You can barely find anyone."

"I know. Obviously they know something we don't. Wednesdays are always slow at the store."

Helen chuckled. "That's for sure. We should use their marketing agency."

"I was thinking the same myself." Christen grinned.

"Hi."

Christen turned to the newcomer and blushed. "Hi."

"Am I interrupting?"

"No. No, of course not. Helen do you know Laurel? She worked for us until…" Christen stuttered.

Helen smiled. "Yes, I know Laurel. How have you been? I heard you found a job quickly, I'm pleased for you."

Laurel chuckled. "Andrea told you, didn't she?"

Helen nodded. "Look, I have to go and find Steve. He promised me that he had booked a table. It's our thirtieth wedding anniversary and they can't find the reservation. I guess it's Spagmali's again tonight. Enjoy your evening. Good to see you, Laurel."

"You too, Helen," Laurel murmured.

"Hi, again," Laurel said when Helen left.

Christen's stomach flipped several times at the simple phrase. "Hi again too. Thank you for coming. I'm not sure about the company but I know the food will be great," Christen said softly.

"I wouldn't have come if I didn't like the company." Laurel smiled. "Sorry I'm a bit late. I actually couldn't find anything decent to wear until I rummaged in the ironing pile," Laurel said before laughing.

Christen took in the cream blouse flanked by a red floral print jacket and basic black pants. "You look wonderful."

Laurel shrugged and grinned. "Thanks. For the record, you do too."

Christen felt her heart race. "I told my mother that we would be here but Andrea and David might not know."

"Let's go then." Laurel held out her arm and Christen frowned. "For the sake of appearances."

"Sure." Christen linked her arm in Laurel's and they headed into the restaurant.

As they came up to the maitre d' Christen said, "We are with the Samantha Jamison party."

The man grinned widely and motioned to a waiter.

When the waiter arrived, Christen smiled. "I have friends celebrating their thirtieth wedding anniversary and they are booked in the restaurant. I'd like to send them a bottle of champagne."

"Of course. Of course. Who is the party? As far as I know we have no party of that description that I'm aware off."

"Richardson, Steve and Helen. Want to check?" Christen calmly asked the maitre d'.

"Yes. Yes I will." He flipped a page and coughed. "We don't seem to have…"

"Did you give their table to a regular customer?" Christen asked.

"It's a misunderstanding. We shall offer them another night."

"Forget that. Tonight is the night. Add two more places to my mother's table and find them." She glared at the man, "Now."

"Yes. Yes, immediately." He left the podium and went into the lobby.

"Wow, you were taking no prisoners," Laurel said.

Christen looked at Laurel and saw her smile. *Oh thank God.* "It isn't right. You don't treat people like that," Christen murmured.

The waiter who had been hovering asked, "Do you want me to take you to your table now?"

Christen turned to Laurel. "Do you mind if we wait until they find Helen and her husband?"

"I wouldn't expect anything less. How about I go to the table and let the others know we arrived. I know Andy and David."

"I'm sorry. We will both go." Christen bit her inner lip.

Laurel laid a hand on Christen's arm. "This is good, do what you have to do. I will still be here." Laurel waved at the waiter and left with him.

Christen hesitated as she watched Laurel leave.

"I'm sorry the parties have left the hotel or at least they have not responded to the internal speaker system."

Christen frowned. "If I find them in ten minutes their meal is free."

"I can't do…"

Christen left the restaurant area.

†

Laurel drew in a deep breath as she neared the dinner table and saw Andrea. *I can do this, sure I can.*

Andrea, with her eyes wide, stood. "Laurel? Are you having dinner here tonight too?"

Laurel bit her lip and threw her hands in the air. "Yes, actually I am. With you." Andrea's reactions made Laurel laugh. She couldn't help herself as Andrea's mouth opened and closed like a guppy and her eyes bulged. She wondered if her friend was ever cast as a fish in school plays; she'd be a natural. *God no that's cruel.*

"My dear, you must be Christen's friend. Please sit. Is Christen going to turn up?"

Laurel smiled at the older woman who had spoken and saw the distinct resemblance to Christen. They had the same eyes and mouth. *So this is what Christen will look like as an old lady. Wow.* "Yes, she's being a Good Samaritan at the moment."

"Please tell all, my dear. Oh, how remiss of me. I'm Samantha Jamison and this is my son…"

Laurel smiled. "I know. At least your son. We have met socially once before when he became engaged to Andrea, who is my best friend." Laurel watched as Samantha Jamison gave her a concentrated look and then inclined her head.

"I guess I'm the odd one out then. I did not bring a partner," Samantha said before grinning.

"Mom, you don't need a partner, you have us," David said. "Hi, Laurel. Good to see you again. Where exactly is Chris doing her Good Samaritan bit and for whom?"

"Here actually. Do you know Helen Richardson?" Laurel shrugged. "Sorry, of course you do. It's her thirtieth wedding anniversary and her husband booked a table. Seems that they gave it to…another party."

"She is doing what exactly?" David frowned.

Laurel grinned. "Giving the maitre d' a hard time. It was awesome."

David chuckled. "Typical Chris. Though I thought she would have…"

"Yes, brother?"

"Can't believe you do that to me every time," David said. He stood and hugged Christen. "Interesting."

"Always. Sorry I'm late." Christen looked at Laurel and smiled. "Got held up."

"Laurel told us, darling. Did you find Helen?" Samantha casually asked.

"No." Christen sat down on the free seat next to Laurel.

Laurel reached across and placed a hand on Christen's. "You tried."

Christen smiled. "I did, thank you."

"Well, I think this calls for champagne and not for what happened at the store but my daughter's Good Samaritan act, however unsuccessful. As I've always said…"

Christen and David replied in unison, "It isn't the result but the action that counts."

Laurel laughed and clutched Christen's hand harder. Unaware of the pressure until Christen wriggled her fingers.

"I'm losing circulation," Christen whispered.

"Sorry." Laurel withdrew her touch, feeling bereft when she did.

"My dears, at least you do remember something of your childhood. Now please, let's celebrate."

Laurel watched as Samantha waved the waiter over and decisively asked him to bring a bottle of Moet De Chandon Imperial.

†

Laurel placed a hand on her stomach and sighed.

"You enjoyed the meal?"

"Enjoy…how couldn't you? And the champagne was *wow*."

Christen grinned and then whispered, "My mother always loved a decent tipple and now she's progressed to quality. It's very commendable."

Laurel chuckled while discreetly looking around the table. David and Andrea were talking intently to Samantha. "I like your family…at least the ones I've met in a social situation. Your mother is a superb talker. I swear she could talk the hind legs off a donkey. Not that I'd advocate that but you know what I mean." Laurel blushed. "I meant no disrespect."

Christen smiled. "None taken and yes she certainly can. Thank you for coming tonight, it means a lot to me."

Laurel smiled. "Look, I'm sorry for standing you up Saturday. I have to admit that I never thought you'd contact me again after our conversation. Except we'd probably have to talk under Andrea's gun at the wedding." Laurel watched several expressions cross Christen's features, some she figured out but there was one that had her puzzled.

"No problem. I understand you have a partner. I'm a bit surprised you are here tonight."

Laurel bit her lip as Christen's gaze moved away to the tablecloth and she was unable to see her expression.

"Okay, I'm fascinated. What got you two together? David and I thought it was a no-go," Andrea interrupted. "What about Fiona? Did you finally see sense and show her the door?"

Laurel turned to her friend. "We finished tonight. Are you satisfied? We'll talk about this another time, okay," Laurel whispered and frowned.

Christen quietly remarked, "How can a friendship be a no-go? We are friends, right Laurel?"

Laurel smiled and her heart soared as she stared into a warm chocolate-brown gaze. I'd take Christen home in an instant if she were a stray. *Oh crap, what a thing to think.* She cleared her throat. "Yes, that's right. Friends."

"Wonderful, this will make life so easy for us won't it, darling." Andrea drew David's arm closer and his chin almost collided with her shoulder.

"Absolutely, my love," David said.

"Well, I'm very pleased that you have a friend that you can count on because, Christen, you are going to need the support in the coming months," Samantha said. Her cane rapped against the table as she stood. "If you will excuse me I need to make a phone call."

"Sure, want me to…" David began.

Samantha held up a hand. "I am capable of making a call, my dear, but thank you. Please order more wine. I shall be back soon."

All eyes watched as Samantha slowly made her way out of the restaurant.

"Was it something I said?" Andrea asked, her eyes wide.

"No, my love, of course not. Christen, Laurel do you want more wine?"

Laurel turned to Christen to gauge what she wanted. It was impossible, since Christen's eyes were glued to a table close to the entrance.

"I'm good," Laurel said.

"Christen?" David spoke louder.

"What?"

"Hey, don't be snippy with me." David frowned. "What's wrong? It looks like you've seen a ghost?"

Laurel gazed intently at Christen. She had gone pale and her gaze shifted from her brother to the table where four women were dinning.

"I don't believe in ghosts, brother, you know that," Christen snapped.

"Okay. So do you want another drink?"

"Why not? Laurel likes the champagne. Let's have more of that."

"Well actually…"

"It's okay, David, another glass won't hurt me." Laurel smiled then watched as David waved the waiter over.

"Another bottle and we will have fresh glasses," David said then stood once the waiter had left. "Little boy's room." He grinned at Andrea and left the table.

"Bet he's going to check on his mom," Andrea said with a smile. "Well, I need the little girl's room, anyone coming?"

There was no reply from Christen.

"I'm good, Andy." Laurel grinned.

Andrea stood and winked then left the table.

Laurel waited a few seconds and realized that Christen probably didn't even know she was there.

"What time again do you visit Argyle Market?"

There was no reply. Laurel turned her attention to the table that obviously had Christen mesmerized. She didn't know why but it didn't sit well with her. "Guess no time then." Laurel didn't expect a reply and was surprised when she received one.

"No time? I'm sorry, Laurel, I…" Christen bit her lip.

Laurel reached across and placed her hand on Christen's. "Hey, it's okay. We all have friends and exes floating in the wind out there. Sometimes they even end up in the same place we are." Christen concentrated her stare on Laurel. It was so intense Laurel could feel her body burn.

"How did you guess that…it was a long time ago," Christen said before going silent for a moment. "I thought she loved me as much as I loved her then she left and I never understood why."

Christen turned to her and Laurel saw betrayal in the eyes that held hers. "We believe that, don't we. That people love us as much as we love them. Simple answer is that they don't and we can't do a great deal about that. In fact, there is nothing," Laurel grinned, "other than becoming a stalker, that is."

Christen chuckled.

"Guess that's not your style, right?" Christen nodded. "Thought so, me either." Laurel grinned.

The waiter arrived at that moment, popped the cork of the champagne and poured them both a glass. He smiled and left.

Laurel picked up her glass. "How about we raise a toast to those who have gone before that we have loved and lost."

Christen nodded, raised her glass and the chink of crystal against crystal pealed out.

They sipped the beverage and Christen held up her glass. “Let’s drink to opportunity that is yet to enter our lives.”

Laurel raised her glass and they both smiled as the glasses kissed rims.

“One more from me,” Laurel said. “For those of us who meet the right one down the line.”

“However long it takes?”

“However long it takes,” Laurel said as the glasses chinked one more time.

“I see that your brother has been forestalled by your nemesis’ table. Why not go rescue him? I think it will be good for you,” Laurel said. Her heart on the other hand screamed at her that this could be a bad move.

Christen gave her a frown. “You think so?”

“I do.” Laurel touched Christen’s hand. “Go for it. What do they say…a faint heart never caught the love’s heart or something along those lines. Go.”

Christen smiled and left the table.

Laurel looked around her, seeing that everyone was with someone. They were either talking, laughing, smiling, or even frowning. She was alone and normally that never bothered her but this time she hurt inside.

†

Samantha sat longer than necessary at the lobby phone after completing her call. It hadn’t gone as well as she had hoped. The doctor insisted she return soon to have another operation on her ankle before she damaged it beyond their ability to fix it. The thing was how to tell her children. For some reason a second chance had been given to her to connect again, even with Hank. Though she doubted he thought that at this time. She clenched her fingers as an agonizing pain shot through her ankle. Grimacing she stood up and made her way back to the table.

†

"My dear, why are you alone?" Samantha said as she gingerly sat.

Laurel shrugged. "I'm not alone, you are here."

"That is true." Samantha grinned.

"Do you want more champagne? I'm afraid David took the liberty." Laurel lifted the champagne bottle.

"Thank you, I would love another glass. I have to admit it is my one vice. Drinking. My eldest daughter Frances does not approve. However, I have allies in France," Samantha said with a smile.

Laurel poured the bubbling liquid into the long-stemmed glass. "To be honest, I've never had proper French champagne before. Just the cheap version. I have to say the real thing tastes wonderful."

Samantha sipped her drink. "Then, my dear, you are discerning. How did you meet my daughter?"

Laurel reached inside her head for something simple, but effective, that explained their relationship. It wasn't easy, or was it. "I worked for the store for fifteen years. I was laid off a few months ago. It was a shock. Anyway, I have a great job now," Laurel said, fidgeting with the napkin on the table.

"You were a *casualty* as my late husband used to say," Samantha replied absently.

"Well yes, I suppose you could say that." Laurel glanced over to the table and saw Christen in deep conversation with one woman in particular. *Maybe she's just an old friend or worse the love of her life that she mentioned.*

"This new work you have, exactly what do you do, Laurel?"

Laurel reluctantly dragged her gaze away from Christen and smiled at Samantha. "I work for a small bakery on Essex Street. You probably don't know it."

Samantha beamed. "I know it very well and the owner. I'm assuming she's still there. Maisey Clayton is my old friend. Is she still getting up at four in the morning to bake that marvelous fragrant bread of hers?"

"Yes, but we take turns. Maisey is wonderful in so many ways. I wish I'd met her years ago." Laurel sighed.

She then glanced back to the table near the entrance and frowned. Christen and the woman she was speaking with were no longer there.

Laurel nodded at Samantha's next words but hadn't heard them. *Where the hell have they gone*?

"You do know that you should never agree to something that you haven't taken any notice of." Samantha this time interrupted her thoughts.

"I'm sorry, Samantha, I was…sorry that was rude of me. What did you say?" Laurel asked and felt her cheeks glow.

"My mother said that you should never agree to something that you haven't paid attention to," Christen said. She sat next to Laurel and smiled. "Is it interesting what Laurel has missed?"

Laurel's heart did a double somersault. She looked up at Christen and any words she wanted to say stuck in her throat. She closed her eyes as Samantha spoke.

"Laurel agreed to have breakfast with me on Sunday morning and with you of course, my darling."

Christen laughed and Laurel felt the vibrations strum her soul. "I…I'm sure I heard you ask and it works for me. What about you, Christen?"

Christen winked. "We will be there. This Saturday Laurel and I are going to Argyle Market, right?" Christen asked.

Laurel nodded.

Samantha smiled. "I eat breakfast at nine sharp so don't you two lovebirds forget and don't give me all that friend rubbish. Ah, here come the engaged couple. David, for once in his life, has been smart. Andrea is perfect for him."

"Sorry, guys, we…I well— Hey, what have we missed? You all looked positively stunned," David sheepishly said.

"They do not," Andrea took her seat, "it's probably all that champagne we've been drinking. What shall we celebrate now?"

Christen raised her glass. "To family and," she turned to Laurel, "good friends."

Laurel clasped her hands around the thin-stemmed glass and raised it to her lips. *Oh my. I think I'm falling for the Jamison charm.*

†

Christen dragged her coat close to her neck. She and Laurel were waiting in a taxi queue outside the hotel. The line was horrendously long. David had volunteered to drive them home but that would deprive her of any alone time with Laurel and she desperately needed that even if it was only a few minutes.

A car pulled up with a screech of tires.

Christen glanced at Laurel, who was happily chatting with the couple in front of them. Apparently they knew her from a club she frequented. She'd picked up another woman's name, Fiona, but couldn't make out if she was important or not.

Another taxi squealed to a stop.

Droplets of rain began to fall.

"I love the rain," Laurel said with her smiling face turned toward Christen.

Christen, at that moment, wanted to drop her head and kiss Laurel but she held back. This really wasn't the place and she didn't think Laurel would appreciate it. They were friendly acquaintances, no matter what her mother thought. She suspected that being lovers was the farthest thing from Laurel's mind. She had, after all, committed the biggest faux pas when she sacked her. How could she ever come back from that betrayal? Especially now that she knew Laurel didn't deserve it. "Do you want me to go inside and find an umbrella? I can…"

"No, Christen. Let's just feel the raindrops on our face. It's a great cleansing sensation. You know, if I was rich like you I'd live by the sea. Sea spray every morning after a walk on the beach must be marvelous." Laurel slipped her arm into the crook of Christen's and snuggled close.

"I've always wanted to live by the sea too," Christen replied. Her heart thumped as Laurel rested against her body. Laurel grinned and Christen had to hold herself in check as emotions flooded her body. Desperation the only word to describe wanting to kiss Laurel right then.

"Why don't you, or are you married to your job?" Laurel asked.

Christen shook her head. "Not me. I'd go in an instant if I could. I might give the impression, or rather the name does I guess, of being rich. The truth is I'm not."

Laurel looked at her with saucer-like eyes. "You're not?"

"I had a trust fund from my father. Shares in the store. Can't sell them to anyone but a family member and not if it gives that person control of the company. I exist on a salary just like you do. Thank goodness my father allowed me to finish a degree in accounting. It pays well." Christen shrugged and her eyes turned to the line.

Laurel tugged on her arm and they stared at each other. "I'm glad," Laurel simply said.

Christen smiled as her heart soared. "We are getting closer to the front of the queue, how about we share a ride and…"

"No, you live the complete opposite to me. That's ridiculous. Besides, you can't afford it. But I love the offer."

"I'm not that strapped for cash and I'd afford it for you," Christen said. The fingers on her arm grasped in a stranglehold.

"Thank you, Christen."

The couple in front of them caught the next ride.

"I guess the next one is ours…yours," Christen said.

Laurel nodded. "I've enjoyed tonight. Thank you."

"My pleasure. If you don't want to go to breakfast with…"

The tires of a cab squealed on the rain-soaked road.

"Ah, a pig has arrived, at least by the sound of it." Laurel grinned as she reached for the door handle of the cab. "I do and on Saturday too. I will be there this time, I promise."

Christen grinned.

Laurel opened the door and then hooked her arm around Christen's neck gently and placed a delicate kiss on her lips. "Thank you, Christen, I had a great time."

Christen was in shock as she watched Lauren's taxi sail away on the wet, glistening roads. Placing two fingers to her lips she smiled.

Then that pig squealed again.

Chapter Seventeen

Helen Richardson arrived at Jamison's store at five thirty sharp, just as she had for the last thirty-three years. It was a routine she knew and her body did it automatically. She slid her keycard into the reader and entered the building.

"Morning, Ms. Richardson."

Helen nodded at the security guard and moved to the service elevator that would take her to the fourth floor. Exiting the empty elevator, she headed for her office. Compared to some of her contemporaries it was a tiny box, but nonetheless this was hers. Inserting the key, she entered the room. As always, the sight of a polished mahogany three-foot desk with matching bookcase filled with volumes of fashion magazines and books on marketing greeted her.

There were several swatches on her desk and a pile of papers. She switched on the light and moved to her desk. Then turned in surprise at a voice at the door.

"I went looking for you and Steve last night. You disappeared?"

Helen gazed at Christen Jamison. *And they call her the* Dragon Lady. How wrong they are. "Were you waiting for me?"

Christen moved into the office. "Yes."

Helen frowned. "How did you know I arrived at this time?"

"I checked the security log when I arrived. Easy as one, two, three." Christen shrugged.

Helen wasn't sure what to make of this. "What time did you arrive and why is it important?"

"I guess you can count on one hand how many people arrive before I do." Christen winked. "Thirty years is important, Helen."

"I didn't know that you came to the store early."

"Well, sometimes that's good. Right? The unexpected. I have an invitation for you and you are quite at liberty to refuse, but I hope you don't. My mother asked if you and Steve would join her for dinner tomorrow evening. It is her treat."

Helen frowned. "Where?"

"Last night's venue, which is also my mother's choice for a hotel. Trust me, this time there is no way you will be rejected. In fact, you will be receiving a call from a contrite—he'd better be—head waiter. Carlos ensured me that he would personally contact you himself. Will you accept the invitation?" Christen crossed her arms and lounged against the doorway.

Helen sucked in a deep breath and slowly exhaled. "It's a generous invitation but I'm not sure…"

Christen frowned, straightening her posture. "My mother has a great deal of respect for you, Helen."

Helen looked at her desk then at Christen. Tears were welling as she spoke.

"We would be honored to accept the invitation. Can I ask why? We have barely spoken except formally here at the store. To be honest. I'm puzzled." Helen watched as Christen's left cheek slightly twitched and then the normal visage she had seen Christen wear since she had started at the company settled in place. It was unfathomable yet not unapproachable. No, Christen Jamison had never been aloof no matter what the rumormongers said. Of them all, Christen was the one to be trusted.

"The store executive management is changing and I'm not sure what the fallout will be. I want to at least ensure one of our long-term employees gets recognition for the years given to our store. It's very important to me and my mother." Christen glanced at her watch. "I'm sorry to cut this short but I have a meeting at six. I'll forward the details of dinner to you via email later today."

Helen blinked rapidly and nodded. "Thank you, Ms. Jamison." Helen sank into her chair.

Christen gazed at her and frowned. "Christen, I'm Christen. No matter if it's in the store or personal." Christen left.

Helen wiped a hand across her lips and then tried to focus on the work in front of her. She couldn't. She picked up her phone and called home. "Steve, you will never guess what's just happened."

†

Laurel sang along to Bruno Mars on the radio and was so engrossed she failed to hear the bell that indicated someone had entered the shop. As she crooned along with Bruno the brass bell on the counter infiltrated her session. Scrambling to wipe her hands on her apron she entered the main shop area.

"Hi, sorry for keeping you waiting. Are you here for your usual?" Laurel asked.

"Not today, but I do have a list." He handed over a piece of paper.

Laurel glanced at it and then frowned at the man. "You want this now?"

"Nope." He grinned. "I was thinking around one p.m. and can you deliver?"

Laurel glanced at the list. It was for about fifty sandwiches, muffins, and other sundries. This was way out of the small bakery's league.

"I love your food and we hoped that you could cater for this. If you can't I'll ask our usual caterers."

Laurel sucked in a breath. With heaps of work she and Maisey could do this. If it worked out then it might open doors for other things. Maisey needed the boost in business.

"Can you do this?"

"Sure, I'll deliver it myself. You need to pay now though. Sorry."

The man laughed. "Yeah, of course I do." He handed over a credit card.

"Where do I deliver the food to?"

"Go to the staff entrance at Jamison's store. There's an internal phone use it and dial the extension number on the card. I should answer or my boss might. It's a Ms. Jamison if she does."

The man left with a grin and Laurel's heart double flipped. *He works for Christen.*

†

Hank breezed into Christen's office and thumped the palms of his hands on her desk. The ripple sent several papers floating to the floor and her pens rattled in the holder.

Christen didn't glance up from her papers immediately. She kept her head down and, though her pen wavered over a report she was signing, she refused to be intimidated.

"Christen," Hank barked.

Christen breathed slowly and lifted her head. Hank looked flushed and his gray eyes screamed anger. His lips were taut and his cheek muscles flickered as he held her gaze.

"Yes?"

"I'm not giving Jamison's to you or anyone else. Do you hear me. When Mother leaves I'll take back the reins. You are no match for me," Hank shouted.

Christen stood and faced her brother. They were about the same height, although in her heels she had a slight advantage. It had always made her feel confident to be on equal footing with her brother even if it was only in height.

"That isn't your call anymore, Hank. Mother took away your power of attorney over the store. You now own as much as David, Francis, and I. How many allies can you find to take over again? Mother? David? Francis perhaps?" Christen's legs trembled as she spoke and she gripped the corner of her desk.

Hank growled and he paced the green carpeted floor.

"What I want to know is why Mother breezed in and took over. What does she know about business today? Have you been feeding her information for the last decade and told the rest of us you hated her?" Hank snarled.

Christen's heart beat so fast she was sure Hank would see a Muppet thumping her chest with drumsticks. "No. I haven't and I do not hate Mother. There were just issues over her leaving for so long."

"So she's damaging our livelihood and then disappearing back to France and leaving us to sort it out like she did fourteen years ago. Get real, Christen, you are being played." Hank kicked the wooden leg of the nearest chair.

"I don't think so," Christen quietly replied. She closed her eyes for a second, wondering if Hank was right. Why would their mother do that? She was never vindictive in the past.

"I can see it in your face, Christen. You're not sure and with good reason." Hank sidled closer, his demeanor less antagonistic. "I'll take you to lunch and we can discuss this."

Christen felt the draw of the invitation but resisted. "Sorry, I can't. I'm having a staff meeting with the managers and senior assistants. Want to come?"

Hank narrowed his eyes and glared at Christen. "You will regret this. My God you will." Hank left the room, slamming the door so hard it shook on its hinges.

Christen stared at the door and scratched the back of her head. *Maybe I should call Mother.*

The door opened again, preceded by a knock so quiet she barely heard it.

"Are you okay?" Barry asked.

In comparison to Hank, Barry was a total contrast and how welcome that was. She moved away from her desk and seconds later hugged Barry hard. "Thank you."

Barry grinned as they withdrew from the hug. "What was that for? I only went to order food."

"Because from the day I met you, Barry, you have always been exactly who you say you are." Barry frowned and Christen grinned. "Someone I can trust with my life and have. Someone I want to have in my life forever because you are who you are and to hell with the rest. I love you, Barry. Thank you for being in my life."

Barry gave his best impression of puzzlement and then grinned. "Well of course, girlfriend, who else are you going to love better than me."

Christen laughed.

"Christen, whatever he said, you are doing the right thing for the right reasons."

"Were you listening at the door?" Christen raised her eyebrows then smiled.

"Noooo, how can you think that of me…you love me remember," Barry quipped.

Christen stared at the man who had been her foundation for over two decades and her unsteady nerves settled as they always did when he was around. "You know if you and Malcolm weren't so in love I'd have to try and poach you."

Barry giggled. "And how successful do you think you'd be?"

"Zero."

"Precisely. Besides, it would cramp your style if you found a new woman."

"I think I have," Christen whispered.

Her phone rang at that moment and Barry scowled at her. "Later," he mouthed before leaving the office.

†

Laurel parked the Ford Econoline in the Jamison delivery parking area at the back of the store. She climbed out and looked at the red brick building and sighed. She had worked there for so long that it was and always would be part of her life. A big part. Even the bland brick fascia she gazed upon had appeal. It was a lovely building, architecturally one of the best in the area. She fervently hoped it would remain so, protected from the property rats who wanted to build malls on sites such as this one. Whatever was happening with Jamison's and the management overthrow, she hoped it was successful and not lead to the demise of the business and the building.

Her hand reached for the door handle of the 1962 vehicle that belied its age. Maisey loved the minivan almost as much as she did the bakery. She said it was her one impulsive buy of something brand new when she'd begun the business. She traded from the back of it for almost twenty years before buying the building that housed the shop and Laurel's apartment. Gently pulling at the temperamental steel handle of the door it opened slowly accompanied by a sound that she had nicknamed *a grumpy old man in protest*.

She was totally taken by surprise when a bear of a man engulfed her in a hug. "Crap, Frank, I almost had a heart attack." Laurel sucked in a breath then grinned at her old comrade.

"Didn't believe my eyes, young, Laurie." Frank Benson shook his head as he let her go. "What brings you back here?"

Laurel smiled. Frank was barely fifty—okay maybe his midfifties—but he had an ancient face full of lines and craggy channels. He had been the dispatch supervisor for as long as she could remember.

"I'm catering for Ms. Jamison." Laurel's skin tingled at the words. She wondered what he would have said if she said Christen instead of Ms. Jamison.

"Ms. Jamison huh? She doesn't often outsource the catering. In fact, she normally has lunch in the park. Mind there are things going on that haven't filtered down yet, but let me tell you changes are happening," Frank sagely replied.

"For the best I hope. Too many good people have lost their jobs in recent years," Laurel said. She reached inside the van to pull out a tray.

"Hey, let me help you. In fact, I'll do better than that. Just tell me where you want these and I'll have my guys do the heavy lifting." Frank took the tray from her.

"You can't do that, but thank you, Frank."

"I can and I will. It's almost lunchtime and my boys will be doing it in their own time." Frank gave Laurel a harsh stare.

Anyone who didn't know this man would have been scared. Laurel laughed and stood up on her tiptoes to kiss his whiskered cheek. "Thank you. I'm not sure where the food will go. I need to contact Ms. Jamison's office."

"Probably the private room off the canteen. I'll take care of things, let me know if it's a different place when you talk with her office." Frank grinned and walked away toward the goods inward area. "Don't be a stranger," he said before shouting something she couldn't decipher only to see three men appear.

"I'm in good hands," Laurel whispered and supervised the removal of the trays before locking the vehicle and heading toward the staff entrance.

Laurel entered her name in the log and detached the handset of the phone on the wall and called the number on the business card. She held the handset close to her ear and waited.

"Hi, Barry Craig? Great, this is Laurel from Maisey's bakery… sure all taken care of. Where do you want it?... Great it's on the way." Laurel frowned. "I was going to arrange the food for easy selection but I didn't know that you wanted someone here for the duration of the lunch… Well, it isn't about the recompense. Maisey can't cope with the lunchtime rush on her own." Laurel sighed. "… I can't find someone that easily…surely you can use one of your resident canteen staff to help." Laurel heard another voice enter the conversation in background and it was female. *Could it be Christen?* "... I'm sorry I won't let my employer down, it isn't right…You never mentioned this only the purchase of the food… I've done my part the rest is, unfortunately, your problem. I'm sorry…. Yes that is my last word on the subject… Do you want me to organize the food? Otherwise I'll go... Fine, enjoy the lunch."

Laurel replaced the receiver and drew in a shallow breath. Her hands trembled. When she had been working for Jamison's and with Ronnie there had been no bravado just taking whatever people wanted. "Thank you, Fiona, for making me a stronger person," Laurel said. She was unaware that someone was behind her until she turned and her mouth gaped.

"I guess I should meet this Fiona. Is she okay with you spending Saturday morning and Sunday breakfast with me?"

Laurel gazed up at Christen Jamison. Of all the people to be in hearing range. "She has no opinion on the subject. We broke up," Laurel admitted and watched Christen's features for a sign, any sign at all, that it was important. A schooled expression was firmly in place. What had happened to that sexy smile and serious concerned eyes that she entranced her with.

"I'm sorry to hear that. Look, I have to go, I have an important lunch planned. Out of interest, why are you here? I would have thought this is the last place you'd want to be," Christen asked.

Laurel had to think fast. Did she admit to being the caterer of the lunch and probably have the assistant trash her?

Damn. "I was hoping to see Andrea for lunch but she's not answering." *I hope a thunderbolt doesn't strike me dead.*

Christen nodded. "Yes, of course, Andrea. If you want me to find her…"

"No. No, Christen. It's fine. I'm due back at work anyway."

"Me too," Christen said.

Laurel saw the forced smile Christen gave. "I'd best go then as we both have other responsibilities."

"Laurel?"

Laurel gazed at Christen. She could see the tiny flecks of white in the pale gray eyes. "Yes?"

"Do you mind if I call you before Saturday?" Christen dropped her gaze.

"I was going to ask you the same thing." Laurel grinned as her heart somersaulted.

"Thank you." Christen's head shot up. There was that smile Laurel remembered and her heart soared.

There was a loud buzzing. "Sorry, my assistant needs me." Christen pulled out her phone and glanced at the screen. "I'll call tonight. If I miss you I'll call tomorrow."

Laurel grinned.

"Nowhere to go. I'll be there."

Laurel saw the hesitation in Christen and she smiled. "Do you like spaghetti bolognas? I do a mean one. If you are free tonight around seven maybe you'd want to join me?"

"Thank you, but at the moment I can't guarantee that I'll leave the store at a reasonable time. I'm sure you wouldn't want dinner at midnight. I'll call, I promise," Christen said accompanied by a shrug.

Laurel smiled. "I'll look forward to it."

Christen grinned and then with a slight shrug again she let herself into the main building.

"She's incredible. Why hasn't someone snapped her up." With a spring in her step Laurel left the building and headed for the van.

Chapter Eighteen

Christen hooked her phone to the speaker and selected one of her favorite albums. She picked up the glass of Merlot she'd poured earlier and with a sigh sank into the sofa. The meeting today had gone well. Better than she'd thought. She smiled before taking a sip of the wine. Everyone had been grateful for the update on the company but the thing they had enthused about the most was the great lunch. She'd have to find out more about the company that provided the food. Perhaps it could be Jamison's new catering staff.

She'd have to ask Barry about that another day. Her eyes strayed to the red rooster clock on the wall showing nine fifteen. Every time she looked at it there was a tangible reminder of Macy. She'd been fixated on country-style art. It was the only shared thing left behind when Macy left her. Except bitterness. Yet she never got rid of the clock. It was a thread to something she thought should have worked out so differently.

She sipped her wine and contemplated her encounter with Macy at the restaurant…

"Macy, it's good to see you." Christen was amazed when Macy stood up and engulfed her in a hug.

"Chris, I'm so glad to see you. It's been way too long." Macy kissed her cheek and then gave her what she thought was a fond look.

"Yes, over a decade. Barry tells me you've recently become a parent." Christen fell on information she knew.

There was a squeal of delight from Macy. "Chris, it's wonderful you must try it…maybe you have. Barry is a closed book when it comes to you," Macy said and retook her seat.

Christen saw her take the hand of the woman to the right of her. She was ordinary. At least nothing to write home about in the looks department. Plain would probably have covered it. Macy had always been about beauty. Always.

"Barry is a good friend. I don't have children." Christen glanced at their table and saw Laurel retake her seat.

"Well, if ever you decide to go that route it is worth it. Believe me." Macy beamed. "I'm remiss. This is my partner Dawn and our two friends, Ade and Cheryl. We have a mutual friend babysitting." Macy pulled out her cell. "I'll know if Daisy cries. It's an app on my phone, thank God."

Christen smiled at the other three occupants of the table.

"I have to go. My mother is home for a short stay, we're having a family dinner," Christen said.

"I know. David dropped by to say hi. He's still gorgeous looking and engaged too. Good for him. I'm glad you've buried the hatchet with your mom, Chris. It doesn't do much good to bear a grudge," Macy remarked and then turned to grin at her partner.

Christen saw in that small action the difference between her relationship with Macy and the one she shared now. Macy loved Dawn unequivocally. It was in the way she looked at the woman and constantly touched her. They had never shared that closeness except in bed.

"True. Enjoy your meal. I'll let Barry know it's okay to talk about you now." Christen smiled. "I'm glad you found happiness, Macy, it suits you." It had. The woman she had lived with for six years had been all about beauty and money, nothing ever seemed to satisfy her. Now she lit up like a candle when she gazed at her partner who looked like a homely housewife. How time and people change another.

"I want to be that happy," she whispered. She stood and walked over to the wine bottle on the granite kitchen countertop. As she opened it she contemplated her life.

"It's not too late," Christen declared to the bottle in front of her. She walked over to the speaker system and unhooked her phone. Selecting a number she pressed dial. "Hi. Is this too late?" Christen grinned as she walked back to the kitchen area. "I'm sorry I missed dinner. It's just a hectic time right now." She leaned against the countertop and smiled. "I'm sure you did a great job. I was wondering if you wanted to get together tomorrow night. It will not be early probably say eight thirty but… Ah, right, your ex was a nightclub person. Got it… Want me to pick you up… okay, I'll meet you, say at Laschelles Coffee House on Ninth.... I'll be the one wearing the flower in my lapel." Christen chuckled, "… No, not really but I will if… Great… Good night, Laurel, sleep well." Christen grinned as she disconnected the call.

She filled her glass and sat down and reconnected her speaker to the phone.

†

Laschelles was the hippest place in town at the moment having been open for only a couple of months. Laurel glanced around at the establishment. Cozy wheaten-colored chairs and traditional coffee tables, strewn with market magazines, nestled comfortably between the stark metal barstools and tall tables in the middle of the room, leading to the three-barista stations, where people crowded. She glanced at her watch. Eight fifty. A server in a deep purple shirt with the Laschelles logo hovered near her. She'd been by twice already. *I bet she thinks I'm just coming in from the cold and taking up good customer space.* Laurel smiled.

"Your friend hasn't turned up yet?" the server asked.

"No. I'm sure she will real soon. Look, I'll have a small latte. Thanks." Laurel grinned at the server who looked unimpressed.

"Okay," she said and left.

Laurel settled back in the sofa that was closest to the entrance and sighed. *Maybe she's forgotten, or too tied up in business. I should call.*

Laurel pulled out her cell and selected the last call she'd received. She stared at the number. Then she looked up and stared at Christen.

"Sorry, Laurel, I had a hell of a day," Christen said and took the seat next to her. The sofa sighed in response.

"No need to apologize. I'm just glad you made it. If you were too busy you should have called."

"No." Christen frowned. "Sorry, no…I need this. Have you ordered? I heard this was the best place in town right now."

"We shall see. I've just ordered a small latte. Not really that impressed with the attitude of the wait staff. Still I guess they could have thought me a vagrant." Laurel shrugged.

Christen frowned. “Never. Who would think that about you? Damn, I wish we’d gone to Jane’s now. I thought it was unfair for you meeting me close to where I live.”

“Seriously, I love that place. The coffee is great and the food even better. They have the most delicious savory muffins I’ve ever tasted.” Laurel winked. “Don’t tell my boss that.”

“Ah, your friend arrived,” the server remarked. She deposited the coffee next to Laurel and it hit the table so hard that some spilled. “What can I get you?” Laurel, for the first time in her life, actually saw a champion of the weak in action.

“First, shouldn’t you apologize for spilling my friend’s drink and perhaps offer to at least clean up the mess?”

The younger woman gave Christen a curl of her lip. “Do you want to order?”

Christen stood. “That’s it? No, I don’t want to order, the service is atrocious.”

Several people turned their heads and watched the altercation.

“Oh please, it’s a busy night and she’s been taking up space for almost an hour without ordering anything.”

“Where is the manager,” Christen demanded.

The girl threw her head to the left. “He’s the middle barista. Are you going to order or not?”

“No, I’m not. Come on, Laurel, we are leaving.” Christen glared at the woman.

“That will be fifteen dollars.”

Laurel jumped up. “What? It’s a small latte and you spilled some of it.”

“I’m definitely going to see this manager of yours,” Christen responded angrily.

"No. No, it's okay, Christen." Laurel gave the woman a twenty and grabbed Christen's arm. "Let's go somewhere we both love."

Christen frowned. "Laurel, this is poor service not to mention extortion."

Laurel smiled, glanced at the unconcerned waitress and then at Christen. "Then we won't come back again and we can tell our friends."

Christen smiled slowly. "Good point."

They moved toward the exit.

"I'm just glad you turned up," Laurel linked her arm in Christen's.

"Anything to oblige." Christen grinned. "Actually, I haven't eaten since a muesli bar at breakfast. I hope Jane is still open for food."

Laurel tugged at Christen's arm and they faced each other. "How about you come back to my apartment and I cook something nutritious for you that won't keep you awake all night?"

"Oh, Laurel, I don't want you to bother for me."

"I can't make the best coffee in the world but a snack is a no-brainer. Are you game?"

Christen chuckled. "Absolutely. My car is just outside the door. How did you get here?"

"Public transport."

"Right, then you have a very grateful recipient of your invitation. Thank you." Christen placed her arm on Laurel's forearm. Perfect.

†

Laurel mentally drilled herself not to get too excited about Christen agreeing to come to her apartment. Being a tidy freak meant the place wasn't a mess, which was a definite bonus.

"You really don't live far from Jamison's," Christen said as she negotiated the left turn at the lights leading to Essex Street.

"I know. A glutton for punishment, some would say." Laurel chuckled and saw Christen smile. "I even live over my current workplace, Maisey's Bakery. Go figure."

"Thank God I don't live over the store or I'd never have a life," Christen softly said.

Laurel noted that her lips tightened after she spoke. "Oh, there are advantages. I can literally step out of bed and be at work. Though I'd never have traffic as an excuse for being late," Laurel said.

"Maisey's you said? Hmm, now where have I heard that recently. I'll have to think on it."

Laurel bit her lip and then gave a tight smile, glad Christen was preoccupied with driving. Maybe her assistant had said bad things about the service.

"It's right ahead. You can even park in front of the building. There aren't many places you can do that these days, even at this time of night," Laurel replied. "During the day it is wall-to-wall cars and some stay all day while others make a quick dash inside for food."

The Subaru Legacy 2.5i glided to a halt at the curbside.

"I love this car. It's got everything but isn't pretentious. Is it new?" Laurel asked as she smoothed her hand over the shiny black glove compartment.

Christen stopped the engine and turned to her. "Thank you. You are the only person I know who approves of this car. I've been called unpatriotic by my brothers and even my best friend shook his head."

"It's a car, not a state of being." Laurel chuckled.

Christen grinned.

At that moment Laurel knew without a shadow of a doubt she was falling big-time for Christen. It was so different from her feelings and experiences with Ronnie or Fiona. It felt right just being with her.

"Couldn't have said it better myself. I bought it four weeks ago. I wasn't going to pay big bucks for an inferior product," Christen said.

"Well, my sage friend, I agree. Right, let's go. Do you have any preferences for a snack or should I be asking do you have any running-to-the-hills aberration to any foods?" Laurel opened the passenger door and stepped out.

Christen did the same from her side and locked the car.

"None. I'm a good girl. I even ate my greens as a kid. You can ask my mother."

Laurel's body warmed all over at the words. "Excellent, I love Chinese food and I have a great simple lemon chicken recipe. Are you game?"

"I love chicken." Christen smiled and moved to stand beside Laurel. "Thank you for thinking about me in this way. I appreciate it."

Laurel took her hand and winked. "You haven't sampled my food yet." As she led her to the side door for the apartment, she thought, *not strictly true*.

†

Christen wandered around the modest family room. It was decorated in what she could only call an eclectic way, unlike her own place, which was all pastels and nondescript in comparison. A minute sofa took up most of the room with a tiny coffee table and a TV, the size she hadn't seen since college, held on a bracket directly opposite the seating. What she did find fascinating were the watercolors lining the largest surface wall. All of areas of the town. They were excellent.

"Christen, the coffee is brewed and I'm in the middle of the stir-fry. Do you want to pour?" Laurel asked.

Christen smiled as she took a few steps and entered the galley kitchen. Laurel was whipping her wok around the electric heat element of her stove. For a few seconds she just watched and what she saw warmed her heart. Laurel, by her very expression, loved to cook and she could see it in every motion. The coffeepot was close by. "Got it."

"I like mine with loads of milk. I'm not a heavy coffee drinker it always leaves a weird taste in my mouth. Can you believe that?" Laurel giggled.

Christen grinned. *Nope, but I'm happy to learn*. "Each to their own I say."

"What about you?"

Christen poured her coffee into one of the cups next to the machine and moved to within inches of Laurel. "See for yourself." She placed the cup in front of Laurel.

"Wow, you are a real Coffee Joe. How can you drink that? It's like mud." Laurel laughed.

"Easy watch me." Christen held the cup to her lips and sipped the liquid. Then frowned.

"What? I thought you liked it dark and mysterious."

"I do but it was so darned hot it burned my lip."

"Go away, please, or I'll laugh so much our snack will be toast." Laurel shook her head and grinned.

Christen moved a foot away. "Well, that's some sympathy." She grinned. "I like it."

"I'll be done in five. Go sit. Put the TV on or not."

Christen gazed at Laurel's back and smiled. "At your command." She went back to the family room and sat on the couch where she stretched out and relaxed.

True to her word, Laurel brought in a tray with steaming dishes of chicken and noodles.

"Be right back. We need plates and cutlery."

Seconds later, Laurel returned with two bowls, chopsticks, and forks. "Tuck in and enjoy."

Christen looked at the food and wondered how in such a short space of time someone could come up with something so aromatic and appetizing. "I can't believe you did this. Wow, it smells great." Christen picked up a bowl and the chopsticks.

Laurel grinned. "It's something I'm good at. Enjoy."

†

Replete after the meal, Christen settled back in the couch and rubbed her stomach. "I can't thank you enough, Laurel. That was delicious."

Laurel smiled. "That's all the thanks I need if you enjoyed the food. I'll have to really wow you with a proper dinner one evening."

Christen gulped back the excitement those words caused. She felt like a teenager on her first date. *Where is all this euphoria coming from? All she did was mention a meal.* "I'll hold you to that. I'm not sure what talents I can bring to the table if you wanted a meal at my place. It's often takeout or beans on toast. Might try the odd scrambled egg." Christen chuckled. "In the kitchen, cooking isn't my thing but I can clean up afterward very well. Want me to show you?" Christen was about to stand when Laurel's arm stayed her progress.

"No. Please sit. I don't want you getting indigestion."

"I wouldn't dare do a thing like that after that great meal. It would be sacrilege."

Laurel laughed. "I like you, Christen Jamison."

Christen's heart leapt and she sank back down next to Laurel. "Well, the feeling is mutual." Laurel turned to gaze at her and Christen could see the tiny freckles that crossed the bridge of Laurel's pert nose. It was cute.

"Christen, I don't want you to get the wrong idea about me."

Christen's heart dropped like a dead weight in her chest. *Damn, I knew it. She isn't really interested in me.* "I don't think I have. Why do you say that?" Christen held her breath.

Laurel drew her legs up and hugged them tight. "I don't want you to think I'm fickle in relationships."

Christen frowned and was about to speak when Laurel continued.

"When we first met, actually when you laid me off, I'd just finished with my long-term partner." Laurel gave her a tiny smile. "I'm not bitter; in fact, it was probably the best thing that anyone has done for me in years."

"Really," Christen said.

"Don't look so shocked, Christen. Sometimes we have to have a dramatic change to make us realize that life has a lot more to offer us." Laurel grinned. "I think it's working out perfectly. Anyway as I was saying. I'd just broken up with Ronnie. We'd been together for eight years and lived together for five."

"I'm sorry."

"Yeah, well, I should have known better. For the last couple of years we'd been drifting apart. Ronnie liked women, lots of different ones. She didn't think infidelity was a problem. I came home one day from work and she'd changed the locks. It was a shock and relief at the same time. I guess that doesn't make any sense."

"It does." Christen took Laurel's hand and held it.

"Thank you. I met someone a few weeks later and she was good fun at first. I needed to feel wanted and loved again. Fiona was good for me after the whole losing the girlfriend and the job at the same time. We had a good few months together and split up the night you called me to have dinner with your family. Great timing, by the way." Laurel gave Christen a watery gaze. "I just wanted you to know that I'm not someone who treats a relationship lightly although you could be forgiven for thinking so."

Christen's thumb stroked Laurel's hand as she digested the explanation. "I've been alone now for about thirteen years and celibate the whole time." She shrugged. "My ex, Macy, was the woman I was speaking to at the restaurant the other evening. She ditched me, packed her bags and left a dear Jane letter. Well, I can't even call it that. It was a few short words on a Post-it. I never forgave her for breaking my heart until I saw her and realized what she has with her partner is something we never had. I wish someone would look at me like that, as if I was the only person in the room." Christen sighed.

Laurel turned and they faced each other. "Seems we have some things in common then, because that's exactly what I want. Monogamy along with it would be good." Laurel chuckled.

"Maybe together we can find that someone." Christen leaned in and kissed Laurel's cheek.

"Yeah," Laurel softly replied.

Christen jumped up from the sofa and looked at Laurel. "I think I said I was a great dishwasher." She began to collect the dirty dishes.

Laurel giggled. "You certainly did and I'll help."

†

Christen sighed as she and Laurel nestled into each other on the sofa. "I guess I had better get going."

Shifting to face Christen, Laurel ran her tongue over her lips and smiled. "Why not stay? It's late and it will be at least an hour before you finally get to bed."

"Thank you, but I don't want to wear out my welcome. You've already gone out of your way to feed me." Christen smiled.

Laurel held her breath for a few seconds then exhaled slowly and drew Christen's head closer and kissed her lips.

Christen groaned and responded with a more voracious kiss, gently prizing Laurel's lips apart, allowing her to trace and entangle her tongue with Laurel's. Her hands moved over the puce cotton shirt Laurel wore, drawing her close.

When they came up for air, Laurel grinned. "Will you stay?" She wrapped her arms around Christen's waist and fingered the waistband of the black pants she wore.

"I shouldn't…but."

"No buts. Make love to me, Christen."

Christen lost all sight of anything but the need in Laurel's eyes and her own burgeoning drive to love her. She grazed her teeth on Laurel's neck and sucked in the smooth skin as her hands moved around to cup generous breasts. Her fingers encountered pert nipples waiting to be loved. She deftly unbuttoned the first four buttons and revealed the skin-colored bra that opened in the front. Christen snapped the fabric apart and fleshy breasts with brown nipples begging for her touch popped out. She nestled her face into the skin and breathed in the musky smell of the woman in her arms and began to trail kisses over each one until Laurel cried out.

Laurel's hands feverishly released Christen's blouse from the pants she wore and then unzipped the trousers. Her hand followed and hooked into her panties and slid past her navel to the hair that protected her mound.

"Oh, God, Laurel, please," Christen groaned.

Laurel's neck arched as Christen bit gently on her left nipple.

Christen almost jumped off the sofa as Laurel's hand snaked past the hair and her fingers slid along the wet, velvety folds. When Laurel's fingers circled her clit and pinched it gently Christen reacted immediately as jolts of fire tore through her body.

As Laurel massaged the swollen nub Christen knew she wasn't going to last long. "Go inside please," she begged.

Laurel smiled as her free hand gently pressed Christen's head against her breasts. Two fingers slid easily inside and she bent them slightly. Just as she was about to get into a rhythm Christen began bucking wildly and groaning in pleasure.

Christen collapsed against Laurel.

"Are you okay, Christen?" Laurel softly asked.

Christen couldn't speak for a few moments then she looked at Laurel and smiled. "Oh, my God," she whispered. "It was perfect." She reached for Laurel.

"Let's go to bed and I'll show you how wonderful I feel." Christen moved and picked Laurel up.

"I'm way too heavy."

"Not to me. Now which door?" Christen grinned and kissed her passionately.

"Second on the right," Laurel groaned.

Chapter Nineteen

Samantha wandered around Christen's large apartment, glancing out of the window, fully expecting to see speedsters racing up and down the street as they did in the old days. When Christen had mentioned the locality of her new home purchase years before she had nearly caught the next plane back to the US. Her youngest child living in the worst place in town was unacceptable. How had that happened?

Now, as she gazed at the refurbished street lighting from the turn of the century she noticed that they'd kept all the classical features only updating the actual lighting components for today's standards. It was beautiful. Patches of grass and the tree-lined street brought back so many memories of her early days in the city. Of all her children, Christen had been the most elusive to understand. She had an external beauty that could have made her a model, yet her child had never used it to her advantage. Quite the contrary. She recalled that vulnerability when Christen was ten years old…

"Mom, why do people hate me?" Christen sobbed.

Samantha drew her ten-year-old into her arms and soothed her. "Christen, don't be silly. Who hates you?"

Christen snuggled into her shoulder. “I just wanted to be friends with them and they said they wouldn’t be seen dead with me. Why didn’t I go play with the other pretty girls?” Christen cried.

Samantha smoothed down the sparkling chestnut hair. “Who are these girls, darling?” She kissed the top of Christen’s head.

Christen gulped and drew away, and with enormous eyes filled with tears she spluttered, “The cool kids. They love science and physics and oh, Mom, all the stuff I like.”

Samantha smiled. “The cool kids…right I see.”

“I have a brain, Mom, not just a pretty face. Do you think if I can get rid of the pretty face they will like me?” Christen asked, rubbing at her cheeks.

Samantha drew Christen close. “One day, my darling, you will be happy you have the beauty. Believe me, it will help when you are older.”

“Really?”

Samantha grinned. “I think we shall arrange a science fair for the school at Jamison’s and we can use the canteen. Do you think that might help?”

Christen’s eyes glowed and then she threw her arms around her. “I love you, Mom.”

“I love you too, darling. Will you sleep now?”

“Yep.” She snuggled down into her bed and soon was fast asleep.

Samantha drew herself out of reverie of the past and brought it to the future and the hectic morning punctuated by Hank’s angry outburst in the middle of several of the store’s manager meetings. That prompted Christen to take her to her apartment for a break from the business troubles.

The room was stark in its furnishing. It had none of the comfort of a home that she was used to. Frances was a collector of almost anything, a trait she had obviously acquired from her. Christen was the exact opposite and had always been. Samantha frowned.

"Why are you frowning, Mom, is something wrong?"

Christen entered the family room and deposited a tray on the glass coffee table.

"No, darling, I was thinking about the area and how it's changed for the good." Samantha moved to the red sofa and slowly sat down. A couple of cushions would be good for her at the moment. Her back was going to give her hell without the support.

"I made the tea you like. Jasmine right?" Christen hovered.

Samantha breathed in the aroma of the scent and smiled. As always, Christen's attention to detail amazed her. "Yes, thank you. I didn't think you'd remember after all this time."

Christen laughed and sat down. "Mom, we called it stinky Sunday for a reason and it was always that tea."

Samantha shook her head and smiled. "Busted. Do you like it?"

"No way. It's like being made to eat sprouts as a kid. You never get over that." Christen grinned.

"Ah yes, the dreaded sprout. The only vegetable you refused point-blank to eat." Samantha looked at the teapot and leaned over to pour a cup.

"No, let me do that. Do you need a cushion or two? I know this beast can be hard on the back."

"I'd love a cushion. Two would be better. Unfortunately old age is not very forgiving."

Christen sprang up from the sofa and left the room.

"As always, thoughtful to everyone, my darling. You have a tender heart," Samantha softly said.

Christen returned moments later and gave Samantha the cushions.

Repositioning them in the most comfortable way Samantha sighed in satisfaction. "Thank you, my darling."

Christen nodded and bent to pour the fragrant tea into a cup before pushing it toward her. Then she picked up a mug next to the teapot. "It's coffee for me. Salute."

They sipped their drinks.

"There is something else that I need to tell you, and in light of what's happening it really isn't a good time." Samantha bit the inside of her upper lip as Christen stared at her.

"Tell me," Christen said.

"The accident to my ankle…it's not healing well, according to my doctor. The last x-rays I had a day before I left were supposed to be a formality. Apparently, the injury is worsening and I need an operation." Samantha sighed heavily.

Christen remained silent and simply sipped her coffee.

"I will postpone it if you need me, I have abandoned you for far too long."

Christen placed her mug on the coffee table and shook her head. "Mom, thank you for coming back, for lots of reasons but mainly for Jamison's staff. David and I miss you, that's plain to see, but we haven't been exactly the best children."

"Don't say that…"

"No Mom, it needs to be said. We earn enough money to have a holiday in France or any of the other places you've lived in Europe in the last fourteen years—we didn't. We were selfish. I've even been worse, not telling you about my breakup with Macy."

"So you are okay with me returning to France sooner than expected?" Samantha frowned.

"Perhaps not okay, but understand. Got to say you are leaving with a bang and I'm proud to be your daughter," Christen declared.

Samantha smiled. "Will you come visit me in France, please? You will love it. I so want to show off Miss Pompadour. Your dad never liked animals so we didn't have pets when you were young…sorry I'm an old woman rambling on."

Christen grinned. "I'd love to come over. If I bring a friend, is that okay?"

"I like Laurel. How long have you been dating?" Samantha asked with an impish grin.

"We've only just started. Its early days yet. Not sure it will work with this current workload I have, but I hope it does." Christen frowned. Then smiled as she recalled their passionate lovemaking from the night before. Tingles ran through her body as she recalled Laurel's fingers on and inside her.

"Do you want it to work?"

Christen hugged her mug to her chest. "Yes, I like her."

"I do too. She's honest. What you see is what you get I believe is the phrase. What does she think about your workload?" Samantha looked at her daughter.

"To be honest I don't know. It isn't something we've talked directly about."

"Perhaps you should. Then it's one less problem. There are always problems aplenty in budding relationships. Look, if I'm prying please tell me."

"No, you aren't. In fact, it would be good to talk. I usually only say this stuff to Barry." Christen sipped her drink.

Samantha smiled. "Barry is your best friend, it goes without saying. However, sometimes a female point of view would be nice. To be honest, I always wondered why you chose a man as your friend rather than a woman."

Christen shrugged. "That's easy. I wanted a friend for life. Every woman I met who might understand me always wanted more. You once told me that my beauty would be an asset. Trust me, in my life it's been a burden I'd have preferred not to carry. Life is difficult enough."

Samantha put down her cup and touched Christen's cheek. "My darling, you have a tender heart and that is the most important. What do you really want out of life?"

Christen smiled. "I want to live by the sea, walk with the spray on my face and wake with someone next to me who will love me for the rest of my life." Christen laughed. "That's like asking to win the lottery, right?"

Samantha thought about the words. There had been a time way before she had met her husband when she had thought similar things. "Not the lottery, my darling, just a dream that can be reality. Because you want what everyone does and I believe you will find what you want."

"You do?"

Samantha moved and kissed Christen on the cheek. "You are my daughter and nothing is impossible. Remember that fake volcano?"

Christen spit out the coffee she was drinking. "Mom, what a thing to remember."

†

Laurel watched Maisey walk from her chair in the office to the counter and peer at the produce there. She looked pensive, even worried.

Removing her latex gloves she sauntered to stand next to her boss. "To the best of my knowledge they will not bite, egg, lettuce, and onion have yet to grow teeth. Unless, of course, you know something I don't?" Laurel grinned and watched a smile crease Maisey's lined face.

"No silly, although I believe a chicken can peck you with its beak…that's like a bite," Maisey replied and straightened. As she did Laurel thought she saw her wince.

"It might not be my business but you look pensive. Is something wrong?" Laurel asked and rested her elbows on the glass countertop. Maisey frowned then drew in a shallow breath as she exhaled. Laurel was sure a decision had been made.

"I'm thinking of retiring, Laurel."

The simple words sent a shock wave through Laurel. *Oh no. I love working here*. "Is it the arthritis?"

Maisey nodded. "As always, very astute, Laurel. I saw the doctor last week and she said if I wanted to see any of my retirement with any kind of comfort it was time to hang up the apron."

"Well then you should. Besides, you've gone way past the retirement age. It's time for you, not getting up at four most mornings for the bakery." Laurel placed her arms around the older woman and hugged her tight. "There must be something you have on your bucket list that's a must-do." She withdrew her arms and smiled.

Maisey grinned. "I have plenty, but I love working here. This is my life." She glanced around the small shop.

Laurel watched her and could, in part, understand her reluctance to leave something she knew so well. Her own exit from Jamison's had incited a little of that dilemma in herself for a short time. "I don't want this to sound like a crass question but are you going to close up or sell the business as a going concern?" *God, I sound like a piranha.*

Maisey frowned. "I think that is the difficulty. I only want to sell if someone has the passion I have for the business. Someone like you."

Laurel's heart jumped at the statement and she knew her cheeks were red as the heat scorched her skin. "I wish so much I could even consider that as an option. I wouldn't have the finances or the financial credit to go to a bank with a proposal." Laurel shrugged.

Maisey caught her gaze. "Who said anything about a bank? Are you interested in taking over from me?"

Laurel tried to speak, sure her mouth gaped like a guppy.

Maisey giggled. "Ah, lost for words at last. I knew I'd catch you one day."

Laurel chuckled. "You have big-time. I don't understand though. If you want to retire and do things, you need capital."

"You think after working over fifty years in the food business I don't have a nest egg? Shame on you." Maisey gave Laurel a hard stare, then winked.

"I still don't understand. Why not make me a manager or something? I would happily run the bakery for you if you trusted me."

"I trust you like family and as you know I have none. This is the perfect solution for me, but what about you, Laurel?" Maisey waited for an answer.

Laurel wasn't sure she could give one. *I need good advice, hmm.* "I have a friend who I'd trust to give me and you great advice on this. Let me call her and maybe we can have dinner or a coffee and see what we can work out. What do you say?"

"I say you must have a wonderful friend. The answer would be yes." Maisey smiled and nodded to the office. "Best go and finish the month end accounts."

Laurel smiled. "Yes I do. She's an accountant by trade. My friend that is."

As Maisey left the shop area, Laurel pulled her phone out of her pocket and punched in Christen's number and hoped she would agree to this meeting. Then her mind drifted to the lovemaking of the night before. The experience had been exhilarating. Never before had she succumbed to so much emotion as she had when Christen brought her to an orgasm throughout the night.

"Hi."

†

Christen flicked her pen across the desk, hitting her pen holder, before bouncing off the desk onto the carpeted floor and rolling until it stopped by the leg of the conference table. She sighed heavily. Right now would be a good time to give notice and simply leave all the crap behind. She hadn't wanted the responsibility and frankly wasn't up to the job. Her mother was right—she needed to speak with Laurel about the workload, because after their lovemaking she wasn't going to lose out to this place. It had taken its pound of flesh over the years and she didn't wish to give it any more.

Her internal phone rang.

"Yes," she growled. "Sorry, it's been a long day… Yes, I know it's only lunchtime… What do you want, David… I'm having a grumpy day. Why would you and

Andrea want to have dinner with me tonight?... Right, right, okay, let me call you back… Yes I know, and I promise if dinner is doable we will. Okay."

She replaced the phone and her cell rang. Without looking at the caller ID she barked, "Hi... Sorry, I'm sorry, Laurel, it's been one of those days… Yes, I know, and thank you for understanding. How can I help?" Christen listened intently and frowned. "I have a great idea. David and Andrea have invited Mom for dinner at David's place tonight and they invited me. How about we kill the proverbial two birds with one stone. You and Maisey come over too. What do you say?... Great, let me text you the details later… okay, you catching up with Andrea for the details is great… Thank you for understanding… See you later."

The call ended and Christen focused on the pen on the floor. She stood and picked it up. "Right, my friend, we have work to do." She chuckled. "Did I actually say that. The day just got better, exponentially."

†

Christen rang the bell of David's apartment. She looked around and saw the signs and trappings of a newly developed neighborhood. She'd had that but not in such a salubrious area. What she paid for her three-bed apartment was peanuts on what David had paid for this place. He was probably up to his eyes in debt.

The door opened and Andrea stood there in a floral dress that was a little over the top for her liking, but the woman inside of it she liked.

"Hi, Christen, you're the last one." She flipped back her head and shouted, "David, you can put the main course on now, Christen's here."

"You said eight, sorry I'm late." Christen bit her inner lip. "I tried hard to leave on time but people kept hassling me. Still eight thirty isn't too bad, is it?"

"No problem. For you we would have all waited until midnight," Andrea said before breezing back inside the apartment.

Christen stood in the doorway, entered, and put the lock on the door. *I guess I come under the category, you are not a guest, just family.* She smiled as she shook her head. Then her heart throbbed as Laurel snuck her head around David's family room door.

"Hey, did you have a good day?"

Christen smiled. "I've had better but right now it's looking up."

Laurel grinned. "I think the same way too. You can come inside, we don't bite."

Christen rolled her eyes "Are you sure? I have marks," Christen said. She winked when Laurel blushed.

She entered the room and watched as Laurel took a seat next to an older woman and smiled before heading toward her mother. "Mother." She bent and kissed the smooth cheek.

As Christen straightened, her mother smiled. "I'm glad you could make it. I know things are terribly difficult right now. However, Laurel being here must be a bonus."

Christen's cheeks reached melting point at the reference to Laurel. She looked around and saw an empty chair opposite Laurel and her friend and took it.

"Christen, this is my boss and friend Maisey, who I told you about earlier." Laurel grinned at Maisey, who smiled at Christen.

"Pleased to meet you, Maisey. Laurel thinks very highly of you."

"As she does you too, Christen, if I may call you…"

"Yes. Yes, there's no ceremony here."

There was a shattering of a glass and Christen rolled her eyes. "Be right back."

She headed toward the kitchen. "Is everything okay?"

David gave her an exasperated look and blew away the hair that had fallen over his eyes.

"Well, my dear brother, you look frazzled. I hope the meal isn't the same. Where's Andrea?" Christen looked around the sleek stainless steel kitchen area.

"She needed the bathroom. Look, Chris, can you get the dustpan and brush from the laundry and clear up this mess. Damn. I didn't think when I pulled the dish out of the warming oven without an oven glove."

"Sure, be right back." A minute later, Christen quickly cleared away the debris of the shattered vessel. "At least it didn't hold any food."

"I think I've been a bit overambitious asking so many to dinner. The roast will be okay, but I'm not sure if I've made enough veggies."

"Sorry, my fault. Look, if it's too much we can always call for takeout and…"

"I can't give my mother and guests takeout. What will they think of me? Besides, Andrea will kill me."

"I will? Why?" Andrea asked as she entered the room.

"Nothing, love. Why don't you take the hors d'oeuvres out and socialize?"

"Don't you need help?" Andrea frowned.

David grinned. "I have things under control, trust me."

"Okay." Andrea didn't sound convinced and slowly left the room.

Christen remained in the kitchen and leaned against the counter. "Are you sure? I can help if you like."

"And pigs might fly. No, go have some leisure time, you need it."

"I won't disagree with that." Christen turned to leave.

"Chris, I'm glad you've decided to move on. Laurel is a lovely woman."

Christen turned back. "Yes, she is." She returned to the family room where she could hear the others laughing.

†

Laurel leaned back on the chair on the balcony and groaned. "He said he wasn't sure there was enough food. Wow. Does he think we are starving? He could have fed twenty." Laurel chuckled. "Thank you for tonight and the talk with Maisey."

Christen gazed at Laurel.

"You are welcome on both counts. It must be a family trait—overcompensating for company, although I have to admit he did a great job. The beef dropped off the fork."

Laurel didn't shrink from Christen's intense gaze and smiled. "Do you overcompensate around invited company?"

Christen narrowed her eyes. "Sometimes. Not everyone is given the gift of confidence. Most of us just wing it when we have to. I remember the first time I took home a girlfriend. I don't know who was more nervous, her or me. My dad wasn't very happy about my choices and decided to take a golfing weekend in Barbados and Hank took a last-minute holiday. It should have been easier but it wasn't."

Laurel nodded and reached out and took Christen's hand and held it. "Why?"

Christen stared toward the half-moon in a blue black sky. "Because the ones you love the most are sometimes the hardest to convince you are happy."

The quietly spoken words resonated in Laurel. Her mind immediately went to her differences with her father. *God. Dad, it's time we worked things out.* "Your mother and David seem okay with your lifestyle."

Christen turned back and smiled. "Always have been. David in particular. My mom was my confidante over relationships before she left for France." Christen chewed her lip. "Time takes its toll on a relationship and somewhere in the last fourteen years we've drifted apart as a family. Shouldn't happen, but it did. God knows I've missed her. I think that's why I was so angry." Christen rubbed her forehead. "Sorry, you don't want to listen to me and my baggage."

Laurel squeezed the hand she still held. "I do. In fact, I feel privileged that you want to share it with me. It's getting late or I'd open up with my baggage and I have a ton of it. You'll be running to the hills once I start."

"I wouldn't," Christen simply replied.

"Good, but you might regret that statement." Laurel chuckled. "You really think Maisey isn't selling herself short with her ideas for me and her bakery?" Laurel watched several expressions cross Christen's face and one had her worried.

"No, she believes, and I do too, that you are a solid upright citizen."

"The nerve." Laurel lightly smacked Christen on the shoulder.

"Okay. I haven't seen any numbers so I don't know the score for sure but I think if it's something you want, then this weekend, if Maisey will release them to you, we can go over the financials and I will give you my best opinion. Though you will need to see a professional in this area before you finally decide what you want to do." Christen shrugged.

Laurel waited a moment to reply. “Right now, your opinion is the most important, as strange as that might sound to you.”

Christen gazed at Laurel and leaned forward and kissed her.

Laurel’s heart stopped and started and raced in what could only be called a roller-coaster ride as their lips entangled into a full-blown kiss.

When they parted they were both breathless.

Before they could speak the sliding door opened and Andrea poked her head out. “Guys, it’s freezing out here. Have you finished your business talk, because Maisey and your mom want to leave?”

“Yes.”

“Sure.”

They replied in unison and Andrea frowned at them. “Okay. Christen, your mom said you offered her a lift. Thanks, that’s really cool of you. I’m bushed.”

Laurel and Christen stood and looked at each other and grinned.

“Guess that’s our cue to leave. Saturday morning at nine. It’s still on, yes?” Laurel asked.

“Absolutely, if I get the chance…”

“No, you concentrate on business. It’s only another day. I promise I’ll be at the East Argyle Street entrance, come hell or high water.”

“I’ll look forward to it.”

“Me too.” They reentered the family room.

Chapter Twenty

East Argyle Street on a blustery morning was something to see. Stalls and their awnings were moving, if not exactly in sync with the wind, they were trying hard. Flapping tarps and the odd crash echoed around Laurel as she stood in the doorway of a building giving her the view of the street and affording her protection from the strong gusts.

She was trying to tamp down the excitement flowing in her veins at the prospect of seeing Christen. No one she had dated had ever induced the reaction Christen did. As soon as she was in the vicinity of Christen she became the most important person around her. She'd thought she had been in love twice in her life. Kay Glassly in high school, her first kiss and grope if she put it down to the basics. Then there had been Ronnie. The excitement and unexpected actions Ronnie brought into her life in the beginning had been exhilarating and she'd thought it love. Now she wasn't so sure she had ever been in love. Until now.

The wind struck again and there were angry expletives in the air as things flew around.

Laurel settled back against the red brick wall. *Am I in love for the first time in my life?* Surely they needed to spend more time together, not just have the odd meal and one night of passion before making that decision. She was being stupid, for it couldn't be that quick. Then she looked across the street and her heart hammered in her chest as she saw Christen step onto the crossing heading her way.

"I love you," she whispered. As Christen moved closer, Laurel ducked into the main street and tapped her on the shoulder.

Christen jumped, then grinned. "Hell, you scared me."

"Whoa, I don't want to do that. Is this better?" Laurel stood on tiptoe and gave Christen a fleeting kiss.

Christen seemed lost for words and nodded.

Laurel hooked her arm in Christen's. "Let's go. You said there was a stall you wanted to show me."

"Yep, this way."

They walked at a slow pace through the packed stalls, occasionally stopping when merchandise caught their attention.

"Oh damn," Christen said.

"What?" Laurel looked around.

Christen pointed to an empty bay where a stall usually stood. "They aren't here this week."

"Okay, well I'm sure they will be next or the week after. We can stop by another time," Laurel said, holding her breath for the reply.

Christen pursed her lips.

Laurel swallowed hard. It wasn't a good sign She moved too fast in saying they would have other weekends. What could she say now. Christen's words caught her attention.

"I really wanted to show you something," Christen said. "But you are right, we can do it another week. Did you delay breakfast?"

Laurel's chest lightened immediately and she nodded and rubbed her hands. "Actually, I'm starving."

"Great, I know the best place here to eat. Come on, it's on the next row."

A few minutes later, Laurel frowned as they stopped at the worst-looking stall in the area. Laurel couldn't believe that Christen would like food from a place like this. It might kill them with all the germs floating around. Christen was an enigma, that was for sure.

Christen turned and said, "I know it looks like a rat trap but trust me, please. The food is wonderful."

It was Christen's *please* that was Laurel's undoing. "Okay, but if I get food poisoning I'm sending you the medical bill."

Christen grinned and moved closer. "Not going to happen." She dropped her head and planted a kiss on Laurel's lips.

Before Laurel could respond or even think she heard Christen talking to the stall person.

"Hey, Gina, I want my usual and my friend will decide in a minute." Christen cast Laurel a look.

"Ah, is this the friend who couldn't make it the other week?"

Laurel watched as Christen scratched the back of her left ear. Then she coughed.

"Yes, but she's here now and that's what matters. I'll have coffee, black." Christen turned to Laurel. "Coffee, tea, or something else?"

"Coffee is good, milk, and a spoon of sugar please."

The woman behind the stand winked. "I do the best bacon and egg roll you will ever eat," Gina said before turning to attend to her grill.

"Laurel, let's sit. There's a bench free."

They sat a few feet away from the enclosed hut housing the stall.

"Is she really that good? Let's face it, bacon and egg on a roll is not something you can describe as cordon bleu."

Christen laughed. "I used to think like that…no…maybe not. I've known Gina for over twenty years. She took over from her mom and dad when they retired. This has been a family business for years. It probably was here when Argyle Street Market started. The Edwards have always had a stall. Sorry, getting to the point…"

Laurel leaned closer and smiled. "No, please go on. I love it that you know so much about this."

Christen blushed and Laurel sank even deeper into her love for the woman.

"Okay. I'm what you would call a nerd when it comes to something I'm interested in. Did you know that at least half of the stall owners here are related to the original purveyors of good food and quality merchandise from 1910 when the market started?"

Laurel shook her head.

"Yes, that's over a hundred years of history. I remember the first time my dad brought me here and he said something I'll never forget."

"Chris, has your friend decided? It's getting busy," Gina bellowed.

Laurel laughed. "Hey, I'm going to try the house special, the bacon and egg roll."

Gina winked.

"It's my favorite," Christen said.

"So tell me more of the history of the market. I'm fascinated, and more importantly, what did your dad say?"

"Really?" Christen furrowed her brow.

Laurel grinned. "Yes. Really."

†

Christen hooked her arm into Laurel's. "So now that you have partaken in the delights of Gina's delicacies what do you think?"

Laurel laughed and hugged Christen's arm closer. "She's right, what else can I say?"

Christen chuckled. "Yep. Maybe you and she should get together, if you decide to take up Maisey's generous offer."

"I have that tabled in my app. Seriously, Christen, do you think I can take over Maisey's business without putting forward any capital? It doesn't seem right."

Christen frowned. "Under normal circumstances it wouldn't be. A little collateral always helps."

"I'm seeing my lawyer in a few days about a settlement I'm negotiating regarding Ronnie. Hopefully that will help."

"You want to do this?"

Laurel remained pensive for a while. "My dream is to live by the sea, my hopes are that I can with the right person. In reality, happiness in the here and now is the closest someone like me will ever achieve."

Christen stopped walking and turned Laurel so that they faced each other. "That's my dream too. Please don't say that about yourself, Laurel. Everyone, no matter who they are, should always have hopes and dreams. I, for one, know that you will achieve both."

Laurel sucked in a deep breath and smiled. "You say the nicest things. Why on earth are you still single?" It was meant as a compliment but the shadow that crossed Christen's face indicated that it hadn't, or at least she thought it hadn't, worked out that way. "I'm sorry, I didn't mean to be…"

Christen shrugged. "Want to walk along the riverbank? It's the closest to the sea I can manage on this date."

Laurel gave a silent prayer of thanks. "I'll take any walk if it involves you."

Christen moved her head to the side and simply stared at Laurel.

"Do I have ketchup on my chin? You are staring?"

Christen blushed. "Sorry, and no you don't. You might not want to do it…but this *single* business. How do you feel if I said I'm no longer a single girl because I want to have you in my life?"

"You are asking me to be your girlfriend?" Laurel looked around. People were weaving around them as they stood in the busy street.

"Yes, please."

Laurel disregarded everyone and everything around them and reached up and kissed Christen. Their lips locked for seconds, yet eons passed as far as Laurel was concerned.

"Hey, get a room," someone yelled.

Christen guiltily pulled away. "The river walk is only ten minutes away. Are you still game?"

"Well, I am, but I'd rather go back to your place. We only have a couple more hours before you need to go back to work, but I know a few things to relax you before you go."

Christen grabbed Laurel's hand and at speed began to walk away from the market.

Laurel chuckled. *Guess she does. Yeah.*

†

Jamison's frontage had changed over the years sure but generally only the window dressings. The signage was still the same. Faded a little but still the bold red lettering depicting the name shone brightly. There had been mutterings in the last couple of years to update or even change the name. The town wouldn't be the same without the Jamison store and yet right now it was teetering on the edge.

Christen frowned and then drew her mind to her morning with Laurel and tingles went through her body, especially the sight of Laurel in her bed needing and wanting her touch. She clasped her hands to her face and the heat of her thoughts generated to her cheeks.

They had gone their separate ways an hour ago and it seemed like a lifetime.

Christen locked her car and headed to the side entrance and entered with her key card. About to press the button for the elevator her cell rang.

"Hi, David, what's wrong?"

Christen paled. "I'll be there in," she checked her watch, "fifteen, if traffic is friendly." She held the phone in her hand as she disconnected and simply stood in the small vestibule of the entrance. Then she turned and exited the building, reaching her car in seconds flat, the words David had solemnly said ringing in her ears. "Christen, there's been an accident.."

Chapter Twenty-one

Chester Methodist Church was beautiful as the trees in the courtyard swayed with spring growth. The numerous cars arriving struggled to park in the already overflowing tiny parking area. Looking across the grassy area one came face-to-face with the formidable spires that jutted out on all four corners with a handsome tall spire in the middle. To the left was the graveyard, no longer able to take remains unless a family plot had been purchased before 1980. It was kept in exemplary order as was the church itself.

People who had arrived at the last minute quickly made their way into the church as the hearse arrived and the pallbearers, six in all, flanked the coffin.

As the coffin entered the church the congregation stood and the strains of "The Last Time I Saw Paris" filled the building and several sobs managed to permeate through the music. As the coffin came to rest at the altar the minister stood and began the ceremony.

An hour later another musical number from the forties drifted into the room, "Whatever Will Be Will Be." The pallbearers took up their positions and walked with solemn faces out of the church toward the graveyard. The mourners followed.

†

Christen watched Laurel busying herself with the caterers; fussing would be an apt term. She looked frazzled.

"Hey, it was a nice ceremony don't you think?" Andrea said.

Christen reluctantly removed her gaze. "Yes. Strange, the music choices people make for their funeral," she said absently.

"Haven't made any for mine yet, have you?"

Christen frowned then shook her head. "No, Andrea, I haven't. Where is David?" Christen glanced back to where she last saw Laurel. She was gone.

"He needed to take a call. Said it was important. How are things, Christen?" Andrea asked with a serious expression.

Christen took a deep breath, contemplating her answer. How could she answer a question like that after someone dies? "Doing is good. Getting up in the morning, making that first coffee, having a shower and trying just for a moment to make sure that everything is as it was a week before."

Andrea touch Christen's shoulder. "Thank you for being so strong."

David arrived at that moment and Andrea gave him an evil look. "Hi, I've switched the darn thing off, love, I promise. Christen, I was thinking after the wake we should get together. What do you say?"

Christen glanced around and still didn't see Laurel. "Sure. Look, I need to find Laurel. I'll see you both later."

She was about to leave them when Andrea said, "Check out the back room."

Christen looked at Andrea, who smiled. "Thank you." She left and walked toward the area Andrea mentioned.

†

Christen saw Laurel with her back to the office door and her fingers threading a paper handkerchief. "Hi, need a friend?"

Laurel turned, her eyes red and swollen. "I didn't know her for long but, Christen, I loved her. She was like family. Why did it happen to her? Why couldn't it have been someone else."

Christen took an unconscious step back at the vehement words. Instead of a reply she moved closer to Laurel, took her in her arms, and held her close, kissing the top of her head. "Accidents happen, Laurel. The van's brakes failed, the hospital doctor said she died instantly. I didn't know Maisey as well as you but she wouldn't want that, Laurel. The woman I met wasn't vindictive."

Laurel sobbed into Christen's shoulder. "It isn't right, you know. It really isn't. She worked so hard and she deserved her retirement. What am I going to do now? I just seem to go from one disappointment to another."

Christen held Laurel and took a deep breath for them both. "Am I one of those disappointments?" She held her breath.

"No."

The answer was so adamant Christen had to stop herself from smiling at the ferocity. Instead she hugged Laurel closer. "I'm here always for you. Maisey was right you know…with her last piece of music."

Laurel frowned and then shrugged. "Whatever Will Be, Will Be?"

"Yes."

"How can you say that?"

"Because I love old forties musicals." She saw Laurel frown. "No, I do. Life is like that…we have to move on or become lost in what was."

"Christen, I keep making all kinds of mistakes in my life with jobs and relationships. I just wanted to get something right for once. Even my dad doesn't want to speak with me and right now I could do with his support. I don't think he realizes how much I love him." Laurel nestled her head into Christen's shoulder.

The need to kiss Laurel almost overdid Christen's fortitude. It wasn't the right time or place. "Hey, will it make a difference if I said people love you and want you in their lives."

Laurel sobbed.

"Your dad loves you no matter what issues you have." She lifted Laurel's chin with her fingers. "Believe me, I know. Take my problems with Mom. She sends her apologies, Laurel. She had to go back to France for an operation on her ankle. Seems it didn't repair as well as she thought and we thought it would be better if she convalesces with Frances. Besides, that's her home now."

"I wish I'd said goodbye to Samantha. She was really nice to me." Laurel's lips drooped.

Christen nodded. "We'll go see her together next year. Does that sound like a plan to you? I've never been to France, have you?" she asked.

Laurel sobbed. "I would love to. I do still make a mess of things and I might in your life too," Laurel replied with her head downcast.

"Andrea thinks everything you say is gospel."

Laurel lifted deep red eyes and said, "What about you?"

"From the words of Stan Smith, *you are the one designed for me*. I'm here for the long haul if you are interested."

Laurel cried and Christen held her tight. Kissing the top of Laurel's head she whispered, "I love you."

Laurel produced a tremulous look her lower lip quivering. "You do?"

Christen nodded and smiled. "I do. Remember when we first met?"

Laurel glumly replied, "Yes, you fired me."

Christen chuckled softly. "That was the second time. The first was waiting for the elevator that day."

"You remembered me? Wow, why?" Laurel's eyes widened and she gulped back a sob and waited.

"I was impressed." At Laurel's look of astonishment she laughed. "Actually I wanted to laugh too. You almost, and I say almost, looked at me in horror. You did a brilliant job of masking that. For the record, most don't. They usually look away or leave before the elevator arrives. You were a bit slow but you did take that ride with me. Besides," she grinned, "you were cute. What more can I say?"

"You think I'm cute? You thought it when you first saw me? My goodness. I couldn't tell," Laurel said, shaking her head.

Christen laughed. "And have a lawsuit for sexual harassment? I'm sharper than that."

"You most certainly are." Laurel smiled. It was weak, but nonetheless it was there.

Andrea snuck into the room and smiled. "Hey, how are you doing?"

Laurel smiled slightly. "Better. Thanks, Andy."

"I knew Christen would make you feel better. There's a guy here named Sylvester Pascale and he wants to speak to you. He wouldn't give me any details other than he was Maisey's lawyer. I can send him away if…" Andrea began to say.

Laurel moved away from Christen's embrace. "It's fine, I'll speak to him."

Christen watched Laurel take a deep breath and move toward the door as Andrea backed out.

Laurel turned to gaze at Christen. "I love you too." With a drifting smile Laurel left the room.

Christen grinned. She knew she must look goofy and at a wake too, but right now those four words meant the world to her. She left the room and shut the door behind her.

†

Christen hung her head as she poured boiling water into the daffodil motif mug filled with a lemon balm tea bag, one of her mother's parting gifts. The fancy box had several different teas all attributed with helping to solve some kind of dilemma of the human spirit. In this instant it was a calming remedy. Right now Laurel needed it in spades. As she steeped the tea in the water she closed her eyes and wondered when Laurel's problems would be over. Ever since she had met her there had been one disappointment, as Laurel called it, after the other—at least she wasn't one of them.

Peering into the pale liquid she frowned. Then stirred it a couple of more times and lifted the stainless steel tea leaf holder out of the mug and left it in the sink. Picking up the mug she walked back to the lounge and stood for a few seconds looking directly at the dejected expression on Laurel's features—it almost broke her heart, she dearly wanted to take the pain away. Walking into the room she stopped beside the sofa arm closest to Laurel.

"Hey," Christen softly said. "I've made you some lemon balm tea. My mother swears by this herbal tea stuff. The label says this one has a calming effect." She held out the steaming mug.

Laurel gave a her a weak smile and listlessly took the proffered ceramic.

Christen smiled and took a seat next to Laurel and watched her closely as she sipped the drink, fully expecting a grimace. Instead there was a tiny smile.

"Do you like it?"

Laurel turned. "It's very pleasant. I didn't know you liked herbal tea. I've always figured you for a coffee girl?"

Christen chuckled. "Believe me I am. I hate tea, and those flavors…please. Mothers think they know best."

Laurel's tears flowed and she placed the mug on the coffee table in front of them and attempted to wipe the tears away with the sleeve of her sweater.

Christen bit her lip and reached out to pull Laurel into a hug. "I'm sorry, Laurel," she said, kissing the top of her head.

"I miss my mom, Christen, so very much, especially now. She would have had all the answers." Laurel whispered through her sobs.

"I know you do, love, I know. I wish I could help you more. If I could turn back time for you I would, even if it was for a few minutes to make you feel better." Christen hugged Laurel close and then gently gave her several kisses on the top of her head.

As the sobs subsided. Christen released Laurel and bent to pick up the mug.

"You can share my mom, she likes you, and Mom would insist you drink this to help," Christen said with a smile.

"I like your mom too," Laurel gravely said.

Christen settled back in the sofa as Laurel sipped the tea. They stayed like that for a few minutes in silence.

"I'm going to see my dad, like you said," Laurel declared.

Christen nodded. "Not that I'm good at family differences and resolving them but I think that's great."

Laurel stood up and walked over to the window shrouded by a puce curtain, shielding them from the outside.

"My dad isn't the problem you know, it might sound that way with what I've said…"

Christen stood and walked over to Laurel and took her hand. "You are a free agent right now. The lawyer Pascale said the bakery was forfeit for Maisey's debts. Why not go stay with your dad and mend those invisible fences?" Christen said, her heart clenching at the thought of not having Laurel to come home to now. This week with her at the apartment had been so right, and this was the worst of circumstances she figured.

Laurel gazed at her and after a few seconds smiled. "You really are something dreams are made of, Christen. It will mean that I won't see you every day. My parents' home is a couple of hours outside of Chester."

Christen's throat went dry at Laurel's words. Mom was right, dreams can come true. Laurel thinks I'm made of dreams, how much better can my life be.

"Hey we can Skype anytime you want, talk on the phone, and there are the weekends. Whatever the obstacles, Laurel, we will make it work." Christen sucked in a breath and closed her eyes.

"I love you more than I ever thought I could love another person," Laurel said, leaning in to kiss Christen.

When the kiss was over Christen pulled Laurel into her shoulder and they nestled into the sofa.

"Want my car to go see your dad tomorrow?"

Laurel shook her head against Christen's chest. "No, I'll take the train. When the time is right, will you come over and meet my dad?"

Christen moved so that she could see Laurel's eyes. "I'd be delighted. I want to meet the man who had a hand in making the woman of my dreams."

Chapter Twenty-two

The house was larger than expected.

Christen craned her neck to look over the immaculately cut front lawn with a neatly trimmed hedge going up the driveway. She stopped the car outside the address Laurel gave her where they were to meet. It was a prestigious home. She decided not to park in the driveway in case it wasn't the right house. Stepping out of the Subaru she walked confidently up the red brick drive. The black door had an elaborate doorknocker with the face of gargoyle. "I've always wanted to do this," Christen whispered and giggled as the iron hit the wooden surface.

She was smiling broadly when the door opened and a stern-faced man stood in the doorway. Taking a step back, she licked her dry lips.

"Yes."

The equally stern word had Christen on her back foot. "Hello, Mr. Rogers, I'm Christen Jamison, a friend of Laurel's, and she asked me to meet her here, I'm an hour early." Christen gathered all the inner courage she summoned for business meetings that she found difficult to handle and allowed it to radiate around her. There was a steady stare from cool blue eyes reminiscent of his daughter's and that helped calm her nerves. "You are, Mr.

Rogers…Laurel's father?" Christen glanced at the number on the wooden panel next to the door.

"I am. Come inside, Laurel has just gone to the supermarket for provisions. She will be back anytime." He moved out of the doorway and held the door.

Christen frowned and then sucked in a deep breath and entered the house, flashing the man a smile. He was short and stocky with a flawless skin tone that any woman would die for, never mind a guy. His nose was squat but it suited him. The rest of his features were average—not ugly exactly but not handsome. Interesting; his features were interesting.

Entering the house, Christen's first impression was a long passage with white walls and white furniture to match. A hall stand and white spindle chair adorned the left side. A tiny table to the right held a bowl of lilacs to give a hint of color. The light was marvelous as it streamed in through a side window and glanced off a crystal chicken strategically placed, she figured, to refract the light, sending a rainbow effect over the black-and-white tiled floor.

"Wow." Christen couldn't hold back her delight at the clean, crisp, and heavenly feeling this entrance gave her.

"Yes, most strangers say that," the man replied.

Christen turned. "I'd say it every time I opened the door and entered. It's so calming and wonderful. You must think the same?"

"My wife was the decorator…I just keep up the theme."

The toneless way Laurel's father spoke his homage to his wife's talent was sad to Christen's ears. "It's ageless. Your wife was very perceptive."

There was a grunt in reply and Laurel's father moved past her and opened a door to the left.

Christen followed and, entering the room, was blown away again. White walls with a magnificent Edwardian style mirror at least three feet wide adorned one wall. Eclectic furniture looked as though it was scattered around but as she focused on the two wheaten sofas opposite each other, switching to a bright red recliner complete with footstool to the right, it tuned her senses. A black coffee table in an octagon style took center stage, complete with coasters that didn't match. A large-screen TV snugly fit in the corner. It reminded Christen of Laurel's place. *She must have inherited the talent from her mom.* "Family room?" Christen asked with a smile.

"Yes. Do you want a coffee, tea, or something else?"

"Sure. Coffee. Thank you," Christen said.

Mr. Rogers left the room and she glanced around, taking in family photos on the right wall flanking the mirror. She walked closer and smiled as she saw the Rogers family.

"Got to ask Laurel about that one." She grinned, tracing a finger over a photo of Laurel from high school. She had huge bunches in her auburn hair. Then she scrutinized a picture that was center stage. Laurel with her parents at, she presumed, her graduation. Christen smiled. Laurel looked so much like them. She also had her mom's gorgeous hair color and smile. Switching her gaze to the opposite wall she saw small art pastels of buildings and public places that reminded her of the art at Laurel's home.

"Coffee, not sure how you like it so I brought milk, it's skimmed. I have saccharin if you need a sweetener; we don't do sugar here."

The gruff words didn't surprise Christen, her observation of the photos told its own story. He was always a step back from the event in the pictures but his eyes hovered over his family with pride and definitely love. She was certain of that. "I like it black, thank you."

The coffeepot and two mugs were placed on the table.

Christen took one of the mugs. It was plain white—true to the décor—and poured herself a cup of coffee and moments later sipped it. She grinned at Laurel's father. "I love this…oh all those caramel notes in it are wonderful. Thank you."

"Starbucks premium."

Christen smiled again at Laurel's father. "What do you think of their French blend?"

"Haven't tried it, this was Laurel's mother's favorite."

"Wonderful taste. It shows in everything I've seen so far and I've barely gone past the hall," Christen said.

She turned and looked at the expression on Laurel's father's face. So proud. Definitely the look in the photos. "Who painted the pastels?"

Deep red smattered across the man's cheeks, he coughed, and poured himself some coffee. "I did," he finally replied.

Christen opened her mouth then closed it. She was speechless.

"My wife loved those. We came together because of them. She was a struggling art student who was into pottery." He pointed to what could only be called grotesque in every manner a twelve-inch tulip-shaped vase, or was meant to be.

Christen nodded and smiled.

"I was struggling too. I had a market stall on Argyle Street to sell my paintings on a Saturday. She saw one and loved it. She couldn't afford it though. She barely had a cent to scratch her head with."

"I love going to Argyle Street Market every Saturday that I'm not working. There's still an art stall there," Christen said with a smile.

Laurel's father nodded and smiled.

Wow. The man had an amazing smile that added an extra dimension to the otherwise plain features.

"Haven't been there since Anne became sick." He shrugged. "Afterward it never had the appeal."

Christen nodded. "I can understand that." She sipped her coffee. "I took Laurel there on our first date. Real date, that is. Now I love the place more. Did Anne ever persuade you to part with the painting she liked?"

There was a deep chuckle and Christen watched as the stern features she had witnessed when she arrived cleared completely and a deep groove creased each cheek as he smiled.

"Pretty girls get their way. I did make a bargain. She had to have breakfast with me at Gino's, best—"

"Bacon roll in town," Christen interrupted excitedly. "I know. I know. I took Laurel there. She didn't believe me until she tried one." The coolness in the man's gaze warmed significantly. Christen liked him although she knew little of him. In a subtle way it was exactly how she had felt about his daughter the first time they'd met.

"I wasn't very welcoming when you arrived. I'm Don. It's a pleasure to meet you." He stood and Christen followed suit as he extended his hand.

They shook and Christen was surprised at the smoothness of the hand she held. "It's a pleasure to meet you too, Don." Glancing around she focused on a two foot by three foot pastel of a seashore. It looked so real. It portrayed a young woman holding the hand of a child of about five paddling in the froth of the incoming tide. She pointed at the picture. "I love that one. It captures a perfect moment I suspect."

Don nodded and walked over to the wall and Christen followed. He gently traced the plain white frame. Then turned and grinned. "Yes, it did. Laurel always wanted to see the sea. We had a wonderful weekend in a cottage in Fernandina. I'd sold a couple of paintings to make it happen. Every penny and every second was worthwhile."

Christen saw tears welling in Don's eyes and she wanted desperately to hug the man but clenched her hands instead. "I've never been there though I hear it's beautiful. Laurel still loves the sea. She wants to live there one day. By the sea that is. Something else we have in common; it's one of my dreams too. The memories you made have etched themselves in her heart for sure." Christen wished she could have meet Laurel's mother, Anne. They must have been an awesome couple. Unlike her own parents.

"Laurel always follows her heart so I suspect one day she will get her way. I hope you're ready for that."

"Yes, actually, yes I am. As I mentioned we have the same dreams pretty much on what we'd like to have happen in the future," Christen replied immediately.

"Good. It's time my girl found someone who deserves her."

Christen's heart felt like bursting, and throwing caution to the wind she hugged Don and whispered, "Thank you. I promise to always take care of her."

"Hey, Dad, sorry," Laurel said before her eyes bulged.

†

Standing in the doorway, she would have dropped her shopping had she not already deposited it in the kitchen. As she gazed bug-eyed at the two most important people in her life embracing she couldn't believe what she was seeing. It was incredible and an overwhelming happiness filled her at the sight. "Is there room for me?" she finally choked out.

"There's always room for you, Chipper. Come here." Don winked.

Christen moved away a little.

Laurel grinned at Christen as her dad hugged her close and kissed her cheek.

"Right, I just need to check something in the root cellar. I'll be gone fifteen minutes then we'll get to know each other better. I was thinking about not making dinner and going to Fernando's on Tenth instead. It's my treat." Don released his daughter and headed out of the door.

Her dad left so fast that Laurel couldn't think with any clarity what to reply. She blinked rapidly then turned to Christen. "What have you done to my dad?"

Christen chuckled and wriggled her eyebrows. "I can be charming you know."

Laurel shook her head and wrapped Christen in a bear hug before kissing her deeply, their tongues exploring each other's mouth. Breathing heavily, Laurel took a step back and rested her forehead on Christen's. "I think you are incredible. In fact, I don't think, I know," Laurel whispered.

"Love you too, Chipper. Now that is a new one," Christen said and chuckled as they broke apart.

"Don't please. You know how you hate it when people shorten your name? I'm that way with the nickname."

Christen laughed, snatched a kiss, and winked. She flashed a finger across her lips. "My lips are sealed unless you decide to unlock them."

Laurel's heart somersaulted at the teasing. How had she ever thought of Christen as the Dragon Lady? She was the furthest from that description ever. "Well, you can unseal them and tell me why you and my dad were in a hug? Cripes, I've never seen him hug any other person expect mom, me, and grandma. He would only shake his brother's hand when he lost his wife and they are kin."

Christen shrugged and moved to the couch. "Your dad and I were having a great discussion about your mom and you. Somehow, it just happened. I even get to call him Don. You never told me his full name."

Laurel opened her mouth and scowled. "He talked about Mom to you? How long have you known him? Ten years? He never talks to strangers about Mom…sorry, but you know what I mean."

Christen smiled as she picked up her coffee cup and sipped the tepid liquid. She pulled a face.

"Is it cold?" Laurel asked.

"No problem. It's still good even if it's cooler. Would you believe that your dad and I have things in common?"

Laurel nodded. "Sure you do. Me right?"

"That's one thing yes."

Laurel pouted.

"Okay, you are the most important." Christen grinned. "We both love Argyle Market, and yes, I know he doesn't go there anymore. He told me he met your mother there so it will always be important to him."

Laurel gasped. "He told you that? Are you sure you haven't met him before? Wow."

"I love these pastels on the wall and he told me that he painted them. We talked about the sea and about you."

Laurel was amazed at her dad's unfolding. "I've brought girlfriends home before—Ronnie in particular—and he spoke about ten words to her before he left the room and never came back. They had art in common."

Christen nodded. “He wasn’t that way with me, thank goodness.” She smiled. “Oh, and your dad loves bacon rolls from Gina’s. He, of course, got them from her dad, but the recipe is the same.”

Laurel sank down next to Christen and threw her head against the sofa. Then she took Christen’s free hand. “My parents always used to say that there was a certain special person in the world made just for you. I used to laugh because it sounded ridiculous. Their relationship was what dreams are made of, and yes, I wanted that but figured life was more complicated these days. Seemed I was right for a long, long time.” Laurel glanced at Christen, who gazed at her intently.

“Then I met you, really met you. We both had baggage and you simply ignored or forgave the past as if it didn’t happen. I still don’t get it that someone as beautiful as you, with a tender soul and well connected, could ever love me.”

Christen squeezed Laurel’s hand. “I told you and I have never lied to you. I noticed you the first time we met. Circumstances were unkind at first. I believe that our life experiences have led us to each other at this time and place. It isn’t about physical beauty or connections but two people who are meant to be together, like in our dreams don’t you think?”

Laurel inwardly gasped at Christen’s summation. She turned and pulled Christen closer and kissed her. As they moved apart for air Laurel said, “I love you, my dream girl.”

†

“I’ve never seen an art studio before,” Christen said, frowning at Laurel’s reluctance. “Of course, I want to see it.”

"My daughter is shy," Don said. "Some of her earlier works are still in the studio. She never believed in her talent." Don swung a key in the air.

Christen's eyes flared. "You paint? Why haven't you told me? I bet those paintings on the wall in your apartment are yours right?"

Laurel grimaced. "Not all of them. Most of them are Dad's," she gruffly replied.

Christen grinned and reached out to take Laurel's hand. "I promise if it's something you did when you were five not to laugh."

Laurel sighed. "This is worse than the baby pictures I was always told parents showed to prospective loved ones."

Christen laughed and kissed Laurel's cheek. "I'd love them as I do you. Now are you going to go willingly?"

Laurel chuckled. "Sure."

Don smiled and unlocked a door at the end of the hall.

The first thing that caught Christen's attention was the kaleidoscope of lights that bounced around the room. Dust particles floated in the air like a dreamscape. There was a long table filled with all manner of paints, pots, cloths, and several palettes, some filled with paint. A folded easel stood to the side and a large one stood almost in the center of the room. Brushes were in abundance by the easel and on the table. As she gazed past the easel she saw an enormous picture window that looked onto the expansive garden and to the hills in the background.

"It's incredible. There's so much peace and scenes in here. It's the perfect place to paint, I suspect." She turned to look at father and daughter.

Don nodded. "Well, it normally is." He winked at Laurel.

"Now, Dad, you were the one who wanted me to try my hand. It wasn't my fault I like music to paint to." Laurel cuffed her father on the arm.

"Do I get to see the canvases which are yours?" Christen asked.

Laurel walked over to a stack leaning against a wall in the left corner. "Now remember these were done long ago now," Laurel said. Then placed the first one on the easel.

It was a mirror image of the hillside, perfectly proportioned as far as Christen could determine. She simply gazed at it in awe. When Laurel showed her several more paintings of different landscapes and rooms in the house she was lost for words.

"What do you think?" Laurel asked, crossing her arms and looking pensive.

Inner depths had nothing on Laurel as far as Christen was concerned. She had as much talent as her father, possibly more. *Talk about the wow factor.*

Laurel looked at her with anguish as she remained silent, unable to formulate the best way to say what she thought. Then Christen pulled her close.

"You said something about beauty, tender soul, and connections to me. I'm going to say talented, loving, and awesome. Why do you want to be with me, a dour accountant?"

Laurel blinked rapidly and Christen was sure she was surprised at the statement. "If I said I love you, would that work?"

"Every time. Perfect, in fact. I couldn't think of any better words myself. Except that I love you more."

"Please, can you leave this for the bedroom. I think I said dinner was on me. Let's go, shall we," Don said, giving them a wry grin.

†

Laurel watched Christen from the inside of the door to the conservatory. She looked totally relaxed and happy. A tiny smile graced Christen's full lips and the worry lines that had been etched on her face for the past couple of months had disappeared. It was good to see and even more remarkable it was here at her family home. Things hadn't changed much—it was just as her mom had decorated and arranged the furniture in the house before she succumbed to the final stages of cancer. They'd had some wonderful conversations in this 'garden room' as her mom called it. Watching the season change from spring to early summer and with it the abundance of flowers that filled a strip of garden along the miniature wall leading to the lawn. Nature had a way of simplifying the hardest of times and her mom had loved this place. A bolt-hole when life wasn't working out as planned. Christen had been right about coming home to see her dad, he'd simply welcomed her home with a hug.

"I know you're watching. Is there a reason you don't want to join me?" Christen said, turning and flashing a brilliant smile.

Laurel grinned and took the few easy steps to sit next to Christen on the wicker two-seat sofa.

"You looked like you were miles away?"

Laurel smiled and shook her head. "Not miles away. Here, in fact, but I was recalling the last times I was here. Mom used to love this room. She called it the nearest to heaven on earth."

Christen stared at Laurel then reached out and touched her cheek gently. "I think she might be right. It's an incredible house, Laurel. Every room that I've been in so far has a wonderful ambience about it. Makes me want to stay, close the door, and keep the world at bay. Kind of an odd thing to say from a sage accountant don't you think," Christen said with a chuckle.

Laurel moved to wrap her arms around Christen and gently kissed her until they were both breathing heavily. "For the record, I doubt sage accountants kiss like you do and it isn't odd at all to me. Do you want to stay tonight? I've missed you. The phone calls and Skype just don't tick those boxes."

Christen frowned and rested her head against Laurel's. "I would love to stay but…"

"Yeah, I know. Work calls your name," Laurel said and softly smiled.

Christen sighed and moved away. "Sorry, I know it's interfering with us being together. I spoke to Mother this morning before I came here. She's promised me that I only needed to continue to take the helm of Jamison's for a couple more weeks. Hank is coming around at last and I think he'll take over again under a new management system that won't allow him to do what he did before."

Laurel shifted on the sofa and leaned against Christen's chest. She could hear the steady heartbeat and it soothed her. "It isn't a problem, Christen. We talked about this. We both have, or in my case had, commitments that proved annoyingly predictable in keeping us apart."

Christen laughed and traced a fingertip over Laurel's lips. Laurel nipped the finger and grinned. "I'm sorry the bakery closed. Have you had time to think about what you want to do next?"

Laurel shrugged. "I've been doing some painting here…just simple stuff. Before you ask, no you can't see them—yet. Not until they are finished. Dad said I could stay as long as I needed."

"From what I've seen, you could make a great living out of your artwork. Why did you end up at Jamison's with all that talent?" Christen asked with a frown.

"Oh, I worked with paint in the hardware department, just not applying it." Laurel chuckled and winked.

Christen snatched a kiss and laughed. "Hmm, not quite the same. Why?"

"Rebellion. I figured I was never good enough to compete with Dad. Then later there was Ronnie. She used to mock my paintings, saying that they were more like technical drawings that anyone could do with a bit of aptitude," Laurel said, before hanging her head.

"Ronnie was a fool. I hope I never meet her because I'd have choice words for her," Christen said with her face set in determination.

"My champion." Laurel snuggled into Christen's body.

"I have a feeling you would do the same for me. We've become great friends and learned a lot of good things and bad about each other over the last few months. How you've put up with me and all my problems I'll never know, but you do and I love you more for it. We will be together soon, I promise. If we aren't, then I'm going to give up the damn job. Hell, I'm tired of crossing my legs when I'm talking to you."

Laurel burst out laughing. "Did you really say that?"

Christen wriggled her eyebrows. "Don't you?"

"Well, yes, but…oh come here and kiss me, you temptress, you."

Chapter Twenty-three

Barry knocked on Christen's office door and entered. He grinned broadly and sat down.

Christen raised her eyebrows and waited.

He fluffed up his polka-dot tie and flicked back a stray bang that crossed his forehead. "I've got news." He flourished a hand in front of his face.

"That would be?" Christen clasped her hands in front of her and stared at her friend.

Barry giggled. "I'm getting married this weekend. What could be better news than that? You are still going to be my best woman right? No changes to the plan?"

"If I changed my mind the filing cabinets would be in such a disarray that I'd never find anything for a week."

"Three months more like it," Barry quipped.

Christen chuckled and grinned at her friend. "I have the whole weekend off. Hank needs to take back control at some stage and he's desperate. I figure it's the perfect time. Friday night at six I'm off the clock and ready to take you out on the town. Aren't we meeting some of your friends at Alexander's at nine?"

"Girlfriend, we'll probably add more 'friends' when we have drinks at Cesar's beforehand." Barry wriggled his eyebrows.

Christen laughed and picked up her pen and began to doodle box shapes on her notepad. "Malcolm won't be impressed by that remark and your days of sowing wild oats are gone my friend."

Barry shrugged then winked. "Wouldn't think of it. You know me, the life and soul of the party. An entourage always follows. What about your girlfriend? You've been very cagey about her. She's invited, if I hadn't mentioned that already."

At the mention of Laurel Christen's stomach knotted in anticipation of seeing her next.

"You've gone all goofy on me, love. Please, why haven't we met yet? I swear I'll be good with your dirty laundry." Barry leaned forward in anticipation.

Christen laughed and leaned back in her chair.

"Soon, I promise. I did ask her to join us. Unfortunately she and her dad will be away and won't be back in time. She's living with her dad at the moment in Breckenridge. It's a sixty-mile commute and with my schedule we haven't seen each other for almost two weeks. I figured if I could spend the last couple of weekends tying up all the loose ends Hank could take over quicker, and I'm almost at the finish line."

"Crap. That wouldn't work for me. If I couldn't see Malcom every night once we met I'd have died," Barry bemoaned.

"I doubt that. When you get back from the honeymoon we'll have dinner together, the four of us," Christen said.

"She's coming to the wedding though, right? You're not going to be alone. I'd be devastated," Barry stood up melodramatically.

Christen shook her head. “She can’t make the ceremony but she will be at the evening party for sure. You’ll meet her briefly.”

“Why only briefly?” Barry raised his eyebrows.

“Because, as you said earlier, you are the life and soul of the party and how many guests are going…at least one hundred and fifty last time we went over the list. Briefly works.” Christen smiled. “Right, Mr. Craig, I do believe I have a management conference in,” Christen glanced at her Rolex, the roman numerals bulged out at her, “five minutes. Are we done?”

“Sorry, boss.” Barry bowed with a flourish of his hand.

Christen grinned and shook her head at him. “Barry, I’ll be there for the Friday party, Saturday as your best woman, and until you and your new husband leave for your honeymoon. I have your back always, just as I know you have mine.” Seconds later she was engulfed in a hug and kissed on the cheek several times. As she pushed Barry away she saw tears streaming down his face.

“Don’t forget if…no when I get married you have to stand up for me, okay? It’s a pact.”

Barry threw back his hands. “I can’t wait to meet her now. You’ve never mentioned the M word before, even with Macy. Wow, I love it.” He chuckled and gravitated toward the door.

“When Macy and I were together there was no such opportunity. Go, I need the financials from five years ago.”

“Be with you in two minutes as you leave the office,” Barry said as he exited the room.

Christen was left to consider his last personal remark. Even if the opportunity existed she wouldn’t have considered marrying Macy. Laurel—the lovely, unpredictable Laurel—

in a heartbeat I'd kneel down and ask her to marry me now. Crazy, I'm crazy.

The phone ringing dragged her back to the reality of her day. "Hank, wonderful, I will see you in a few minutes in the conference room." She took out her personal phone and sent a text.

†

Christen sank down on the park bench and threw her head back as the air whispered past her face. The breeze cleansed her. She'd missed her daily visits to the park since she'd taken the reins of the business. In the beginning she was thwarting Hank and his cronies, keeping the staff, and the most important people, the customers happy.

Unwrapping the sandwich Barry had given her she took a bite and almost spit it out. She looked at the chicken roll. It looked similar to the ones she'd had before but this one was tasteless. "Damn, has he changed where he buys from? I will have to fix that." She looked at the wrapper—it was a local fast-food place. "Probably didn't have time to go to the regular place with all the wedding plans in his head," she muttered. After sniffing the package she placed it on the bench next to her.

Observing the people who were close by she saw two couples walking hand in hand from different directions. One of them in particular was affectionate, stopping every few feet to snatch a kiss. The other couple was talking animatedly and laughing, which was always good to see.

A young woman with a stroller, dressed in shorts and T-shirt, multitasked as she jogged along. When she came closer, the woman grinned at Christen. The child in the stroller was fast asleep. *I guess that's one way of doing it.*

Her thoughts strayed to Laurel. When didn't they? She smiled and her heart fluttered as she recalled the last kiss they shared and she placed a finger to her lower lip. Then a familiar voice spoke her name.

"I knew you'd be here." Laurel grinned and slid down on the bench next to her.

Christen gaped at her lover. "Wow, this is a wonderful surprise." Christen shifted to pull Laurel into an embrace and kissed her lightly on the lips.

Laurel rested her head against Christen's shoulder. "Surprise is good."

"Absolutely, but how did you know? I haven't been here for over a month?" Christen hugged Laurel to her and sucked in the wonderful aroma of the light fragrance she used.

"I called your office and your assistant might have mentioned that you were taking a stroll in the park. However, I know you, and a stroll means a chicken roll on a bench in Ridgeway Park." Laurel kissed the underside of Christen's face.

"True, but the chicken roll isn't up to scratch. Barry has changed where he gets it from. I'm going to have to have words. It tastes foul."

Laurel laughed. "Well it would, darling, being a chicken roll."

Christen narrowed her eyes and shook her head. "Hmm. Well, it isn't the quality then of what I'm used to," Christen grumbled. She pointed to the offensive roll. "You try it."

Laurel shook her head. "Sorry, I know that place. I wouldn't buy anything from there, especially chicken."

Christen's eyes widened. "Oh no, don't tell me it's dog or horse or rat." Laurel stared at her and Christen could see the twinkle in her eyes.

"Okay, okay, not those. Just basic fast food," Laurel said. "Cross my heart and hope to die."

Christen's heart went off the chart. "Please don't say that, please."

Laurel gazed earnestly at Christen. "It's just an old expression. I promise never to say it again."

Christen pulled her closer. "Laurel, I know I said about the right time…"

"Christen, I came into town because I wanted…no you go first "

Christen gulped back her next statement. "No go for it, you first."

Laurel smiled. "I hope you're going to like this."

"I like anything you tell me. No, there's one thing I wouldn't but I know it isn't happening," Christen said. She kissed Laurel's lips for a few seconds.

"When you do that I can't think."

"Another good thing." Christen laughed. "Go for it, darling."

Laurel shuffled away and stood. "I wanted you to have something important to me and hopefully you'll always remember me no matter what happens."

"Okay."

"I dropped it off at Andrea's apartment."

"I'm sorry, Laurel, but I can't wait another minute more." Christen stood and gently took Laurel's jaw and turned it so they faced each other. "Marry me, Laurel Rogers. For the good things and the bad but most of all because we love each other. I'm done with all this waiting. What about you?"

Laurel couldn't believe what she was hearing, had in fact heard. Out of the fog her mind was in she heard Christen speak again.

"I'm sorry." The deflated voice and the withdrawal from the warmth they shared had Laurel hesitating.

"Look, it was a bad idea, I'd better go back to the office." Christen turned away.

Laurel drew in a huge breath. "Don't go."

Christen held her head up high and her facial expression was bland, pretty much like the first time they had met. That catalytic morning her world changed forever when she met this woman.

"Yes."

Christen's expression didn't change.

"You and I, Christen, we are like a ball in soccer, passing from one to the other without aim. Today you hit the goal, my love. Believe me, you are my love. I've never felt this way about anyone and I mean that. I'd be honored to be your wife," Laurel said.

Christen's whole demeanor changed and she half laughed and half cried.

"Yes?"

"Yes." Laurel rushed at the taller frame and hugged her tight, kissing her soundly until they needed air.

"I…we need to arrange a dinner to celebrate," Christen babbled.

Laurel shook her head. "No, we need to get married. Any chance your friend wants a tag on?" Laurel grinned. She couldn't have stopped grinning if she wanted to. This must be how it feels to be on top of the world.

Christen chuckled. "Possibly not at this late stage. Besides, you promised your dad you'd go with him to see your mom's dad." She glanced at her watch.

Laurel pursed her lips and tugged at her chin. "You have to go right?"

"I'm so sorry. I have a meeting with…"

Laurel leaned in closer and kissed the full lips that tempted her and had earlier spoken such wondrous words. "I don't need to know. We're going to celebrate later though. I'll stay in town and meet you at your place. What time?"

Christen frowned. "I won't finish until after nine and I know you need…"

"Sounds great. I'll be waiting at the door shortly after nine. Do we have a date?"

Christen laughed. "Absolutely, you adorable witch." Then she fished in her pocket and withdrew a set of keys. She selected one and took it off the chain. "Here you go, let yourself in. My place is yours now."

Laurel gasped then kissed Christen again. "Thank you. I promise not to wreck anything."

Christen laughed. "The only thing I'd care about you breaking is my heart."

Laurel opened her mouth to speak and then closed it. Trying again, she whispered, "Never."

Christen smiled and kissed her tenderly. "Great news."

"I'll keep Andrea company this afternoon, she's sick, and pick up my surprise for you. I'll call Dad and he can pick me up from your place in the morning for the plane trip to Denver." With a wide smile and a jaunty wave, she whispered, "I love you." Laurel turned and headed off in the opposite direction to Christen.

Christen stood there for a few moments lost in the memory of one word—*Yes*.

Chapter Twenty-four

The streetlamps glowed as Christen parked her car in the garage. It was nine ten and hopefully Laurel wasn't too upset at her being late. Reaching out to the passenger seat, she collected the packages sitting there and then climbed out of the vehicle. A couple of minutes later she used her spare key to let herself in.

Entering the narrow hallway she shouted, "Hi, it's me."

Laurel came out of the kitchen door. "Wow, have you been buying out the store?"

"No, not quite," Christen said. "I'd appreciate a hand, though."

Laurel quickly took the flowers that had covered Christen's face.

"These are beautiful and they smell…" Laurel pushed her nose into the flowers and squealed, "are not real."

Christen shrugged. "I decided that I wanted them to last forever as I didn't have a chance to get a ring yet. It's a new type. Don't you think they look like roses? They are flax and those silk white orchids make the perfect contrast."

"A bit like us you mean?" Laurel laughed. "I love them, thank you." Laurel stared at Christen and then gave her a kiss. "I'm glad you're home."

"Me too," Christen throatily replied. She placed her other packages on the hall table.

"Oh, before I forget, remember I have something for you too." Laurel took her hand and dragged her to Christen's study.

"Ah, you found my bolt-hole, not as glamorous as your mom's." Christen's mouth gaped as she looked at a painting propped up against her desk. It was the one from the market. *It's my painting.*

Laurel chuckled. "I thought it was perfect as it's Jamison's a few years ago. If you don't like it…" Laurel was pulled into a hug and kissed thoroughly.

"This is the painting I wanted to show you at the market. Talk about fate," Christen whispered, shaking her head.

"Really? I took it off the market after someone was interested in buying it. I gave it an exorbitant price to hopefully scare them off and it worked." Laurel shrugged. "I felt a bit guilty, but my heart was telling me to keep it until the right moment and this is it. Do you really like it?" Laurel turned expectant eyes to Christen.

"I was that buyer. I love it. I'm not sure I can accept it though, Laurel, or should I say Harley." Christen knew tears weren't far away.

"Harley is my painting name, also my middle one, and, wow, what a coincidence. It can be my engagement gift to you, Christen. Please accept it." Laurel smiled.

"I love you," Christen said and pulled Laurel in for a kiss. When they broke apart they left the study.

"Whoa, what smells delicious?" Christen's nose was twitching.

"Chicken casserole with crusty French bread. Wasn't sure if you might be hungry or not. I know it's late."

Christen pulled Laurel into a tight embrace and kissed her again. As their tongues meshed, her heart rate went off the chart before they reluctantly broke apart.

"I'm starving."

"Great, so am I. Want a glass of wine?" Laurel asked. She headed for the galley kitchen.

Christen smiled, watching Laurel sashay through her hallway. *I wonder if she knows she does that? Talk about sexy.* "Wine sounds good. Thank God it's Thursday. I just have to get through another day and then I have a whole weekend off. Can't remember when that ever happened."

Laurel's reply was barely distinguishable. She caught the odd word, time, good, at last. Christen collected her packages and took them to the family room. She placed them on the coffee table and walked over to the door leading to the kitchen and entered. "I'm not going to sit around while you do all the hard work."

Laurel turned with a spoon to her mouth. "Caught me. I was testing the flavor."

Christen smiled and wandered around the counter and placed her hands on Laurel's hips and pulled her gently closer. "Any good?"

"Try it."

A spoon hovered close to Christen's mouth and she sipped the liquid. She pulled away. "Hey, that was hot."

Laurel winked. "Well, you wouldn't want me to serve you cold food would you? What kind of chef would I be."

Christen narrowed her eyes. "I don't care if it's cold, tepid or as hot as hell if you made it."

"I love you too," Laurel said and relaxed into Christen's hold as she stirred the casserole.

Christen smiled and closed her eyes, allowing the loving emotions to seep into her body. This was so different to what she had ever experienced before. She dropped her head, snuggled into Laurel's neck, and felt her pulse race as her lips touched the smooth skin.

"It's ready," Laurel said huskily. "Can you fetch the dishes?"

Christen dropped her hold and walked over to the cupboard. Five minutes later, they were seated opposite each at the kitchen counter with steaming casseroles on their plates and a fragrant French loaf cut into several rounds.

Christen took a mouthful of the casserole and allowed the delicious taste to sizzle every taste bud. *I'm going to get fat loving this woman but who gives a damn.*

"What do you think? I know your lunch was dire," Laurel said as she spooned the casserole into her mouth. "You know the reason why, don't you?"

"Nope, why?" Christen asked.

"Because your lunch for years was bought from Maisey's. In fact, I bet some of the ones you've eaten in recent months I actually made. What do you think of that?"

"Wow, now that is taking the small-world syndrome to another level. Can I coerce you into making me lunch every day for work in the future?"

Laurel chuckled.

Christen picked up a piece of the pliable fresh bread, dunked it into the juices of the casserole, and munched on it.

"That good then." Laurel giggled.

"When I said I was starving I meant it. I think I had twenty meetings today and achieved nothing. What kind of day is that?" Christen asked.

"So you're going to marry me for my cooking skills," Laurel said and ate more of her supper.

Christen watched Laurel eat and smirked.

Laurel caught her gaze. "That's it, isn't it? Food. Works every time."

"Does it? Did it with Ronnie…in the beginning?" Christen seriously asked.

Laurel put down her spoon and stared intently at Christen. "In one word, no. Ronnie permanently watched her figure. She liked women with 'big bones' as she called it, but she had to be fit. Went to the gym every morning. I thought it was great for a couple of years until I found out she went there to bed as many of her fellow keep-fit colleagues as she could. I guess I was a fool to stay as long as I did. In the end, she had to throw me out. It sounds pathetic doesn't it?"

The quietly spoken words permeated Christen's mind. Laurel sounded resigned, guilty perhaps, and something else. "Macy, my long-time, only ex, because, of course, as I mentioned before you came into my life I'd given up on love, was an achiever. I think she must have thought getting in with a Jamison was a kudos thing. She chose the wrong Jamison. Needless to say she left me eventually. I wasn't what she expected. I hate parties, I loathed the social activities we were invited to because of the name. In a nutshell, I liked the quiet life. She left me one day with a scribbled note. It said…"

Laurel placed a hand on hers.

"No, let's today wipe the slate clean. We both have old baggage, and it is old, and we are going to discard that, shredding all those old notes and lies of the past, deal?" Laurel said.

Christen squeezed the hand that held hers. "That's my kind of love."

Laurel stared at her for a few moments and began to cry.

"Hey, I'm sorry, what did I say," Christen said. She moved off her stool and went around to hold Laurel close.

A few minutes later Laurel looked up and sniffed. "Nothing. Everything. I'm sorry for crying."

"I'm not. What do you need me to do?" Christen asked, kissing the top of her head.

"I said *yes* today."

Christen frowned. "Yes, you did."

Laurel snuggled into Christen's hold. "Take me to bed and let's seal that promise."

Christen's heartbeat raced. "I need a shower after work and..." She picked Laurel up. "To hell with it. This is exactly what I'm starving for." She nibbled Laurel's ear. She rapidly ate up the distance from the kitchen to her bedroom and placed Laurel gently on the king-size bed.

"I love you." Laurel kissed her hard.

Christen did not reply, intent on only one thing—divesting Laurel of her clothes as hastily as possible and showing her how much she loved her.

†

Laurel lay replete in Christen's arms, their naked bodies swathed by a cream silk sheet, legs entangled like twins and Laurel's head rested against Christen's breast bone. Their lovemaking had been frenetic and exciting with the aftermath the opposite—gentle and tender. Kissing the silky flesh beneath her lips, Laurel sighed.

"I wish I didn't have to leave tomorrow," she whispered.

Christen held her closer and kissed the top of her head. "You'll be back Saturday afternoon and then I'm not letting you go again."

Laurel listened to not only the words but the rumblings the spoken words generated in Christen's body. "You sound so alive."

There was a fierce rumble as Christen chuckled. "Hope so, or you'd be rather strange in your tastes of who you take to bed."

Laurel giggled. "I didn't mean it like that. I'm not into necrophilia. I just mean…I love to feel you breathe and the sound you make when you speak and…oh, everything that makes you alive and mine."

Christen sucked in a breath that was audible in the quiet room. "I'll do my very best to keep it that way just for you. I've been thinking, Laurel, about you living with your dad and all the work I've been doing lately. What do you think about a vacation? A long one. Just you and me?"

Laurel leapt up and rested her elbows on Christen's chest, who protested with a squeal of pain.

"Sorry love. Of course but where and when?" Laurel eagerly asked.

Christen grinned. "There's a place I've been looking at before we even met. You know my friend Jane, from the café?" Laurel nodded. "She has a small cottage at Wentover Beach. It has two bedrooms, a shower room, and a living area that includes the kitchen. I can vouch for the great sunsets and sunrises on a clear day."

Laurel kissed Christen thoroughly. "My bags are packed."

Christen laughed and held Laurel's face in her hands. "I love you. Hank is in charge at the end of next week. I think then it's time for you and me."

"How long can you take away from work?"

"As long as I need. In fact, I was thinking about going to live there. It's a huge step and you might not…"

"Yes, yes, yes," Laurel screamed her delight.

Christen smiled and pulled her close. "Now, I think it's time I did something to you that makes you that vocal with action rather than words. I can't quite recall if you screamed that loud when you came last time." Christen sucked on Laurel's left nipple and trailed her tongue over the tender flesh. Laurel groaned and lost herself in the sensations that throttled through her body.

Do dreams come true? Sure. All you need is faith.

The End

About the Author

JM Dragon

JM Dragon is a New Zealand citizen, living in the beautiful Canterbury countryside. JM Dragon loves to garden, travel, write, take care of her animals, family, and pursue her business interests—Affinity Ebook Press.

A keen reader of sci-fi, crime/mystery, classic and romance, which helps to feed the imagination for her own stories.

Currently published by Affinity Ebook Press NZ Ltd, her books include, *Fix It Girl, In Name Only, The Destiny Series, Circus* and 2015 GCLS finalist *The One*.

You can contact her by email at jm1dragon@yahoo.com or on Facebook at http://www.facebook.com/julie.dragon.

Other Books from Affinity eBook Press

Return to Me—Erin O'Reilly Renowned microbiologist Sydney Tanner left work as normal for her trip home but never arrived. Ellie Scott her wife of ten years franticly to the point of obsession attempts to find her—the only evidence there is something amiss is Syd's crashed truck then the clues go cold. Ellie refuses to believe that she will never see Syd again but realizes many months later with nothing solid to go on, it's time to attempt to move forward with a life without Syd. Leaving her home town she accepts a new job at Salvation aptly named for Ellie's predicament. There Ellie meets beautiful Maya Rojas who is the director of Salvation a rehabilitation hospital. Although she hasn't given up on finding Syd, Ellie finds herself increasingly drawn to Maya.Will Salivation bring just that to Ellie allowing her to find peace and happiness again or will it have her questioning all that she believes in? A wonderful romance cloaked within an intriguing mystery.

Terminal Event—Ali Spooner Tally Rainwater was born with the gift of second sight. A near fatal accident, at age twelve, brings her visions to her more clearly. As she matures, a spirit enters her visions to guide her in using her gift. When Tally uses her gift to locate the body of a murdered teen, she realizes her gift is to help lost souls find their peace. When it's discovered a serial killer murdered the teen, the FBI is involved. Blaire "Spooky" Cooper is the Agent in Charge assigned to the case, and a task force of local detectives and FBI forms to track the killer. Together with the team, Tally helps them piece together the puzzle of murders spanning twenty years throughout the Deep South.

Arc Over Time—Jen Silver Dr Kathryn Moss has job offers flowing in after her exciting archaeological discoveries at Starling Hill the previous year. Now she has choices to make that could jeopardise her relationship with Denise Sullivan, the fiery journalist, who has become her lover. For Denise the choice seems obvious. She thinks they have moved beyond the casual sex stage to something more like a true relationship. However, she's not sure how to handle Kathryn's continuing infatuation with Ellie Winters. Ellie's new career as a promising artist proves to be a catalyst for the simmering tensions in relations between her wife Robin, Kathryn, and Denise. Will Denise persevere in her pursuit of the reluctant professor? Does Ellie have anything to fear from Kathryn's fascination with her art, or is there another motive behind the professor's obsessive interest? This wonderful romantic continuation with the characters from *Starting Over* ties up loose ends. But the question is—does everyone have a happy ending? A must read.

Presence—Charlene Neal After catching her husband red-handed in bed with his secretary, Kayleigh Gibbs takes her daughter and her Jeep and flees across the country. She opens up her own veterinarian practice, and they move into an old, secluded farmhouse in Hoekwil, South Africa. At her best friend's housewarming party Kayleigh meets the beautiful and enchanting Rebecca Steward. Rebecca is instantly drawn to Kayleigh, but is still recovering from a breakup—her girlfriend left her for a man. She's afraid of a repeat performance with Kayleigh, and won't pursue a romantic relationship with her, preferring instead to develop a platonic friendship. When odd, inexplicable things start happening on the farmhouse, a terrified Kayleigh turns to Rebecca for comfort, only to find herself developing unexplainable feelings for her new friend. Rebecca, despite her best intentions, is falling in love with Kayleigh. But when Rebecca moves in with Kayleigh to help her get to the bottom of the haunting, she finds more than she bargained for. Can Rebecca and Kayleigh overcome ghosts from the past and their own insecurities, or will a presence from the past tear them apart?

A Walk Away—Lacey Schmidt Kat and Rand's daily worlds are 2,100 miles apart, but something about their meeting on the magical shores of the nation's oldest national park east of the Mississippi sparks questions that neither woman can just walk away without answering. Sometimes chance brings you to the right person to help you resolve some of your baggage, and you learn to like yourself a little more. Kat and Rand are smart enough to recognize this chance in each other, but they also find that there is a catch to every opportunity—walking toward something is always walking away from something else.

Love Forever, Live Forever—Annette Mori No one forgets their first love. For Nicky, that's Sara, who abruptly disappears one day, leaving only a cryptic letter. That day scarred her soul. When the pain starts to diminish, Nicky begins to get her life back on track until it is derailed once again by an unimaginable twist. Changed forever, Nicky becomes a careless, womanizing nomad known as the Little Wild One, until she meets Annie. Thirteen years later, Nicky's finally settled and happy. Fate intervenes and puts her directly back into the path of her first love, Sara, and the corresponding events send her into a tailspin. Now she must decide—who will be the person she ends up living with and loving forever?

Possessing Morgan—Erica Lawson New York City, in the height of summer. Crime seems to have taken a holiday, and Detective Morgan O'Callaghan is bored, bored, bored. Paperwork is mating and multiplying on her desk, and even a jaywalker is starting to look good. Anything to get her out from behind her desk! Enter Andrea Worthington, Charleston socialite and all-around rich girl, right down to the wealthy fiancé. She's also the new Assistant District Attorney assigned to Morgan's precinct. Their first meeting is like two freight trains crashing head on. Then a high profile, career make-or-break murder case throws them together again. The investigation has barely begun when Andrea becomes the target of a nearly fatal hit-and-run. But was it really aimed at her? Can she and Morgan find the common ground they need to solve the case and stop the attacks, or are the gaps just too wide to bridge?

Twenty-three Miles—Renee MacKenzie Talia Lisher has a long family history of lying, about anything and everything. With her father dead, and her mom gone on a quest to start a new life, Talia struggles to keep in touch with her only remaining family, her incarcerated brother. When Talia sets her sights on Officer Shay Eliot, she vows to stop lying. She starts watching Shay, waiting for just the right circumstances and amount of courage to talk to her. Talia might be watching Shay, but someone in a dark van is watching Talia. Is the mystery driver a dangerous part of her family's past, or is it all just a coincidence? Shay Eliot has left the police force because of what she perceives as a hostile work environment. When a brutal double-murder on the 23-mile-long Colonial Parkway puts the FBI's magnifying glass squarely on her, her alibi comes from an unlikely source – a young woman who has been stalking her. Shay wants to keep her distance from Talia, but once she gets to know the younger woman she can't keep feelings from developing. This is a story about community, and how it comes together in dangerous and devastating times. When you don't know who to trust, you better have friends who will rally around you. Will Talia and Shay find the answers they need to the mystery of the murders on the parkway, or will justice be elusive? Will they survive their quest for the truth?

Confined Spaces—Renee MacKenzie Andie Waters spends her days pulling waste samples for environmental testing and at night, she tends bar at The Cave, a popular hangout for straights in a small Georgia town. Serial monogamy has grown stale for her, so she's content working to pay off her debts and hanging out with her old hound dog. Or so she thinks, until a beautiful lesbian drops by The Cave. Andie suspects her involvement with the woman will be only temporary. Little does she know no part of her life will be left untouched. Kara Travis likewise anticipates nothing more than a brief fling upon meeting Andie, especially given her reputation as both a personal ice princess and a corporate hatchet wielder for Royal Environmental. What luck to find a hot lesbian bartender in nowhere rural Georgia. Andie and

Kara spend a passionate weekend together and find that their notions of no strings attached are far from accurate. Their supposed short-term ideal diversion of a commitment-free romp hits a major complication when they come face-to-face with one another at Royal Environmental's offices Monday morning. While carrying out her duties, Kara discovers crimes being committed by and against Royal Environmental employees. Will Kara be forced to shut down the Georgia Division of the company? If she does, Andie will lose her job. Worse yet, Kara may lose Andie before she's really even sure she's got her. Corporate politics, complicated romance, and long distances conspire to keep Andie and Kara all boxed in. Can love triumph despite the Confined Spaces?

Reece's Star—TJ Vertigo Reece Corbett watches over the dancers in her gentleman's club with the blue, razor sharp eyes of The Animal. Few know that resting comfortably in her office is her newest love, a tiny MinPin named Smudge. What happened to The Animal, known for her rapacious appetite for women and danger? Faith Ashford is what happened to The Animal. Faith and Reece have been together a while now and they have settled into something resembling domestic bliss. This bliss alarms Reece. It's one thing for Faith to see her softer side, that's vulnerability enough, but to let her friends see it…no. Not the best plan. Under Faith's guiding, loving hand, will Reece successfully traverse the rocky road of emotion and embrace the positive changes in her life? Or will she panic and be unable to control that Animal part of herself? Will she take that next step to declare herself fully capable of love and devotion? This third installment in the popular series that began with *Private Dancer* continues the passionate and often hilarious romance of Reece and Faith as they both grow in love and in trust.

Flight—Renee Mackenzie It's 1983 and Kate Hunter is a student at a small, private college in Virginia. When Lana coaxes her onto the back of her beat-up scooter one night, Kate's education starts to encompass more than just her pre-vet studies. Kate has always done as expected of her, so when she starts staying away from home on weekends to spend time with her new lover it's way out of character for her. Lana is secretive, but Kate accepts things as they are and gives Lana her space. When she feels the sting of betrayal, will she be able to continue giving Lana her privacy? Kate's sister April is a high school student playing with fire as she parties with her older boyfriend, Boyd. After finding someone overdosed the morning after a big party, April grows weary of all the drugs and alcohol. Will she be able to convince Boyd that they should slow down? Will she be able to pull it together before it's too late? Kate and April are forced to face up to events from their younger years, their mother's desertion, and their long-deteriorating relationship with one another. Some lives will be lost and others changed forever when the sisters' lives intersect. Will they be consumed by the wreckage, or will they be able to pick themselves up and take flight?

Reflected Passion—Erica Lawson Where passion, reality, and destiny combine. Dale Wincott is a 27-year-old woman born into Bostonian wealth and groomed to marry into the social hierarchy. Her mother is a hard-hearted society matriarch, but her father feels for his daughter and helps Dale find a life on her own as a furniture restorer. Françoise Marie Aurélie de Villerey is a 28-year-old Countess, born into the French aristocracy and forced to marry a count much older than herself. For ten years, she was his trophy wife, forced to endure his perverted desires, until the day he finally died. He had broken her emotionally and she no longer cared for what life had to offer, slipping from one sexual partner to another as often as she changed her clothes. Until... that one night when Françoise looked up during a sexual encounter and saw Dale watching her from the mirror. A veritable angel, full of innocence and curiosity, who touched her very soul. Through the mirror, Françoise embraces life anew, while for Dale it is a powerful awakening, forcing her to discover not only her sensual nature, but the inner strength she possesses.

The One—JM Dragon Phil (Philomena) Casters loves her work as a pilot, above everything else in her life except Ming, her married lover. Phil needs to enhance her status in the community before asking Ming to leave behind her wealthy husband. Rosa Moran a teacher, raised by missionaries in China after the death of her parents. She loves the country of her birth and the people. Her English grandfather desperately wants her to live with him to atone for the guilt he feels about the death of her parents. He sends her a letter requesting her to come home. When Phil flies to the mission to deliver the letter to Rosa, neither can envisage the chain of events about to take place. It starts as a collaboration to save four children, leading them to the surreal private paradise of Langshow. Could this be the perfect place for the children and Rosa to settle? Phil is not so sure. Chang, an old friend from Rosa's childhood lives in Langshow and makes no bones about the fact that he wants Rosa. All thoughts of Ming disappear as Phil tries to fight her attraction to Rosa. However there is the little matter of an innocent misunderstanding—Rosa thinks Phil is a man. *The One* is a romance with everything, love, intrigue, misunderstandings with a happy conclusion—the only question—who gets the girl?

The Chronicles of Ratha: Book 2 A Lion Among the Lambs—Erica Lawson It has been three years since Jordana Laren's path first crossed the Noorthi's - three years since she's had a drink, had sex and a life of her own. Her only excitement has been spent keeping up with her two year-old daughter, Rice, who is definitely a chip off the old block. All has been peaceful until one of the colonists becomes sick. Bad news shifts to worse news when the disease spreads through their community. Unable to get proper medicine, Jordana is forced to rely on the Noorthi healers to come up with a cure. Soon the herbs run out, leaving her with no choice but to search for more on the Noorthi home planet. What is supposed to be a simple pick-up flight turns into a nightmare. Can Jordana believe in herself like her Noorthi sisters do? Only then can she fulfill her destiny as The Chosen One. Follow the colorful cast of characters in this action-packed adventure sequel as they traverse the galaxy. Of course, nothing ever goes smoothly when Jordana is involved.

Cowgirl Up—Ali Spooner When the new ranch hand, Coal Bryan, arrives at the MC2, the last thing she's looking for is love. Her co-workers are surprised when Coal turns out to be female. Coal, used to the reaction, quickly earns the respect of the crew with her work ethic and skill with horses. Coal uses the strenuous work and friendship of the ranch hands to try and forget her broken past. Melissa Conway, owner of MC2, offers Coal a place to live in her home. They both are shocked to find they are linked in a way neither of them imagined. Mary Leah, Melissa's sister, arrives at the ranch to recover from a recent tragedy. The attraction between Mary Leah and Coal is instant and mutual. Can the three women survive their personal dilemmas? The love and friendship they develop certainly helps but will it be enough to bring them together. Ride along with the MC2, for boot scootin', butt kickin', dirt eatin', rodeo adventures, with a love story thrown into the mix.

If I Were a Boy—Erin O'Reilly Katie McGuire appears to have it all. A devoted husband, a job she loved, and a comfortable lifestyle. Helen Swenson is a successful financial director of a prominent investment firm, with an unfaithful husband, and few friends. Their husbands' annual trip to Padre Island National Seashore to reunite with their air force pilot squad becomes a pivotal point for the two women. Their lives take on a completely new meaning when an undeniable magnetism between them draws them together. Passion and secrecy becomes the norm, as they have no choice but to succumb to their attraction. Can the vacation love affair continue? When they leave for their respective homes, will they regret what happened? Life is not that easy to change and the people around them are the hardest to convince. There is no more powerful motivation than love. Except hate and there are plenty of people who want to see their relationship destroyed. Will Katie and Helen be able to make a life together work or succumb to doubts and the pressures of family? This story will fill you with the thrill of passion and the tenderness of love.

The Chronicles of Ratha: Book 1 Children of the Noorthi—Erica Lawson Jordana Laren is a hard-drinking, hard-fighting womanizer, who works as a freighter pilot in her spare time. Her latest customer drugs her, steals her ship, and abandons her on a desert hellhole called Rigeus, infamous penal planet for the worst women criminals. Her chances of survival aren't looking good. She has no food, water, or weapons, and the nearest bar is a million miles away. Just when she's ready to write her last will and testament, Jordana is rescued by a group of barely-clad women. Has she found nirvana? Her own personal harem seems like a possibility, until the intercession of their enemy, the Velkren. Their leader, Vel, remembers Jordana well, and not fondly. But why is Vel on this planet, surrounded by murderers, thieves, and bad-tempered bitches? Jordana knows Vel isn't a prisoner, so why is her nemesis on Rigeus mining mud, of all things? Jordana knows only one thing. She has to get off the planet before Vel kills her. Unfortunately, the women who saved her reveal themselves to be holy. They are the Noorthi, and Jordana's dream of endless debauchery becomes a nightmare of eternal servitude. The Noorthi make her one of them, marking her with a wrist tattoo, and leaving her no choice but to protect them with her life. The last thing Jordana wants is to become involved in galactic politics or heroic actions. But the tattoo ochre in her body is suddenly giving her morals and scruples, not to mention a better vocabulary! And she really can't pass up a chance to outwit Vel, whose megalomaniac plans are endangering not only the Noorthi, but the civilized galaxy itself. But Jordana is torn. Does she stop Vel at all costs, or does she get out from under the thumb of the Noorthi while she can? Some things were never meant to be easy…

Nesting—Renee MacKenzie Macy Stokes, a divorced mother who is struggling with her sexual identity, jumps at a once-in-a-lifetime opportunity to help her friends. She doesn't foresee it will put her in jeopardy of losing her son,

Jeremiah. Fresh out of high school, Cam Webber travels to Augusta, Georgia, to reconcile with her aunt. When she learns that's impossible, she determines to gain acceptance from her aunt's partner, Sharon. Meanwhile, Cam sets her sights on Macy, but Macy has other ideas. Kenny Brewer is a good old boy who loves his wife, Dorianne, even when he thinks she's gone totally off her rocker. Dorianne gets it in her head that a local woman is her long-lost half-sister. But soon, her obsession with that is eclipsed by medical problems that involve them all. Set in Augusta, Georgia, *Nesting* explores the age-old issues of guilt, regret, and redemption, and the part they play in driving people to create and protect family-at any cost.

Reece's Faith—TJ Vertigo In the return of the main characters from the bestselling novel ***Private Dancer***, we see the blossoming relationship of bar owner, Reece Corbett and actress, Faith Ashford. The two women explore new, uncertain territory together, using sexual intimacy as a glue of comfort, helping them become strong and whole. A trusting Reece shares with Faith the sordid tale of how she became ***The Animal*** and Faith finds herself newly empowered by Reece's ongoing trust and support. Jealousy arises when Faith has to kiss a man on her TV show and two amorous women stalk Reece. When Faith is outed on her television show, things get crazy. With the arrival of her parents on the scene, the craziness escalates. As Faith tries to justify her lifestyle and defend her love for Reece, she discovers that nothing about her parents is as she once believed. This, not to be missed passionate and erotic romance, will have you begging for more.

E-Books, Print, Free e-books

Visit our website for more publications available online.

www.affinityebooks.com

Published by Affinity E-Book Press NZ LTD
Canterbury, New Zealand

Registered Company 2517228